A long time ago, when the Kings of England were always named George, and any light at night that wasn't the moon or stars came from candles or magic, there lived four silver-tongued siblings called the Belles...

To my family

First published in the UK in 2023 by Usborne Publishing Limited, Usborne House, 83-85 Saffron Hill, London EC1N 8RT, England. usborne.com
Usborne Verlag, Usborne Publishing Limited, Prüfeninger Str. 20, 93049 Regensburg, Deutschland, VK Nr. 17560

Text © Peter Bunzl, 2023

Photo of Peter Bunzl © Michael Hayes.

Cover and inside illustrations by Katarzyna Doszla
© Usborne Publishing Limited, 2023

Title lettering by Leo Nickolls © Usborne Publishing Limited, 2023

A CIP catalogue record for this book is available from the British Library.

ISBN 9781801313681   7629/1   JFMAMJJA OND/23

Printed and bound using 100% renewable energy at CPI Group (UK) Ltd, Croydon, CR0 4YY.

PETER BUNZL

GLASSBORN

USBORNE

The Fairy Queen

Otto Glass · Tempest

Robert Glass · Anna

Eliza · Kisi Fremah

Cora · Bram

The Family Tree

"Can you keep a secret? I wonder if you can.
Once an evil curse was set by the Queen of Fairyland.
Now six lost souls must remember their true names.
A five pointed crown must be won in riddling games.
Four wooden soldiers must help cast magic spells.
Three Glassborn children must sing like ringing bells.
Two Fairy twins must hide a magic key,
and the child who is the chosen one must set their
family free."

Traditional Fairy Nursery Rhyme

PROLOGUE
20th December, 1799

Once upon a time, five days before Christmas, at the thirteenth stroke of midnight, on the night before the Winter Solstice, a wolf named Thomas leaped across the moonlit sky, springing from cloud to cloud in great, long leaps.

The wolf wore a stone with a hole in it, called a hag stone, and a yellow tooth on a string around his scraggy neck. His long snout sniffed the snowy air. His eyes – one green, one blue – twinkled in the silvery moonlight, searching for a Fairy Tree that grew in an old churchyard, beside the walled garden of a crumbling cottage.

A Storm Sorceress named Tempest rode on the wolf's

back. Her eyes – one green, one blue – were full of wisdom and cunning, and her determined, wrinkled face was as rugged as a cliffside. Her leaf-green cloak and her loose white hair streamed behind her like the banners of a marching army. She was not afraid of the wolf, for though he was known to be wild he was also her brother.

A red robin named Coriel flew beside the Storm Sorceress and the wolf, gliding on the midnight winds to keep pace with them. Her coal-black eyes glanced ahead in the dark, as she chirruped out the occasional direction. She was the first to spot the Fairy Tree, and she landed in the tree's branches as the wolf and the Storm Sorceress touched down in the frozen grounds of the churchyard, beside the tree's great trunk.

The Storm Sorceress climbed from the wolf's back and brushed snowflakes from her hair. The wolf crouched among the gravestones and began to dig among the tree's roots. The snowy earth squelched between his scrabbling paws.

The Storm Sorceress put a wizened hand in the pocket of her cloak and took out a carefully folded handkerchief. From it she unwrapped a little sparkling key with wards like gold teeth. She placed the key carefully in the hole and the wolf pushed the earth back over it.

The robin flew around gathering moss and twigs to drop over the bare ground.

When they were done, the Storm Sorceress grasped the cloud-shaped piece of bone and a carved wooden boat that hung round her neck, and spoke a spell.

"Tree that's wise, earth that knows, keep this secret down below."

Tufted grass and spiked branches sprouted over the patch of freshly turned earth, and each new blade and twig that grew crackled with frost. Soon the spot where the key was buried looked no different from the rest of the clearing around it.

The Storm Sorceress smiled. Her work here was done. There was no more reason to remain. The magic would take care of the rest. She felt the heaviness of her eighty-seven years. Life would be lighter soon, of that she was sure. She pressed her palm to her necklace once more and spoke another spell.

"Fairy Tree, tall and grand, open a path to Fairyland."

A sparkling, silver web grew from the tree's branches. Its threads twined together to become a doorway, which floated in the air a few inches off the ground. On the far side of the doorway was a separate shimmering world, ever so slightly different to our own. It was daytime over there and rather than the glow of the full moon everything was bathed in sunlight.

"Remember what I told you," the Storm Sorceress

advised the wolf and robin. "The Chosen One is coming for the key. I'll see you again when you bring them to me. Whatever you do, don't let the Fairy Queen get to them first, or else doom will befall us all."

She stepped through the magical doorway. "**Close!**" she commanded, and it shut behind her. One moment she was there, the next she was gone, as if she'd never existed.

Then all that was left was the red robin sitting in the Fairy Tree, the wolf pacing around its trunk, and the magical key buried deep underground.

ACTON BELLE
20th December, 1826

A long time ago, when the Kings of England were always named George, and any light at night that wasn't the moon or stars came from candles or magic, there lived four silver-tongued siblings called the Belles. Their surname was Belle like their papa, but people sometimes called them the Glass-Belles, because their mama's family, who'd been glassmakers, had the surname Glass, and because each of the children's voices was pure and true, like the chime of a glass bell.

The four children were storytellers. When one of them lost the thread of a story, another would take it up and complete it for them. That's how close they were. So close they stood on each other's toes, shared each other's hopes and dreams, laughed at each other's jokes, cried each other's tears, or accidentally poked each other in the ribs after an especially egregious argument.

It was five days before Christmas, one day before the Winter Solstice, at around four in the afternoon, and the four Belle children were shivering in blankets in a horse-drawn carriage hurrying through the frosty Greenwood Forest. Black clouds threw large snowflakes across the sky, and in the wide-open spaces and long shadows a chilly grey twilight was falling.

One Sunday last winter, almost a year ago, the children's mama had become suddenly and violently ill. A few days later, she had died of influenza at their home in Miles Cross. Today they were taking a long and winding road with their papa to their new home in Tambling village: a house called Fairykeep Cottage.

Acton was the youngest Belle. The last to get the hand-me-downs, and to be told what was going on. Eleven years old, with eyes as blue as a summer's day, delicate features and auburn hair that rippled like the ocean. Acton loved games, adventures, magic, and stories – especially the old fairy tales Mama used to tell. His brother said those weren't true, but Acton knew better. In his heart he was certain he would always believe in Fairies.

Elle was the next youngest. Twelve, with a round face, green eyes bright as spring, long scruffy yellow hair and slim earth-stained fingers. Elle adored nature, and could name every insect, plant, tree and animal. Acton loved it when she took him out on expeditions in search of undiscovered organisms. When they found one they'd always name it. Usually something like: the "Ellesian Moth" or the "Ellestoa Tree". Never, Acton noticed, the "Acton Bush", or the "Acton Flower", which was a pity.

Bram was Acton's older brother. The one who didn't believe in Fairies. Bram's full name was Bramble, which he hated. He was thirteen going on thirty, with eyes grey as winter and ginger hair that was scruffy and tangled. Bram loved battles. The uniforms, the muskets, the medals and the cannons. Whenever he could, he read military history, in case he got caught in a skirmish and had to kill in cold blood. That meant with gore, guts and bone-curdling screams, he explained to Acton with a chilling *ha! Ha! HA!* and a punch to the arm. Bram was also very good at riddles. He collected them like most people collect conkers. He'd recently thought up a new one, which he told to the others now.

"Today, as I went down to the Dead Lands, I met an old troubadour with a lute in his hands. Dancing behind him were sixteen brown bears, twelve moles and one vole, and a brace of grey

hares. Prancing with them were thirteen black cats, and fifty white mice in the tallest tall hats. Waltzing about them were eighteen young brides and eighteen young bridegrooms with tears in their eyes. Each traveller waved, with a paw or a hand, but how many were going down to the Dead Lands?"

Acton had no idea. "All of them," he guessed.

"Wrong!" Bram crowed.

Elle bit her lip, thinking. "Ten?" she suggested.

"The answer's one," interrupted Cora, the oldest of the four, looking up from her book. "Just you, Bramble. Isn't that so?"

"How did you know?" Bram asked.

"You're the sole soul heading towards the Dead Lands," Cora explained. "Everyone else is heading away from them, in the opposite direction."

She'd worked it out and guessed correctly. Acton was impressed.

Cora was his favourite sibling. Fourteen, with a resolute chin and matted brown hair. She had small hazel eyes the colour of autumn, that were glazed with the far-off expression of a dreamer, and over her dress she wore a long red hooded cloak – a family heirloom.

Cora was the best at telling Mama's fairy tales, but she also fashioned stories of her own, about a magical place called Glasstown. She wanted to be a writer when she grew up and write epic novels like Mary Shelley, whose book *Frankenstein* she was halfway through reading. When Acton had asked her what it was about, Cora had said it concerned a monster and a man, and nobody was entirely sure which was which. She'd said this with a wry smile as thoughtful and clever as Mama's. The smile made Acton miss Mama even more.

Acton glanced at Papa, slumped in his seat. Papa's name was Patrick; Pat for short. He liked poems, tricks and riddles. Long ago, he'd taught his four children how to write their names backwards. He did the same for Mama when they were courting, to make her laugh. Papa's name backwards was *Tap*. Acton's was *Notca*. Cora's was *Aroc*. Mama's was *Airam*. Bram's was *Marb*. Elle's was *Elle*, a palindrome that read the same both ways. Elle's whole name *ElleBelle* was a palindrome too, which was the reason Mama and Papa, who both loved word-games, had chosen it.

Papa's stubble looked grey this afternoon, and his mourning suit was patched and ruffled. His once-red hair had turned white overnight after Mama's death. His shoulders were hunched in his high-collared shirt, and his eyes were scrunched shut. His head bounced lightly against the headrest and Acton realized he'd fallen asleep.

Since Mama had died Papa was always tired. He'd lost his job as a vicar, when his sadness became so intense he was barely able to function. Soon he was staying in bed all day. And when he did get up, he didn't wash, shave, or dress, instead he'd sit in Mama's old rocking chair in his nightshirt and dressing gown and stare out of the window. Acton wondered if he was imagining the summer walks he used to take with Mama, or the day trips they'd made as a family.

Mama was buried in Tambling Churchyard. Acton, Elle, Bram and Cora had not gone to her funeral. Papa said it would be too much for them. They hadn't even visited Fairykeep Cottage – Mama's childhood home, and the new house where they were going to live, since they'd lost their old home in Miles Cross from Papa's neglect.

Fairykeep Cottage was owned by Mama's sister, Aunt Eliza. Over the years, Mama had told her children many tales about her family and the house. Cora was the one who remembered most of them. Acton decided he would like to hear one now. It would pass the time on the long journey. "Tell us one of Mama's old stories, Cor," he said.

"All right," Cora agreed. "I'll tell you one you've not heard before, that Mama told me when the rest of you weren't around."

Acton felt a pang of jealousy that he had no similar stories Mama had told only to him. He was desperate to hear this one. He leaned forward and listened carefully. He didn't want to miss any detail that might be drowned out by the rattle of the carriage.

"Once upon a time," Cora began, "a hundred years ago, two ferrymen, named Prosper and Marino, lived in a house called Ferrykeep Cottage, which sat beside the Tambling River.

"Prosper kept a boat called *Nixie* that had a scratch down her starboard side, where she'd once scraped a hidden river rock. Marino carved wooden toys from fallen branches and driftwood. The two ferrymen shared their home with their adopted children, a Storm Girl called Tempest and a Wild Boy called Thomas."

"Our great-grandma and great-grand-uncle!" Acton exclaimed.

"Precisely!" Cora said. "Tempest and Thomas had magic powers…"

"What kind of magic powers?" Elle interrupted.

"Thomas could turn himself into any animal he liked," Cora said, "and Tempest was a Storm Sorceress who could control the weather." She paused, thinking a bit. "Plus, they could both talk to birds and cast spells.

"The village children nicknamed their home Fairykeep Cottage because of their powers, and because they had come to England from Fairyland, and were the son and daughter of the Fairy Queen…"

"Does that mean *we're* related to the Fairy Queen too?" Acton asked, astonished.

"She was our great-great-grandmother," Cora explained. "She was also a tyrant, who inflicted terrible harm on her family. Even saw to it that her own sister was killed, but that's a tale for another day."

Acton hated the idea that his great-great-grandmother had been so evil she'd murdered her own sister. It's only a story, he told himself, and stories aren't always true.

"When Tempest and Thomas came to England to live with Prosper and Marino," Cora continued, "the Fairy Queen tried to keep in contact with them. After all, the only reason she had let them go in the first place was that they'd promised to stay in touch.

"But Tempest and Thomas couldn't bear to see her any more, because of the many evil things she'd done. They wrote her a letter to tell her to stay away. When the Fairy Queen received their letter, she was so angry she vowed to get her revenge.

"For weeks, she tried to think of a punishment evil enough to satisfy her furious anger, but she couldn't, and so she sent bad luck spells instead. Meanwhile, she stewed for months and years about the glorious retribution she would dish out to her children one day, when the time was right..."

Acton shivered. What a horrible way to live, stewing on revenge all the time.

"Back in England," Cora continued, "an enchanted Fairy Tree grew in the churchyard beside Fairykeep Cottage." "Anyone who ate its apples would dream of Fairyland. Marino carved gifts for Tempest and Thomas from the fallen branches of the tree: four colourful hand-carved wooden soldiers – guardians and lucky charms to protect the children from their mother's growing wrath."

"You mean these soldiers?" Elle asked, taking a Green Soldier from her pocket. "Passed down to us?"

Cora nodded and took a wooden Red Soldier from her own pocket.

Acton put his hand in his pocket and pulled out a Blue Soldier. Bram didn't get out his soldier, but it was the yellow one. Acton knew he always kept it in his pocket too, just like the others. The toy soldiers were a gift from Mama. Each was the size of thumb and each carried a musket and sword, just as real soldiers did. The feel of the little Blue Soldier in Acton's palm gave him comfort when he was scared, like today.

Cora put her Red Soldier away and Elle and Acton followed suit, then she continued the story.

"Prosper altered Fairykeep Cottage to add four upstairs rooms, painting them in the same colours as the toy soldiers.

There was the Red Room, the Green Room, the Yellow Room and the Blue Room. Tempest filled each room with Weather Magic, as a reminder of her and Thomas's old home in Fairyland, where the weather was always wild, indoors and out.

"In the Red Room there were glorious sunsets. In the Green Room rain dripped through the ceiling, as if Fairykeep Cottage was crying. The Yellow Room was warmed by a sirocco wind. The Blue Room was dingy in the daytime, but at night a thousand stars shone bright on its walls.

"Years passed and Tempest and Thomas grew up, but the Fairy Queen never forgot her vow to get revenge on them. One day, she finally came up with a plan that was suitably horrible and would punish them for ever."

Acton gasped, but didn't interrupt. He needed to know more.

"The Queen cast a cruel and venomous curse over Tempest and Thomas," Cora explained. "It said that when they died, their souls were doomed to spend eternity in an afterlife called the Dead Lands, serving a ruler known as the Dead King. They would work for the King for ever in his dark tower that overlooks an underworld beneath Fairyland, stretching further than the eye can see or the mind comprehend."

"How awful!" Elle exclaimed, her eyes wide with horror. "No one deserves such punishment!"

"There's worse," Cora said. "The Fairy Queen had miscalculated... Because of their magic and because they were immortal Fairies, who could never die of natural causes, Tempest and Thomas were not affected by their mother's curse. When the Fairy Queen realized her mistake she tried to overcome it by vowing to capture and kill them herself.

"But Tempest and Thomas used their powers to keep her at bay, and, finally, when they grew weak with age, they went into hiding. And thus, they were kept safe from the Queen." Cora paused for a long time and bit her lip. "But there was one more thing...the Fairy Queen's curse remained unfulfilled, and, as a result, it was passed down to Tempest and Thomas's family instead which is..."

"Us!" Elle whispered, anxiously. "We're all cursed!"

Bram gave a snort of derision. "This story makes no sense. Why didn't Tempest and Thomas use their magic to end their mother's curse for good?"

"Because the Fairy Queen wove a condition into her spell that her children could not cancel the curse themselves," Cora explained, "All they could do was avoid its consequences. But that avoidance caused the curse to fester and linger and so its septic remains were passed down like an infectious disease, spreading down the branches of their family tree, affecting their children, and their children's children, and everyone born since, and yet to come for ever after."

"Poppycock!" Bram scoffed.

"It's true, Bramble," Cora said. "It's why Tempest and Thomas left behind the magic soldier charms for their family, to protect us. But those don't always work," she added, tearfully. "Which was why the curse aggravated Mama's illness, and helped hasten her death."

"Mama died unexpectedly because she was grievously unwell," Bram snapped. "You know that as well as I do, Cor."

"It was the curse," Cora insisted. "The bad luck from it passed to her, as it will to us in time."

Acton felt sick. He hated it when Bram and Cora argued, but even more than that, he hated the thought that the curse was sewn so deeply into his family line that it had caused all their misfortune.

The journey was getting bumpier. The road grew rutted and the trees crept in. Frosted branches scraped the windows as the carriage slowed.

Finally, they left the Greenwood Forest and crossed a white stone bridge that spanned the gurgling Tambling River.

"Did Tempest and Thomas know that because they'd

avoided the curse, and because it remained unfulfilled, it would cling to their family for all time?" Acton asked.

"They must've suspected," Cora said. "Even while they lived at Fairykeep Cottage, the curse on them affected other people in unexpected ways."

"How?" Elle asked.

"Well," Cora replied, "as Tempest's and Thomas's adopted fathers grew older, Prosper lost his sight. Whenever he went out on the River Tambling in his boat, his children had to go with him as navigators. Then Marino started to lose his memory.

"The pair of old ferry keepers died on the same day – the summer solstice. The very next morning their boat *Nixie* sank, and the toys they'd made vanished, never to be seen again."

"Except for the soldiers," Elle interrupted. "The curse never got those."

"Except the soldiers," Cora agreed. It had got darker since she'd started speaking and Acton had to squint to see her. "Tempest and Thomas saved those magic charms as protection, and they were passed down the generations of the Glass Family, until, finally, they ended up in our possession as Tempest's great-grandchildren…"

"Eventually Thomas left Fairykeep Cottage and went wandering. Tempest became a herbalist. She married a clockmaker called Otto Glass and took his surname. For their wedding Otto gave Tempest a pocket watch and a grandmother clock he'd made from a broken branch of the Fairy Tree in the churchyard."

"I'd love to see those!" Elle exclaimed.

"The grandmother clock is still at Fairykeep Cottage," Cora said. "The watch, unfortunately, is missing. When Otto died, Tempest disappeared. Then her enchanted Weather Rooms vanished, the Fairy Tree grew weak and the grandmother clock stopped ticking."

"So sad," Elle whispered.

The carriage passed a rusted sign that said:

Tumbling Village

Acton's heart skipped a beat. They were almost there. The dirt track running alongside the fields became straw and wood, and then cobbled stone that shook the carriage wheels and his teeth and bones.

"Otto and Tempest had one son, called Robert Glass," Cora continued.

"Our Grandpa Bob," Acton announced.

Cora nodded. "Grandpa Bob married Grandma Anna. They had two children, Mama and Aunt Eliza. But this new Glass family suffered in the same way as the old one had, from the bad luck of the curse."

"I'm tired of this story!" Bram muttered. "It's such nonsense!"

Cora ignored this outburst. "As you know, Bram, our grandparents died on the winter solstice the year Elle was born." The carriage trundled past a row of low stone houses, thatched roofs spotted with snow. "By now, many years had passed since Tempest and Thomas had left Fairykeep Cottage." They turned off the main road and up a steep hill lined with little shops. "But everyone in the village whispered that the curse still lay strong over their family, and would for evermore." With each shop they passed, the excitement of seeing their new home built like a head of steam in Acton's chest.

"Unless, one day," Cora continued, as they turned off the top of the hillside road, "a special Chosen One comes along who can end it…" She bit her lip. "And that's the end of the story."

"Thank goodness for that," Bram said. Acton only wished there was more. "By the way," his brother added, "there's no such things as curses, or Fairies, or the Dead King, or the Dead Lands, or the Fairy Queen. Sometimes I think, if all the childish fairy tales went away then…"

But Acton never got to hear the rest of that thought, because the carriage pulled to a stop on a narrow, frozen lane, beside an old stone church with a short square steeple and the coachman shouted, "PASSENGERS, DISMOUNT FOR FAIRYKEEP!"

His announcement woke Papa, who yawned, rubbed his haggard face and stared at his children as if in a dream.

"So," he said, in the flat way he'd fallen into since Mama's death. "We've arrived at Fairykeep Cottage." And Acton was too scared to ask whether he thought that was a good or bad thing.

FAIRYKEEP COTTAGE

Acton wiped the condensation from the carriage window and peered out. Fairykeep Cottage loomed above him, a large, grey, miserable-looking, double-fronted house, peering over a high, snow-capped, drystone wall. The dark sash windows that poked through its front were covered in spindly frosted branches.

"Wisteria!" Elle exclaimed. "A climber. That'll bloom with pale purple flowers in the summer."

Acton thought the wisteria looked rather dead. So did the house. But he didn't say so. Not out loud. Mama had always talked lovingly of the place, so he had hoped it would feel more homely, but that didn't seem to be the case.

Perhaps it was the curse at work again.

CLUNK!

The carriage roof juddered loudly.

"W-what was that?" he asked.

"Angry Fairies," said Cora.

"Or nothing," said Bram.

"Or fifty Goblins!" Elle shouted. "Watch out, Acton, they're coming to get you! *By the pricking of my thumbs, something wicked this way comes!*"

"Don't listen to them, son," Papa said. "There are no such creatures. It's the coachman fetching our trunks."

Acton gritted his teeth. He felt embarrassed to have believed his siblings' lies in front of Papa. Especially when Bram had said there was no such thing as Fairies.

As they climbed down from the coach, the Tambling River gabbled in the distance, behind a line of frost-sparkled trees. It sounded like Fairy voices speaking in tongues.

"Need a hand?" Bram called up to the coachman.

"Oh, aye," the coachman muttered, peering over the side of the roof. His face was red from the cold and he had snowflakes in his beard. "I suppose it'll get done quicker that way. Don't want to hang around long at this old accursed place! Not so close to solstice!"

Acton wondered if the coachman knew about the curse. He shifted nervously from foot to foot, trying to shake the cold from his legs, the ice from his toes and the fear from his belly. The brown coach horses fidgeted in their tack, exhaling heavy clouds of breath like nervous dragons. They too seemed scared of the house.

"Mind your heads!" The coachman passed down the first trunk, and Bram and Papa helped lower it. They took it in turns to grab each of the next ones, Papa dealing with the heavier loads.

"Christmas roses!" Elle exclaimed, crouching by a ring of white flowers at the snowy roadside. "I've never seen them growing in a Fairy Ring before. Maybe it's because we're at Fairykeep Cottage?"

"I suppose so." Cora bit anxiously at her nails. When Papa, Bram and the coachman had finally finished unloading, she opened the rusted iron gate in the wall. Everyone followed her through it, along a snow-spattered path that led across a large front garden and up three stone steps to Fairykeep Cottage's green front door.

The others climbed the steps, but Acton wasn't ready to go inside just yet. He felt like he needed to do something brave first. To take a little detour by himself to assuage his fear. Besides, there was something else he wanted to see. Something next door.

He stepped away from everyone, and snuck off through another gate, woven with green copper leaves, that he'd seen on the far side of the garden. Nobody noticed him go.

Beyond that second gate was the dark churchyard, full of gravestones and the grey stone church, where Mama and Papa had married, Cora had been baptized as a baby, and Mama's funeral had taken place.

Acton glanced around the churchyard, looking for Mama's headstone. But everything was so dark and covered in snow, he couldn't see properly. He'd barely gone a few paces when he lost sight of the house behind the high wall and the line of trees. Now he felt truly alone.

"Where are you, Mama?" he whispered, his heartbeat flooding his chest. His body tingled with nerves and cold, and his feet crunched on the snowy gravel around the graves. The Tambling River rumbled in the distance, and Acton glimpsed out of the corner of his eye something watching him from behind one of the gravestones.

For a second he thought it was a grey wolf, but that couldn't be, because there were no wolves in England – not any more. He blinked in shock, and when he opened his eyes again the wolf was gone. Disappearing so suddenly, he wondered if it had been a figment of his imagination. Or perhaps it had vanished by magic?

A stone figure, like an angel with butterfly wings, lay face down before him in the deep drifts. Acton stepped carefully over it, heading towards a gnarled, bare tree growing on the churchyard's far side. The tree was covered in buds, despite the cold weather. Acton felt sure it was the Fairy Tree from Mama's stories. He wished he had Elle or Cora with him to confirm his suspicions, or Bram for his bravery.

He placed his hand carefully on the tree trunk. At once, the air seemed to shimmer, and falling snow swirled excitedly around him. He felt a sudden hum of energy under his palm, and pulled his hand away in shock. When he looked up, a red robin was watching him from a branch above.

The robin angled its head, as if it was from one of Mama's stories and, with a soft rustle of feathers, swept down and landed on his shoulder. It trilled softly, as if it was trying to tell him a secret.

"I know," Acton said. But he wasn't very satisfied with that answer. He didn't know, not really.

The robin didn't seem satisfied either. It spread its wings and, with a sharp little chirrup, glided further off.

With trepidation, Acton trailed after it, into a great thicket of frozen thorns further round the tree. He brushed aside the prickly stems and saw that the tree's branches were clumped in a pattern that spelled out the word:

SECRET

Beneath this, three twigs made the shape of an arrow that pointed at the ground.

The robin hopped beneath the arrow and pecked at something poking up through the snow between the roots: a tarnished metal ring. The robin snapped at the ring, as if it was a worm. It swooped to Acton's shoulder and dipped its head. Acton could barely believe what he was seeing. It was all very odd… and yet, at the same time, he felt sure the bird wanted him to take the ring.

He crouched down and tugged hard. He'd expected the ring to come away easily, but it was stuck in the soft ground between the tree roots. He felt around it.

The ring was not a ring at all, but something else entirely. There was a thin metal shaft attached to it, buried deep in the snow. Acton dug round it as best he could, making enough space to loosen the object. The cold earth pinched his fingers as he curled them round the shaft and pulled.

The object came out of the ground with a sound almost like a…

POP!

Acton was shocked to discover it was a key.

CORA BELLE

Cora, Bram, Elle and Papa climbed the three steps to Fairykeep Cottage. The coachman trailed behind them, his arms loaded with bags and trunks, as the front door swung open to reveal Aunt Eliza standing in the flagstoned hallway, holding a lantern.

"Happy Christmas, little Glass-Belles! Merry Winter Solstice Eve! Welcome to Fairykeep Cottage!"

Her voice was flute-like and clipped. Her hair was blonde and her cheeks, mottled with the cold, were dusted with rouge. The flickering lamplight made her smile look sharp as a broken mirror. She was only a few years younger than Papa, which put her at around forty, though her black mourning dress made her seem older.

"Good evening, Eliza," Papa mumbled.

"Good evening, Pat! Good evening, children! Put those things down over there, would you, please?" she said to the coachman. Then to Papa, Cora and the rest, "I've waited so long for this moment. I'm so glad you're finally here. It'll be nice to have family about the place. A chance to forget the sorrows of the past year. It was hard for me to lose a sister, but worse for you, dear children, and you, Pat. You must be in desperate need of a fresh start."

Cora remembered how Mama used to say: *"There's cosiness in a crisis that some folks enjoy."* Aunt Eliza was definitely one of those people. It'd been years since they'd last seen her, but Cora was already remembering how much of a gossip she was.

Aunt Eliza leaned forward and examined everyone. "You've grown into a fine young gentleman, Bram. And you into handsome young ladies, Cora and Elle... But where's Acton?"

"He was with us a moment ago." Cora looked about. Aunt Eliza was right. Acton was missing. "He must've wandered off."

"He's always doing that," Elle said.

"Head in the clouds," Bram explained.

"Go and look for him, would you, Cora?" Papa said.

"Why must it always be me?" Cora protested.

"Because you're the oldest and most responsible," Papa replied. "Now, hurry up!"

And so, while everyone else stepped into the nice, warm hallway of Fairykeep Cottage, Cora hugged her red cloak round her and set off, following Acton's footprints across the snowy garden to a second gate in the wall, covered in green copper leaves, grumbling to herself as she did so.

She didn't see why she always had to be the responsible one. All she wanted to do was write stories. It'd been different when Mama was alive. Whenever either of them was sad or frustrated, she'd kissed Cora's cheek and called her *special one*. But Papa was so melancholy, and the others so young. They did need her help. Acton especially.

Cora stepped through the gate and Fairykeep Cottage disappeared from view behind a line of snow-coated trees. She looked around and found herself in the churchyard surrounded by frosty gravestones.

"ACTON!" she shouted, but he didn't reply.

Large paw prints trailed beside a child's boot prints in the snow.

"ACTON!" Cora hollered again fearfully, but the only answers came from the church bells in the tower, chiming five o'clock.

She stepped over a fallen stone angel, banged her shins on a low memorial stone and almost tripped.

"Ouch!" she cried, rubbing her leg. Then she noticed the words written on the stone:

"We are such stuff as dreams are made on."

Beneath that quote, a list of names was hidden by compacted snow. She rubbed it away.

Prosper & Marino Ferriman

Otto Glass

Robert & Anna Glass

Her family. At the bottom of the stone, a new name had been freshly carved into the granite:

Maria Belle

Mama! Cora shut her eyes, holding back the tears. How could she have lost Mama so suddenly like that? And her old home and her old friends too? And now just look at her...she'd lost Acton! Was she cursed to lose everything she held dear? It wasn't fair! She had always tried to be so responsible, and yet, somehow, that made no difference to the world. It took everything from her.

"ACTON!" she called desperately, for a third time.

There was only a snow-muffled silence in response. A silence so loud it made her feel as if she'd been sucked away into another world, where she was the only living soul.

Finally, a sound broke through.

SNIP-CRUNK-CRICK!

A handful of swaying roses was growing through the snow around the Glass family headstone. Cora watched open-mouthed as the roses bowed and twisted together to make a flowering frame around the stone. She had thought they were Christmas roses, like the ones Elle had seen on the path. But as she peered closer, she realized they were made of glass.

Each rose shook softly in the breeze, so that it seemed to Cora that the little flowers were tinkling echoes of the church bells. "How curious..." she muttered to herself.

The roses opened slowly. Cora held her breath and stared at the smallest one. A sparkling bloom that grew beside her mama's name. It was prettier and more unique than all the others put together! In all her life she'd never seen a rose so strange and beautiful and spooky. Something so exquisite it seemed to be asking to be picked, but so sharp it might cut you if you did so.

A shiver of fear ran through her, but Cora steeled herself and reached out and plucked the rose just the same. Mama had always said that True Courage was not the bravery of doing something you felt confident about. True Courage was to feel fearful but choose to take a risk anyway.

CRACK!

The rose snapped and came away in one perfect piece.

Cora broke two glass thorns from its stem so it was easy to hold, and pressed her fingers to the petals. They were ice-cold, but gossamer light. She wondered if perhaps she shouldn't have picked the flower, but she couldn't very well put it back, not with a broken stem.

She took a hairpin from her head and attached the glass rose to her dress. She'd just pulled her red cloak over it when she saw a pair of eyes – one green and one blue – appear behind a far-off gravestone.

Cora's limbs froze as the owner of those eyes, a great grey growling wolf, padded towards her across the snowdrifts. Her nervous heart was fluttering so loudly she wondered if the wolf could hear it.

A hag stone and a yellow tooth hung on a cord around the wolf's neck. They reminded Cora of something from one of Mama's stories, but in the whirl of anxiety she couldn't think what. A lump stuck in her throat, as the wolf leaped between tombstones and moonbeams, opened his jaws wide to reveal a mouthful of sharp teeth and gave a loud howl.

AWHOOOOOOOOOOOOOOOOOOOOO!

The noise shivered through Cora's flesh and echoed along the length of her bones. She knew then that she had to befriend the wolf before he ate her.

"What big teeth you have!" she gibbered, too worried to think of anything else. The wolf gave a warning growl and stepped towards her, and Cora turned and ran, clutching the rose to her chest.

She was almost at the gate.

She stumbled onwards and tripped over a tree root, and with a...

THUD!

...fell flat on her face in the snow.

She sat up and brushed the flakes from her eyes. Anxiously, she put a hand to the glass rose, but it wasn't damaged. She glanced round for the wolf, but he was gone. Instead, crouched on the far side of a gnarled old tree, was Acton.

She hadn't noticed him from further off because he'd been hidden by the trunk. Had he seen the wolf...and the glass roses? Something inside her stopped her from asking. "Where were you?" she snapped instead.

"Not so loud!" Acton whispered. "You'll scare my robin."

Now she could see that Acton really did have a robin! It hopped beside him, like something from Mama's fairy tales. It didn't seem scared at all.

"What's that?" Cora asked, staring at something Acton had clasped in his fist.

"Nothing." Acton balled his hand tighter. "It's a secret."

"Let me see." Cora pulled his fingers open and extracted the thing. It was a glinting key, with wards like little golden teeth. She ran her hands over them.

SNAP!

"Ouch! It bit me!" she cried, dropping it. A pearl of red blood gathered on the end of her finger and fell into the white snow.

"That's because you took it without my permission," Acton said. "If it bites, it's definitely magic."

"What does it open?" Cora asked.

"I'm not sure," Acton admitted. "Maybe a door in this Fairy Tree." He grinned. "Wouldn't that be amazing; like something from one of your and Mama's stories!"

Cora looked up at the tree's twisted branches curling across the sky. Perhaps Acton was right. Perhaps this was the Fairy Tree. If it was, it didn't look particularly magical, more…unwell. She waved her hand to relieve the sting of the key's cut. It couldn't really have bitten her. It was sharp, that was all. Sharp enough to pierce her skin.

"We need to get back to Fairykeep Cottage," she told Acton, sucking her finger. "Aunt Eliza was wondering where you were. We should show her your key." *But not my glass rose,* she thought to herself.

"But the key's mine!" Acton protested. "A present from my robin. Promise me we'll keep it to ourselves."

Cora didn't answer.

"Promise me," Acton repeated.

"All right," she agreed, reluctantly. "I promise."

After all, she was going to keep her rose a secret.

She glanced at Mama's gravestone on the far side of the churchyard, and swore she saw the wolf again. It was slinking through the shadows, but she couldn't be sure it wasn't her imagination playing tricks on her. When she looked for a second time the beast was gone, and Acton was already stepping through the gate that led back to the garden.

Cora hurried after him. On the gate's far side, she could make out twinkling lamplight in Fairykeep's fogged windows. Compared to the dark graveyard, the old cottage looked warm and inviting. As she followed Acton towards the house, the robin flitted behind them.

"Your little redbreast is following us," she whispered.

"So it is!" Acton watched the bird with wide eyes as it landed on the gate and strutted about inquisitively on the snow-flecked green copper. "I wonder why."

Cora was asking herself the same question. "I don't know," she admitted, climbing the three steps and knocking on Fairykeep Cottage's front door. "But maybe we can find out."

4

ELIZA AND KISI

"Come this way!" Aunt Eliza trilled, ushering Cora and Acton into the hallway where the Belle family trunks were stacked in the corner. Her wooden overshoes tapped loudly on the flagstones. "You look positively frozen! There's a fire in the living room to warm you! We have another guest with us. She's talking with your father, and siblings."

Cora wondered who it could possibly be, but Aunt Eliza flung open a side door and announced loudly, "Here's Cora and Acton at last, my dear Kisi! Come home to Fairykeep Cottage!"

They stepped into a drawing room hung with colourful Christmas streamers, lit by a roaring fire in the marble fireplace and flickering candles. Elle was perched on a piano stool before a cabinet piano; Papa and Bram were sitting in high-backed chairs at a polished walnut table, beside a glowing oil lamp.

A stranger reclined on a scroll-armed sofa by the door. She wore a fine blue dress, had twinkling brown eyes, dark brown skin and black curls that swept back from her round face.

"Ah, the last two Glass-Belles!" she said, standing. "Good evening, Cora and Acton. My name's Miss Fremah, but you must call me Kisi." Her sparkling voice filled the room like the snap and crackle of the lively fire. "I'm the schoolmistress at the village school up the lane. The four of you will be starting there after Christmas. I've heard so much about the family since Miss Glass and I became heartfelt friends. And from your father, when I first met him at the funeral. It's a pleasure to meet you all, at last!" She shook Cora's hand and Acton's. "I was telling your father, brother and sister how awfully sorry I was for their loss."

"Thank you, Miss Fremah, for your kind words," Papa said.

"A tragedy." Kisi lowered her eyes to the floor, and Cora knew at once that she would change the subject. "As always, I've been admiring your drawing room, Eliza." Kisi waved at a row of shelves dotted with gothic novels and ornaments.

"It's full of such wonderful keepsakes!"

"One, unfortunately, is missing." Aunt Eliza pointed at the empty hook in the centre of the ceiling. "My mother's Wedding Chandelier used to hang there. It had glass roses on it and a one of a kind glass star at its centre. Father made it for Mother as a gift, but it's long gone. It melted into thin air the day she died. Taken before its time, like my ill-fated parents – and your poor dear mama, my unfortunate sister, Maria. But all of that was because of…" Aunt Eliza drifted off into a guilty silence.

"…the bad luck of the curse?" Elle suggested.

Cora held her breath, but their aunt nodded in agreement. She obviously knew about the curse. Her talk of the rose-covered chandelier made Cora remember the patch of glass roses, growing in a frame round the family tombstone. The rose she'd picked from beside Mama's name was still pinned to her dress, beneath her cloak. She wanted to ask if that was connected to the chandelier, but then she'd have to show it to everyone, and it was her secret. Perhaps she'd mention it to Aunt Eliza in the morning, when they were settled in?

"Your family portrait used to hang there." Aunt Eliza pointed at a faded square on the blue wallpaper, where a picture was missing. "The one Maria sent to me. The one she painted of herself with you, Pat, and the children."

Papa gave a deep sigh. "It was her only self-portrait. She looked beautiful in it."

"Where is it now?" Cora barely remembered the picture. She'd been much younger when it was painted, and she'd only seen it briefly before it was packed up and shipped to Aunt Eliza.

"It disappeared when Maria died," Aunt Eliza explained. "That was the curse too!" she added, in a barely audible whisper.

"That stupid story about Tempest and Thomas avoiding their fate so that it fell upon the rest of the family!" Papa snapped. "Such nonsense! And the last thing my children need to hear right now, quite frankly."

"But, Papa," Cora protested. "When Mama was alive, you said all of her tall tales about her family were true."

"You always told us to wear one sock inside out around the solstice," Acton added. "To confuse the Fairies, if they ever came calling." He still adored that story.

"Curses! Socks! Fairies!" Papa muttered. "I no longer believe in such things...or in fairy-tale endings. Real life doesn't work that way. Good doesn't always triumph over evil, people you love die, and there isn't always a *happy ending*."

Bram smiled and nodded, as if he agreed with everything Papa had said. But Cora only felt a pang of disappointment to hear their father express such thoughts. He'd never talked that way when Mama was alive.

"We believe in Fairies," Aunt Eliza said coldly. "And the curse. We've seen too much evidence of them both at Fairykeep Cottage to think otherwise."

"And we believe in happy endings." Kisi put her hand on Eliza's, which seemed to melt their aunt's bad mood.

"We do." Eliza laughed. Her new good humour was only interrupted by Bram's hungry grumbling belly. "But what are we thinking!" she exclaimed. "Here's us wittering on about the past, and you must be famished after your long journey. I've been keeping something warm in the oven for you all. Come on into the kitchen, and you can have a taste of my famous savoury Christmas pie!" Holding her lamp high, she jostled everyone from their seats and led them out through the door. Kisi followed with the second lamp.

Aunt Eliza's kitchen was even more cluttered than her drawing room. There was a washing rack, a green dresser, a stone sink and an iron stove in a sooty fireplace which had brightly coloured paper chains pinned above it. A small window looked out onto the eddying waters of the river that ran behind the cottage garden, on the opposite side to the churchyard. On the far side of the river you could just about glimpse the snow-covered, moonlit Greenwood Forest. A red glass vase filled with a festive bouquet sat on the kitchen table.

"Holly, ivy and mistletoe!" Elle exclaimed. "You've made the whole cottage so Christmassy!"

"I try my best." Aunt Eliza placed her lamp on the mantelpiece. "You won't believe this, but I was in such a state this afternoon, before your arrival, that I forgot to put out a morsel of pastry for the Fairies. Probably why I burned myself on the stove." She stroked her hand. "It's bad luck not to leave a gift for the Fair Folk on the days around the winter solstice, isn't that so, my dear?" She glanced at Kisi, then apologetically at Papa. "I'm sorry. I do go on!"

"You certainly do," Papa grumbled. "And after I expressly said…"

"Smells delicious!" Kisi interrupted, placing her lamp down beside Eliza's, as Eliza took a pie from the oven. It did smell fantastic, and Cora's mouth watered.

"The other trunks you sent ahead arrived weeks ago, Pat," Aunt Eliza continued, setting the pie in the centre of the kitchen table. "I've sorted everything as best I could. There's only three bedrooms, so Cora, Bram, Elle and Acton, you'll have to share."

"Must we?" Bram said. "Elle snores."

"And you smell, Bramble," Elle said.

Aunt Eliza ignored their protests. "You've got the Blue Room, all of you, and, Pat, I've given you the Green Room. I'm in the Red Room. The Yellow Room is barely big enough to swing a cat, but I've put some of your bits and pieces in there for storage."

"The Magic Weather Rooms!" Acton exclaimed. Cora felt excited too. Even though she knew the rooms had lost their weather, she was still looking forward to seeing them.

"Once upon a time they were...before..." Aunt Eliza smiled sadly and trailed off, stopping herself from mentioning the curse again. "A few of your boxes were quite heavy, but Kisi helped me carry them, didn't you, my love? I'll give you the first serving, Pat," she added, as she dished out the pie.

"Actually, I'm not hungry." Papa glanced at the door. "I think I'll go to bed. I can see myself up the stairs." He took one of the lamps, immediately making the room darker.

"Goodnight, children. Goodnight, Miss Fremah. So nice to meet you again."

His shadow faded round the door frame and his feet creaked on the stairs.

"Oh dear!" Aunt Eliza said quietly, when he was finally gone.

"He's always that way," Bram replied miserably.

"We all are sometimes," Elle said.

"He's been so sad since Mama's death," Acton explained.

"Grief-stricken," Cora added.

"Melancholia over his loss," Kisi suggested.

"It'll lift, given time," Aunt Eliza insisted. "But it's a good thing he brought you children here. It will make him step into the world anew."

Cora wondered who she was trying to convince, them or herself.

"Anyway…" Aunt Eliza plastered on a smile. "Have a seat. Let's eat!"

There was only a brief quarrel about who got which chair, and which portion of pie. As soon as Acton, Elle and Bram were tucking in, Cora took a mouthful. Beneath the golden crust was sweet, tasty slow-cooked mutton, gravy, carrots, peas and potatoes. It was wonderfully warming.

Aunt Eliza placed a jug of water down on the table, before serving herself and Kisi. Kisi waved away a seat and ate standing beside her friend at the stove.

"Have either of you actually seen real evidence of Fairies, or the curse?" Elle asked.

"Oh yes," Aunt Eliza replied.

"When exactly?" Bram's face was a mask of incredulity.

"When I was ill as a child," Aunt Eliza explained. "I was lying upstairs in my room, in bed, sweating a fever, and I saw the Fairy Queen in your mama's old hand mirror. She called to me through the glass, but I threw a cloth over it."

"I've seen similar," Kisi said, "though only in dreams, not through mirrors. But my grandfather saw Fairies in the flesh, when he lived at Fairykeep Cottage."

"Your grandfather lived here! When was that?" Cora asked, astounded. This was a tale she'd not heard.

"A hundred years ago," Kisi answered. "But only for a short while. My grandfather's name was Kwesi. He was a sorcerer and friends with Tempest and Thomas. Together they fought the Fairy Queen, and then came here, where my grandfather lived with the old ferry keepers, and Tempest and Thomas, for a few months. I myself came to Tambling to find out more about that story, and I decided to stay when I was offered the job as schoolmistress – and after Eliza and I became wholehearted friends."

"I don't believe a word of it!" Bram snapped. "There's no such place as Fairyland. And as for the Fairies and the Fairy Queen and her curse, those are just silly stories to persuade little ones to be good. We've put away such childish things."

"If you say so," Kisi replied. "Well, I'd best tell no more of my story!"

Cora felt disappointed. Bram's scepticism had ruined another tale for everyone.

"Our stories are as real as your mama's, Bram," Aunt

Eliza said, sadly. "I only wish she'd lived to tell you more of them."

Cora sighed and stuffed the last of her gravy and pie crust into her mouth, trying to fill the gaping hole she felt inside whenever anyone mentioned Mama. She only wished Bram would speak for himself, and not try to answer for everybody as usual.

"Your pie is delicious, as always, my dear Eliza," Kisi said. "And the company has been most delightful, but I should get going, I have some correspondence to attend to at home. No need to see me out. I'll find my own way. Goodnight, little Glass-Belles. Goodnight, dearest Eliza!" She nodded graciously to each of them and kissed Eliza's cheek, before heading for the door.

Aunt Eliza blushed as she tidied the plates away into the sink. Then she took the remaining lamp from the table. "Well," she said. "You all look jiggered! I'd better show you to your beds."

Cora yawned. Aunt Eliza was right. She did feel tired, but she wasn't quite ready for sleep. She wanted to explore the Blue Room and talk with Bram, Elle and Acton about the events of the day and everything they'd seen and heard.

She'd be sure not to mention the key until Acton did, or the wolf and the glass rose. Those were secrets she'd decided not to share with the others yet. They shared everything

51

else: hopes, dreams, toys, clothes, stories, laughter, memories, grief, but Cora knew the glass rose especially was hers and hers alone, and she'd decided to keep it that way a little longer.

Tomorrow she would show it to Aunt Eliza privately, and ask her if it was some sort of Fairy magic connected to Mama, or the missing chandelier, and whether that meant the rose was good luck, or whether it was bad luck, connected to the family's curse.

The rose didn't *feel* like bad luck. It felt special. Cora couldn't wait to find out more about it, and to see the Magic Weather Rooms upstairs and explore the rest of the cottage where Mama had once lived.

5

BEDTIME STORIES

"Does Kisi have magic, like her grandfather?" Acton asked Aunt Eliza, as he, Cora, Bram and Elle followed her glowing lamp up the stairs.

"Oh no, dear." Aunt Eliza shook her head. "Kisi is a lady of letters, an intellectual thinker, and her magic is of the heart. In here." She touched her chest. "Her grandfather's sorcery died with him, just as Tempest's and Thomas's did in our family."

Acton felt disappointed. If he had magic like his ancestors, he'd banish the bad luck of the curse, solve all the family worries, and make everything right with Papa. But he didn't, so he couldn't. Anyway, he remembered, Mama had always said you couldn't solve other people's problems, only be there to listen with love when they were ready to talk about them.

They passed three painted doors on the first floor. A yellow door and a red door, which were closed, and a green door, which was partially open. Behind it in the Green Room, Papa was sitting on his bed in the lamplight, staring at a shadowy corner of leafy wallpaper. His shoulders were hunched and his shirt wrinkled. Acton had an urge to go and comfort him, but he sensed Papa wanted to be alone.

"Here we are." Aunt Eliza pushed open the passageway's last door, which was painted blue. "The Blue Room!"

Acton, Cora, Bram and Elle looked around. Four child-sized beds were set against four walls that were covered in blue wallpaper and scattered with faded stars. Each bed had a carved star on its headboard and a painted wooden trunk at its foot that matched the colours of their four wooden soldiers, and the four Weather Rooms: red, green, yellow, and blue. The trunks were open and had been carefully filled with their folded clothes that had been sent ahead.

"This was my and your mama's room when we were small," Aunt Eliza explained. "I set it up as a nursery for the four of you, in case you came to stay. And now you have!"

Acton thought they were a little too old for a nursery, but the Blue Room was very pleasant. Heavy turquoise curtains, embroidered with more stars, were drawn across the window. There was a small writing desk with an inkstand in front of them. A sheaf of paper, an hourglass and a little hand mirror were arranged on its blotter.

"That's your mother's old desk," Aunt Eliza explained. "Where she used to write, paint and draw. She would sit there all day sometimes. But she always remembered to take a break every hour, when the sands of time had run through her hourglass. The quill and inkstand were hers too, and the mirror. But the paper is fresh. I got that because I heard how much you all love to write stories. Cora in particular, I believe."

"Thank you, Aunt." Cora smiled.

"Shouldn't the mirror be covered at solstice?" Elle asked. "To keep the Fairies at bay, like in your and Mama's stories."

"You're right!" Aunt Eliza exclaimed. "How did I forget!" She took a small black cloth from the drawer beneath the desk and quickly threw it over the mirror.

Acton wanted to ask more about that tradition, but then he spotted the grandmother clock in the shadiest corner of the room. The one from Cora's story, and he couldn't draw his eyes away from it. The clock was as big as a person, with carved creatures on every corner and thirteen hours on its face.

"It was made by your great-grandpa Otto," Aunt Eliza explained, "along with a pocket watch, as a wedding gift for Tempest. The clock once had a special magical winding key."

"I'd like to see that!" Elle said.

"I'm afraid you can't," Aunt Eliza said. "After Otto died, in the winter of the year seventeen-ninety-nine, Tempest buried the key somewhere secret. But they say just before she buried it, she cast a spell."

"What kind of spell?" With a shudder of fear and excitement, Acton touched the key in his pocket, pressing its teeth between his fingers. It felt heavy with importance, but whether that was from the weight of the iron, or of the story, he couldn't say.

"An enchantment," Aunt Eliza whispered, leaning closer into the lantern light. "It decreed that whoever found the buried key would be the Chosen One; destined to go to Fairyland, defeat the Fairy Queen, and end the curse for ever."

"Crikey!" said Elle. "And if this Chosen One ends the curse hanging over Tempest and her brother, I suppose that would mean the end of its evil effects on the whole family!"

"That's what I believe," Aunt Eliza said.

"What rubbish!" Bram spat. "If this key was as valuable as you say, why did she bury it? Why not just leave it in plain view for someone to find?"

"Because she had to keep it secret from the Fairy Queen,"

Aunt Eliza said. "And she wanted to make sure anyone who found the key would keep the secret too."

Acton said nothing. His words were stuck in his throat. Cora was giving him a significant stare. Did finding the key mean he *was* the Chosen One? As yet, he couldn't be sure. He wondered if he should tell Elle, Bram and Aunt Eliza about it. He'd only shown the key to Cora because she'd forced him to. No harm seemed to have come from that. But he couldn't risk telling anyone else, not when the message in the tree branches had been so clear, and when Aunt Eliza had said it should be kept secret too.

"After Tempest buried the key –" Aunt Eliza was still explaining the story – "she left Fairykeep Cottage for good, but you probably know that part."

"What happened to Tempest's pocket watch?" Bram asked.

"She took it with her when she disappeared," Aunt Eliza said. "A shame because it kept good time. Unlike the clock."

"Why does the clock have a thirteen on it?" Elle pointed to the number thirteen on the clock face.

"To tell the time in Fairyland," Aunt Eliza said. "Time has thirteen hours there. When a clock strikes midnight in England that's thirteen o'clock midday in Fairyland. On tomorrow's winter solstice that's the most dangerous time of all."

"How so?" Bram asked.

"They say that's when Fairy magic is at its strongest," Aunt Eliza said. "And the borders between Fairyland and England are at their weakest. Then the Fairies open enchanted doorways to England, and come through to cause mayhem."

Acton ground his teeth. "Why?"

"As punishment for Tempest and Thomas avoiding the curse," Aunt Eliza replied.

Acton shivered. He had heard more about the curse and Fairy magic this evening than he had in the rest of his lifetime and his head was spinning with all of it.

"We're not at risk though, are we?" Elle asked Aunt Eliza, worriedly.

"The Fairies cannot take you if you stay in bed during the midnight witching hour," Aunt Eliza replied. "And you mustn't worry about that grandmother clock either. It hasn't struck thirteen since it ran down years ago."

She put the lamp on the table and kissed Cora, Bram, Elle and Acton goodnight. "Well, my dears, there'll be no more fairy tales tonight. I don't want to scare you too much before bed. I'll leave the lamp here for you while you get settled in, but I'll lock the door, just to be on the safe side."

After she left, Acton heard a key turn in the lock of the door outside. Then her wooden overshoes crossed the hall

58

and her own bedroom door creaked shut a moment later. The noise echoed across the landing and through the Blue Room door, making Acton shiver.

"Did Aunt Eliza just lock us in?" Elle asked in shock.

Acton nodded. He watched Cora and Bram search through the trunks for their nightclothes. He didn't feel like getting ready for bed yet. He touched the key nestled beside the soldier in his pocket, again. It felt safe there. It hadn't slipped off, as magical things sometimes did in Mama's stories. He hoped it *was* magical. And that he was the Chosen One. He deserved to be special after all he'd been through.

He watched Elle rifle through the green trunk for her nightdress, while Bram changed into his night things on the edge of his bed. Cora took off her red cloak and dress. For a moment Acton glimpsed something sparkly hidden in their folds, before Cora bundled up the dress and cloak with the "thing" hidden inside them, and placed the entire heap under the blanket at the foot of her bed.

Acton got into his own night things also and, finally, everyone was ready for bed.

As the others climbed reluctantly under their covers, he hid the key beneath his pillow. He'd use it to open the clock tomorrow; perhaps doing that would reveal more about its magic and how to end the curse. But, right now, he was too tired for any of that. And if he was honest with himself, he was a little bit scared and frightened about it too. He climbed into bed and put his Blue Soldier on his bedside table to keep watch and protect the key.

Looking at his soldier made him think of Mama and what she'd said on the day she'd given it... "These four soldiers are lucky charms, carved by your great-great-grandfathers, Prosper and Marino. Some of the few family heirlooms not to disappear over the years. They've been waiting for the four of you, as your destiny. Keep them with you always, to protect against the Fairies."

Those seemed like wise words now. He missed Mama more than he could say. Missed her stories, her light step and butterfly kisses. Missed the smell of her – oil paint mixed with perfume – and the way she'd filled their lives with joy. He watched the flickering lamplight on the walls of the Blue Room and thought of Papa next door all alone, lost in the dark of this strange new house, just as he was.

Mama had always said: *Home is not the walls, doors and windows of a place, it's where the heart is.* Fairykeep Cottage felt strange, not how Mama had described it at all. Could such a place ever be home for his family? Would his heart ever truly belong here? And could he really be the Chosen One?

He closed his eyes, listening to the familiar sleeping sounds of his siblings. The events of the day: the robin, the key and Cora, Aunt Eliza's and Kisi's stories, tangled in his mind with his worries about Papa and crowded out his good memories as he drifted into a deep sleep.

6

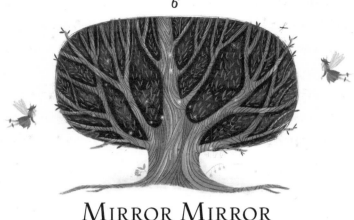

MIRROR MIRROR

Tap. Tap. Tap.

There was a loud noise coming from somewhere in the Blue Room. Acton stood barefoot in his nightshirt in the centre of the floor. Cora, Bram and Elle lay slumbering in their beds. Eyes shut, breathing heavily, asleep.

Tap. Tap. Tap.

The sound was coming from inside the little hand mirror on Mama's old desk. How was that even possible? Not heeding his aunt's earlier warning, Acton pulled away the cloth from it, and peered anxiously into the glass. He could not see his reflection. Only the darkness of the Blue Room without him in it. He leaned in closer to the mirror, wondering what was going on…

"Chosen One!" a voice called softly, like words on the wind. The surface of the mirror rippled like water and a young girl, of about Acton's age, appeared. Her face was pale and wan, her hair white and gossamer as thistledown.

"W-what are you doing in the mirror?" Acton asked.

"I've come to ask for your help," the girl replied. "I've forgotten who I am."

Fear sparked in Acton's chest like a flint striking stone. He couldn't imagine forgetting who he was. The girl pushed against the glass with a ghostly hand, but she couldn't get through. Instead, she pressed her face to its barrier and whispered, "Find my True Name, Chosen One. That's the real key to end all this! Bring it with you when you come to see me."

"Wait!" Acton cried out. "I don't know where you are!"

But the nameless girl in the mirror did not wait. Her image was dissolving fast. Soon no wisp of her remained. The only thing left in the mirror was the reflection of Acton's worried expression.

Acton put the mirror back, face down. The sands of time were tumbling through the hourglass on the desk. Not downwards, as you would expect, but upwards, from the bottom bulb to the top, as if none of what had just happened was real, as if it had all been a dream!

Acton woke up sobbing, thrashing in his blanket. The girl in the mirror had called him the Chosen One, and said her True Name was the real key to end all this, and she'd asked him to come and find her. Aunt Eliza had said the Chosen One was destined to use the key to find Fairyland and defeat the Fairy Queen, but she'd made no mention of a girl who'd forgotten her name. Acton didn't understand what the girl had meant, but he was determined to find out. Even if it *was* just a dream, he needed to know. He grabbed his key from under his pillow, and his Blue Soldier from the bedside table, and sat up.

Cora, Bram and Elle were still sleeping, and the mirror lay face down on the desk. His nightmare was over. Or was it...?

Tick, tick, tick...

went the grandmother clock.

Tap, tap, tap...

went the windowpane.

Probably a tree branch rapping against the glass. The sensible part of Acton told him not to get up and check. But the noise continued with a desperate persistence.

Finally Acton stood and threw off his blanket. It fell in a lump on the centre of the bed, looking eerily like the shape of him asleep. He pulled on a dressing gown and slippers from his trunk, and drew open the turquoise curtains.

The window glass was misted. He wiped it clean. Outside the snow still lay thick on the ground. A near-full moon hung over the church tower. A slim rind of it was missing, like the peeled edge of an apple. Tomorrow, by winter solstice night, it would be full. Acton's worried reflection floated over it. He blinked away the sudden queasy feeling that his dreams were crashing into reality. Fresh air; that's what he needed!

He tugged at the window hasp. It was stiff with age, but eventually he managed to push it open. Immediately, the red robin from the Fairy Tree darted in.

"You're here, my cormorant," she trilled. "Thank goodness! I've been pecking the glass trying to wake you. I tried to tell you before, but for some reason you couldn't understand me. Anyway, my little chick, what I need to say is you're the Chosen One, and that's why you found the key. You're destined to defeat the Fairy Queen, end her curse, and free Fairyland and your family!"

Acton was shocked to be talking to the robin, and that it knew so much about everything, but he tried not to let it show, in case he scared the little bird away. "I know all that," he said. "But…" he furrowed his brow, "how do you know it? Who are you? And how are we talking?"

"My name is Coriel, little siskin." Coriel flitted about nervously. "We're talking because you're finally listening, and finding that key puts you in grave danger! You must come with me to meet my friend and mistress, the Storm Sorceress Tempest, at once!"

Acton was shocked. Tempest was his great-grandmother's name. He couldn't wrap his mind around how his dreams and the family stories were bleeding together into reality. An eerie chiming started in the corner of the room. With a shiver, he realized it was the grandmother clock.

Bong. Bong. Bong.

Acton's skin prickled as three chimes echoed in quick succession.

"Ignore them, my pintail," Coriel pleaded, landing on his arm.

But he couldn't. Three more chimes reverberated in his head.

Bong. Bong. Bong.

"How's it doing that?" he asked, clutching the Blue Soldier and the key.

"An enchantment, my redstart!" Coriel hopped to his shoulder. "It's bad magic. I feel it in my feathers!"

How can magic be bad? Acton wondered, but three more chimes interrupted his thought.

Bong. Bong. Bong.

Coriel fluffed herself anxiously, as the clock chimed thrice more.

Bong. Bong. Bong.

Acton had counted twelve chimes in total, when a thirteenth rang out, louder than all the others.

BOOOOOOOOONNNNG!

As it faded, he found himself standing before the clock. Glowing light flickered out through its keyhole. "Where's that coming from?" he asked. "It should be dark in there!"

"Don't know, my puffin," Coriel squeaked. "And I don't care to find out. Only a fool would do so!"

"I'm no fool," Acton said. If this was a dream, why not take a quick peek inside the clock? That's what you did in dreams, followed the path fate chose for you. He raised the key and put it in the clock's door. It fitted perfectly. Glowing words appeared on the clock face. He clutched the Blue Soldier anxiously, and turned the key in the lock, as he read the words aloud with a shiver,

"Magic Key, I do implore, open up a Fairy door."

Light flooded into the room, along with a wind so cold it made the hairs on Acton's arms stand on end. He gulped, and took his hand off the key. The words disappeared and the door to the clock swung open with an icy…

creak!

Inside the clock was no swinging pendulum, no ticking

clockwork and no bells to make the chime he'd heard. Instead, a thick web of silver threads made a pulsing doorway that framed a great glass tower, which hummed and crackled with magic.

Acton called out to his brother and sisters to come and see it, but they didn't stir. He gasped as he realized he could not wake them. "What's happening, Coriel?" he asked in a trembling whisper. "How can a tower be inside a clock?"

"Not just any tower, my greylag goose," Coriel trilled, fearfully. "When you turned the key in the lock, it became the doorway to the Fairy Queen's Glass Palace. It is here because of the key. But this is not our path. It is not safe to go into Fairyland that way. So, come now, please," she begged. "Step away from the clock at once, and follow me."

Coriel was right, Acton realized. The last person he wanted to meet was the Fairy Queen. Even if he was the Chosen One, and meant to defeat her, he wasn't ready for that battle yet. He needed more time.

He tried to slam the clock's door and pull away, but strange hooks of yearning reached out tugging queasily at his bones, telling him in no uncertain terms that he *had* to step through. It was not a command expressed in words but in a violent pull which cut so deep that at last Acton realized he was not asleep, and all of this was not a dream.

He gasped at this sudden epiphany. Horror kicked inside

him, as a hedgehog man, tall as he was, and standing on his hind legs, with mottled spines that poked through a patchy grey coat, and a gigantic conker shell rammed on his head like a hat, appeared on the far side of the magical doorway. A black raven with clumpy feathers and a scythe-like beak swooped down to perch on hedgehog man's shoulder.

"It's those rascally villains Hoglet and Auberon! Don't let them see me!" Coriel dived into Acton's pocket.

"CRAAR!" carped Auberon, flicking his black feathers and pecking at Hoglet. "What are you waiting for? He's the Chosen One! SIEZE HIM!"

Hoglet blinked deep brown hedgehog eyes – tiny holes in his pinched face – and snuffled his long, grey nose. He thrust a long, pointed hand through the rippling doorway and yanked at Acton so violently that drops of magic spattered everywhere.

"Get off!" Acton screamed, shielding his eyes and fighting Hoglet tooth and nail.

Coriel fluttered in his pocket in alarm.

"He's a feisty feller!" Auberon croaked, his feathers rippling from black to white. "Are you going to come nicely, Chosen One?" He leaped from Hoglet's shoulder onto Acton's head and raked his razor-sharp claws painfully through the boy's hair. His sharp beak tugged at Acton's forelock making the boy's eyes water.

Acton cried out for help, but none came. Hoglet's spiny fingers pinched and snatched at his arms, trying to pull him through the doorway. It took all the strength he had for him to keep Auberon and Hoglet at bay, and all the time he could feel his will waning, leaching out as if it was being sapped from him with each punch and kick, and each blade of sparkling magic light. Then at last…

Snap!

…his fight was gone. And he was pulled, with Coriel in his pocket, through the magical doorway. He screamed as he tumbled head first…

down,

down,

down

…through the insides of the clock, the outsides of a sky, and into the great beyond.

Acton's limbs tangled. His dressing gown and nightshirt tussled with his body, his hair blew in his face. Hoglet and Auberon toppled after him, tumbling in his wake.

Hoglet's arms windmilled and his spines rattled in the wind. Auberon threw his wings wide, surfing the currents like a kite, his feathers whisking magically from black to white and back again. And far above the three of them, in the clouds, the magical doorway, that was also the door to the clock, slammed shut.

An ice-white light lit the edges of everything. Acton cascaded onwards, drifting beyond the realms of understanding. He thought then of Cora, Bram and Elle left behind in the Blue Room, and he hoped that, wherever he ended up, they'd be able to follow his trail and find him.

7

WOLF AT THE WINDOW

AWHOOOOOOOOOOOOOOOOOOOOO!

A far-off howl echoed in Cora's head. It sounded exactly like the wolf from the graveyard. Perhaps it was still out there? That thought gave her the shivers. She rubbed her eyes and glanced around the room. Her brothers and sister were asleep in their beds. The window was open, letting in starlight and moonbeams, and a cold breeze that gave her goose pimples, and made her teeth chatter.

She threw back her covers and crossed the wooden floor. Outside, the winter moon above the church steeple was nearly full. Beyond the frosted garden wall, a handful of tiny sparks glinted in the graveyard, circling the Fairy Tree. Cora wondered for a moment if they were Fairy sprites, but they were probably just fireflies. Did you get those in winter...? Elle would know.

Snap! Crackle! Crunch!

Cora gasped. The grey wolf from the graveyard was prowling in the garden. Shoulders knit, it slunk between snow-covered bushes and across the white lawn, leaving paw prints in the snow. It stopped in the shadow of the house and stared up at her. The wind ruffled its grey fur while its eyes – one green, one blue – seemed to be asking something. What on earth could it want?

The wolf took a few paces back, and bounded towards the open window. Cora held her breath. There was no way it could possibly vault that far! But as she watched, it jumped and took off into the air, gliding across the sky as if by magic; its legs outstretched in a long leap as if it was floating.

It landed with a thump on the windowsill, inches from her face. Its hot breath making clouds in the air, and its tongue lolling over a set of sharp teeth. Cora shrank back as it shook snow from its shaggy pelt onto the carpet. She ran to the door and rattled its handle.

The wolf hopped down to the floor. The hag stone and tooth strung around its neck sparkled. In the flickering of the oil lamp, its shadow looked like that of a man.

"The door's locked," it said in a deep, serious voice. "Your aunt locked it."

Cora gasped in shock. How was this wolf able to speak? And, more than that…how was it even possible that she could understand every word it had said! She bit her lip anxiously and stared at the beast. "How are you doing that?"

"You have magic in you, Cora," the wolf explained. "That's why you and your brother were drawn to the Fairy Tree, and why we can speak. You're in terrible danger because of the curse. So are Bram, Elle, and Acton, who is already missing because of it."

"You know our names!" Cora shook her head in disbelief. "And about the curse! How?" She checked herself. "It doesn't matter. You're wrong about Acton. He's asleep over there." She pointed to Acton's bed by the door, but as she did so, she realized the wolf was right: Acton wasn't in it. What she'd taken for him earlier, in the dark, was merely a balled-up blanket. She threw that aside and stared at the empty bed. How could he have disappeared from a locked room, and such a high window?

"WHERE IS HE!?" she hollered in disbelief. "WHERE'S MY BROTHER?"

Her distress was loud enough to wake Bram and Elle. They scrambled out of their beds in shock. Cora half-expected Papa and Aunt Eliza to come running too, but they didn't. It was as if the entire Blue Room was in a reality of its own, a distant dream-space beyond the sleeping adults on the far side of the door.

Elle's mouth fell open in shock. "What's a wolf doing in our room?"

"Acton's in danger," the wolf explained. "He's been taken through the clock by the Fairy Queen's minions, because he's the Chosen One, destined to defeat her. Coriel's with him. She'll try to keep him safe from whatever the Queen has planned."

"Who's Coriel?" Cora asked.

"The robin you met," the wolf growled. "She'll protect your brother as best she can. But he will not be able to defeat the Fairy Queen alone, for that he will need your help. The three of you must come with me now to Fairyland, if you are to save him."

Cora felt giddy with excitement. *Fairyland - the place from Mama's stories. She would finally get to see it.* But she also felt a little fearful, given that it was the kingdom of the Fairy Queen, who'd caused all this pain for her family.

"How can we be sure that all you've told us is true?" Bram asked.

"I give no guarantees," the wolf said. "But I can tell you this: I'm always as straightforward as I can be, and say things as they are. A lie for a lie makes the whole world blind. But a truth for a truth means every heart sees clearly. Now take the key from the clock – you will need it for your journey. But be careful! Magic keys have a tendency to bite anyone who's not their true owner. They can be wild in that regard."

Cora thought back to when the key had bitten her earlier. The cut still stung. In the top of the red trunk, she found a polka-dot pocket handkerchief. She bound the key inside it and tied a tight knot, so it couldn't bite anyone else.

"You don't have long to fetch your brother," said the wolf. "Fairyland runs on a different time to the human world. Already we have less than thirteen hours until solstice ends there. If Acton and the rest of you cannot defeat the Queen within that time, we will have failed and all will be lost."

"Why?" Elle asked.

"How?" Bram said.

"If you, or your brother fail," said the wolf, "none of you will ever return."

Cora felt sick.

"Preparation is the watchword," the wolf continued. "If the four of you are to face the Fairy Queen this winter solstice together, then you'll need the help of my sister, the Storm Sorceress. I will take you to her in Fairyland, but first you must get dressed and descend the climber."

Cora stepped to the window and peered down queasily. It was a back-breaking drop if they fell, even with snowdrifts to cushion them. The spindly stems of the wisteria didn't look strong enough to take their weight. "Could we not get to Fairyland through the clock, like Acton?" she asked.

The wolf shook his head. "It would alert the Fairy Queen. We must take another path, and to do that you must climb down. Meet me in the garden as soon as possible." He leaped from the window without a backward glance.

The three of them dressed quickly. Bram in his brown trousers and green jacket. Elle in her sky-blue dress, and midnight-blue cloak. Cora in her purple dress and matching red cloak, which hid the glass rose pinned to her chest. Somehow she was sure she still had to keep it secret from the others, and from the wolf. As they put on their thick woollen socks, she remembered Papa's old advice.

"We should turn one sock inside out," she told her brother and sister. "To confuse the Fairies."

Elle did so at once, but Bram hesitated. Cora expected him to protest, but eventually he followed suit. As they laced up their walking boots, Cora stuffed the key wrapped in the polka-dot handkerchief into the pocket of her red cloak, where it nestled beside her Red Soldier.

The three of them stepped to the window once more, just in time to see the wolf down below, whispering to the old climber. The plant's limbs wavered and stretched, growing longer, thicker and stronger, until they grasped the Blue Room's windowsill.

"H-how did it do that?" Bram stared at the wolf in amazement.

"Magic," Cora said.

"Like Jack's Beanstalk," Elle whispered. She tugged at the branches, checking they were safe. All were fused to the wall, frozen wilfully into the brickwork. "The perfect climbing frame!" Elle clambered onto the nearest branch and down its frosted length, descending the wisteria's trunk. Bram followed and, last of all, came Cora.

It was a scary climb. Cora clung on tight, and steeled herself against her nerves. The snow froze her fingers and the wind shook the branch she was on, but if she got frightened by this she'd be no good for the rest of the journey, or for Acton and the others.

"*Hurry!*" the wolf cried, slinking between the bars of the cemetery gate, into the deep snow blanketing the graveyard beyond.

Cora dropped onto the snowy ground to join Bram and Elle, and with heavy hearts and jangling nerves at what lay ahead, they chased after him between the frosty tombstones.

The three of them arrived breathlessly at the Fairy Tree, where the panting wolf was waiting. As soon as they had caught up with it, the wolf licked the stone and tooth round its neck with a long pink tongue, looked up at the tree and chanted a spell.

"Fairy Tree, tall and grand, open a path to Fairyland."

Cora gasped as a sparkling, silver web grew from the branches of the Fairy Tree and its threads twisted together to become a doorway.

As Cora, Bram, Elle and the wolf approached the doorway, it swung open to reveal, not a moonlit view on the far side, but a scene of a bright day. Yellow scalding sunlight flooded through the silver trees, blinding Cora to the dangers that lay ahead. There was a sparkling blurry space beyond the doorway they'd have to fall through to get to Fairyland, and the more Cora looked at it, the further it seemed.

The doorway's edges shimmered and began to shrink inwards.

"Be quick!" the wolf called. "Jump through before it closes!" and with a long, loud howl, he leaped through the magical gap, sailing through the space between worlds, tumbling into Fairyland, and disappeared from sight.

A sudden attack of bilious nerves took Cora, and she stopped abruptly. She, Bram and Elle stared through the magical gap in nervous silence. If they didn't go soon, then the doorway would close for good. Fear rose in Cora. Her bravery had left her. She felt as if she was steeling herself to jump into a fast-flowing river, and if she didn't go now, she wouldn't be able to catch up with their friend the wolf – the only one who knew how to save her brother.

"What are we waiting for?" Elle asked.

"The guts to leap," Cora mumbled, biting her lip. Then she remembered Mama's saying: *True Courage is to feel fearful, but choose to take a risk anyway.*

"It's now or never," she said, trying to persuade herself of that as much as the others.

"Agreed," Bram and Elle said together. Cora took their hands and they jumped.

Everything around them s t r e t c h e d and *smeared*, like the blurred paint smudges on Mama's palette.

Cora felt her thoughts thin and scatter, fuzzy as dust. Her body twisted and somersaulted, her stomach lurched and her skin shivered, but she held tight to her brother and sister as they toppled into thin air while the moon and stars swirled by, whooshing away like water down a drain…

FAIRYLAND

Acton shivered and rubbed his arms. He was alone in a bright, bare, frosty room. For a second he wondered if he was dead…but his chest was moving.

Flutter-thump.

      Flutter-thump.

            Flutter-thump.

He thought that might be his heartbeat. That was there, yes, vigorous and strong. But this movement was more on the surface, in his dressing-gown pocket. He'd put the Blue Soldier in there. Maybe it had come to life?

Then he realized what it *actually* was: the talking robin! What was her name again? Ariel? No… *Coriel,* that was it!

He was not alone. She was with him. He was flooded with a sudden sense of overwhelming relief. "Where are we, Coriel?"

Coriel poked her beak from his pocket. "The Fairy Queen's Glass Tower, my puffin," she trilled anxiously. "We should never have come this way in to Fairyland. I was supposed to take you to Tempest first!"

Acton rubbed his eyes. Her worry made him feel panicky. "Let's go back to Fairykeep Cottage then, and start again," he suggested. "How do we do that?"

"You can't without the key, my guillemot," Coriel said. "And you left that in the door of the clock!"

Acton shivered. That's exactly what he'd done. They were trapped! He hoped his brother and sisters would find the key, so they could come and fetch him.

A sliver of light opened vertically in the wall. A hidden frosted door swung into the room. The walls were made of glass, Acton realized. That was why the room felt so bright. Behind the door stood Hoglet, with Auberon perched on his shoulder.

"The Fairy Queen's most trusted servants." Coriel ducked back into Acton's dressing-gown pocket. "I mustn't be seen by them; they dislike me more than jelly rot."

"Welcome to Fairyland, Chosen One!" Hoglet boomed, as he stepped into the room. "Hoglet Hoghedge, Earl of

Aphids, Duke of White Saddle at your service! May your spikes be sharp, your claws ever-clean."

"Auberon Raven," Auberon croaked. "High Commander of the Crow Army, Baron of Tawny Grisette. May your bill be piercing, your call grating, your flight swift, your nest well-feathered."

Acton didn't understand their titles or their greetings. "What is this place?" he asked, his stomach twitching with nerves.

"A prison cell in the Glass Tower," Auberon rasped.

"A prison cell?" Acton repeated, shocked.

"No need to parrot the raven!" Hoglet's spines bristled. "The journey here took a lot out of you, so we put you in this comfy glass cell to recover, before you meet the Queen."

Acton felt sick. He didn't want to meet the Queen, not like this. He wished he still had the key so he could get out of here, but Hoglet was already pushing the cell door wide open, so they could both step through. "Right this way," he growled.

"It's not far to the Queen's Glass Throne Room," Auberon cawed, shifting on Hoglet's shoulder.

Acton felt very queasy at the thought of how unprepared he was to meet the Queen, especially now that he was her prisoner. If all he had been told was true, and he really was the one chosen to defeat her, how come he didn't feel ready yet? He had no strength or skill or magic; indeed there was nothing particularly special about him. He was such a small boy with so much lacking, how could he alone fight a powerful Fairy foe? He followed Hoglet and Auberon out of the cell anyway. What other choice did he have?

9

STORM SORCERESS

Cora's heart beat sharp as a snare drum, aching for those she'd lost. She thought queasily of Acton, taken by Fairies, of Mama, gone for good, of Papa, drowning in melancholy, and of Aunt Eliza, nervously keeping fort at Fairykeep Cottage. The glass rose battered against her breastbone, as she floated…

up

     up

          up

…and scrambled to her feet on a new pathway. She'd done it! They'd made it to the far side and to Fairyland in one piece! She pulled Bram and Elle upright beside her, and looked around.

The three of them were on the other side of the enchanted doorway. The wolf stood guard, watching. Its grey fur sparkling with magic. There was no churchyard or church here, just bramble bushes and twisted silver trees covered in heavy snow.

It had been after midnight when they'd left England, but in Fairyland the light suggested it was early afternoon on an overcast winter's day. The switch quite disorientated Cora. She examined the remains of the glowing doorway closing behind them. Already the hole was so small it was barely wider than the iris of a telescope. Peering through it, she could glimpse the church tower coated in snow among the rooftops of Tambling village, and Fairykeep Cottage bathed in moonlight. The iris shrank to nothing, the gap closed, and then, worryingly, it was all gone in an instant, as if it had never been.

Cora, Bram and Elle walked urgently along beside the wolf, hurrying through the snowy woods of Fairyland. The wolf marched fast, with purposeful vigour, his tail hanging down and his grey fur fluttering in the wind.

Cora was still not quite over the shock that they were in the place from Mama's stories. A place where, it seemed,

Acton had become dreadfully entangled with the Fairy Queen. "Where are you taking us?" she asked, touching the glass rose hidden beneath her cloak.

"To my sister's home." The wolf leaped over a frozen patch of pearlwort sticking through the snow. "Here we are. This is it, up ahead...in the Heart of the Forest."

Cora caught sight of what had to be the world's biggest oak tree. Despite the winter snow it was still in leaf, and its canopy towered over everything, like a great green umbrella, filling her with calm. The wolf sniffed around the roots, Bram and Elle caught their breath, and Cora wiped the sweat from her brow as the wolf growled another spell:

"Heart of the Forest, with your wood strong as stone, open the door to my sister's home."

With a loud creak, in a sparkle of gleaming thread, a doorway made of bark appeared in the tree's wide trunk and swung inwards. Cora gasped as, behind it, she saw a wooden spiral staircase descending into the earth inside the tree's hollow interior.

The wolf stepped through the doors and hurried down the stairs. Cora, Bram and Elle followed with trepidation, into a space that smelled musty and autumnal and felt as though it was both indoors and out at the same time.

As they descended the spiral staircase inside the tree, Cora's pulse quickened with excitement and her entire body shivered with nerves. She wondered what new stories and challenges they might find when they reached the bottom.

They hurried down the last few steps into a cosy underground home. There was no daylight this deep underground, instead the space was lit by lanterns made of folded leaves that glowed with a magic green light. Each lantern was fixed to a wooden tree-root column. The room was full of them. They held up an arched ceiling criss-crossed with interwoven rootlets that acted like roof beams. Little burrow-alcoves led off from the main room. In one was a bed, table and chair, in another an armchair and a shelf full of spell books and colourful potion jars.

"Welcome!" An old woman who hadn't been there a moment before was suddenly sitting in the chair beside the bookshelf. "You've finally made it!" Her voice was soft and melodious as summer rain. Her unkempt white hair tumbled, like a stream over rocks, and tangled on the shoulders of a cloak sewn from delicate leaves. Her nose was as sharp as the craggiest rock in the river. Her brow furrowed in deep thought, and her eyes, one green and one blue, like the wolf's, and bright as broken stone, took them in.

"I wish I could've come to fetch you, but I've grown frail with age. It's been many years since I left the safety of this home. My legs aren't what they were, and my magic is weaker than it once was. But my brother and Coriel came for you instead." She patted the wolf's head. "Where is Coriel?" she asked.

"With the Chosen One, Acton, their brother," the wolf said.

"Where's he?" the old woman asked.

"In the Fairy Queen's Glass Tower."

"Oh dear!" The woman shook her head. "Already she's one step ahead."

"Excuse me…" Cora felt a little confused by the old woman's appearance. "Are you really the wolf's sister? You both look so unalike… I mean to say, you're different species!"

"I am his sister, and his twin." The old woman stroked the wolf's ears. "He used his magic long ago to become a wolf full-time. His True Name is Thomas, and he is your great-grand-uncle. And I am your great-grandma. Some call me the Storm Sorceress, but my True Name is Tempest."

Cora felt light-headed. These two were her relatives! And the two heroes she'd heard so many amazing tales of in Mama's fairy stories. Up until tonight, she'd been absolutely sure that such magical, larger-than-life beings couldn't ever have actually existed, and yet, here they were, stood before her, as real as real could be!

Her heartbeat skipped giddily in her chest. She glanced at her brother and sister to confirm it was true. Bram and

Elle were gaping at the Storm Sorceress in amazement. Bram's mouth fell open. Elle's eyes went wide.

"But," Cora gabbled, wildly, "if you truly are *that* Tempest and Thomas, then you both must be at least a hundred years old!"

"A hundred and thirteen," Tempest replied, with a laugh.

Cora finally saw how much she resembled Mama's description of her. She wondered if Tempest and Thomas had been watching over the four of them secretly their whole lives. She wondered too if they knew that the curse their mother had placed over them three generations ago was so strong it was still affecting the whole of their family.

"Mama used to tell us stories about you both…" Cora said. She wasn't sure how to put this delicately. "That you were cursed by your mother, the Fairy Queen, and that because the crux of that curse never came to fruition, the bad luck from it passed down our family tree. But I never really thought any of that was true, until tonight." She shook her head in disbelief.

Tempest looked serious. "As Fairies, Thomas and I have lived a long time. Much longer than you humans do. So we never fulfilled the terms of the Fairy Queen's curse. In the last few decades I've begun to realize what terrible consequences that has had for our family. Especially your mother, who left your world too young. I'm sorry you lost her." She hugged Cora, Bram and Elle. "I used to care for your mother, when she was a child and her parents went away. She was bright, inquisitive, and overflowing with art and beautiful stories." She sighed. "I miss that little granddaughter Maria, so full of life, as much as I miss the rest of my family, my husband, Otto, my son, Bob, his wife, Anna, who've all passed on. I hope they all know the blessings of the woods, rivers, trees, mountains, streams, oceans and untamed world are with them, and I hope too that they always remember their True Names."

Cora didn't understand the entirety of what Tempest had said, but it was a wonderfully thoughtful message, spoken with care. She wanted to enquire more about Tempest's memories of Mama, but she didn't feel quite ready to hear those yet. Besides, she needed to ask about Acton. They had to stop the Fairy Queen from harming him.

"You wanted to ask about your brother," Tempest said, almost as if she had read Cora's mind. "Imprisoned in the Glass Tower – it is an unforeseen turn of events, I must admit. I had hoped that Coriel and Thomas would bring Acton here, and that I would have time to teach him all he needs to know to defeat the Fairy Queen. But things have not gone according to that plan, and now it seems that it is the three of you who must rescue *him*. We can still help, by teaching you the skills you'll need to get your brother back."

"How?" Bram asked. "We're only children, what weapons do we have to fight someone as powerful as the Queen?"

"And what strength?" Elle added.

"The magic inside you," Thomas said. "Fairy magic that has always been there, in each of your hearts, but that you have never learned to harness. We'll teach you to use it to create incredible spells."

Cora's heart soared at the idea that she might learn how to do spells. Despite the dangers they and Acton faced, she couldn't wait to uncover more about the secrets of Fairy magic that her newly-discovered relatives Tempest and Thomas possessed.

10

THE GLASS TOWER

"Stop dawdling, Chosen One!" Auberon hopped from Hoglet's shoulder onto Acton's, and dug his claws hard into Acton's collarbone, making him wince. Coriel fidgeted secretly in Acton's pocket, trying to keep out of sight of the raven.

"This way, Chosen One!" Hoglet called, guiding everyone through the freezing, sparkling corridors of the Glass Tower. "It's not far."

The cold seeped up through the floor and into Acton's slippers making him shiver with each step. His breath made grey smoky clouds in the air and his footsteps echoed loudly on the icy floor. The deeper they got into the palace the more splinters of anxiety broke apart inside him.

He wanted to end the curse, for all the sadness and trouble it had caused his family, but he didn't want to risk his life doing it. Perhaps he would claim that he wasn't the Chosen One when he met the Fairy Queen, and tell her that he wished her no harm personally, even if he didn't quite mean it... Papa always said, never tell a lie, if you can tell the truth. But Acton thought a lie would be safer in this case. If the Fairy Queen believed him then, hopefully, she would realize what a terrible mistake she'd made, let him go, and finally end the curse. She might even return him to the Blue Room and to Papa and Aunt Eliza, so they could try and make a home of Fairykeep Cottage.

"CRAAW!" Auberon cried. "Get a move on!" He took off from Acton's shoulder and swooped down the long corridor they were walking through. It was then that Acton noticed that the sides of the room were filled with statues. Glass figures with their mouths open, crying in pain. Each one was so lifelike that Acton had the eerie feeling they had once been living Fairies.

"Who are they?" Acton whispered to Coriel.

The little bird poked her head secretly out of his dressing gown to take a look. "Frozen Fairy servants," she twittered, nervously. "Turned to glass by the Queen. She does that to those she dislikes."

"Who are you talking to?" Hoglet snapped.

"No one…" Acton gulped. "Myself!"

"Liar!" Hoglet reached into Acton's pocket and pulled out the robin in his fist. "Coriel," he snorted. "What are *you* doing here?"

"Let go of me, you hogwarted grunt-weasel!" Coriel squeaked.

"Spying, I bet," Auberon chipped in, landing on a screaming glass statue.

"I was doing nothing of the kind, you feathered floor mop!" Coriel tweeted.

"Squeeze the truth out of her, Hoglet," Auberon snarled. "Crush her until her face is as red as her belly."

"If you harm me in any way," Coriel warned, "the Chosen One will visit the same fate on you tenfold, with a mere click of his fingers."

"As if *this* pathetic Chosen One has that power," Hoglet growled.

"Could you all please stop calling me the Chosen One!" Acton begged. "My name's Acton Belle and yes, you're right, I'm not that special. But please don't hurt Coriel, she's not a spy and she doesn't deserve it." He sniffled and wiped a hand across his face. He was sorry to admit to these three creatures that there was nothing unique about him, but in his heart he knew it to be true. Plus, he reasoned, the smaller

95

and more innocuous he could make himself, the less of a threat he would seem to the Fairy Queen. It was certainly better than fighting her, which he felt sure now, after seeing so much of her Grand Palace, and the many foes she'd turned to glass, that he didn't have the strength to do. They had reached a bright wall at the end of a long corridor. Hoglet stopped and spoke a spell.

"Glassy magic, cold and clear, make the crystal steps appear."

Acton watched in amazement as a flight of stairs made from great round slabs of glass dropped down from the ceiling. Each slab floated in the air to make an ascending row that bobbed one above another. Hoglet pulled Acton onto the first step. Auberon flapped his wings and swooped behind them as they climbed towards a hole growing in the ceiling. They stepped through it and arrived at a set of Glass Doors, etched with strange runes made of winding thorns and ivy fronds.

"This is the entrance to the Glass Throne Room," Hoglet said.

"Don't think about running, Chosen One," Auberon warned, landing on Acton's head, and raking a claw painfully across his scalp.

Acton wasn't intending to run. He had no idea where to go, or how to get home. He feared the Fairy Queen's power;

what she might do when he tried to persuade her to let him go and, most of all, he feared for his own life. He waited anxiously while Hoglet, clasping a nervous Coriel in his hand, pushed open the doors.

The Glass Throne Room blazed with magical light. It flickered and danced over everything, like watery reflections on a sunny day. Hoglet scuttled across the polished floor of erupting stalagmites, clutching Coriel in his clenched fist. Auberon took off from Acton's head and glided about the ceiling that was spiked with stalactites.

Acton stared in shock at the Fairy crowds, noticing their inhuman faces, their tree-bark skin, their deer-snout noses, their ram's-horn ears, their bird-feather hair, their foxy smiles, their dirty muzzles, their sniffing snouts, their wide-smirking jaws, their twiggy claws, their mud-spattered hooves and their stamping cloven feet. Every one of them wore a powdered wig and rich, embroidered fabric robes that were patchworked with leaves, slug slime and sparkling cobwebs. And each of them stared unflinchingly at Acton, with yellow catlike eyes filled with malice.

Acton's heart smashed against his ribs as he glared in turn at their cold predatory faces, trying to work out, but at the same time not really wanting to know, which one of these impossible-looking creatures was the Fairy Queen. He wondered, fearfully, what terrible plans she had for him.

11

ROOT MAP

"I want to show you something that'll help with your onward journey," Tempest told Cora, Bram and Elle, as they stood with her and Thomas in her underground burrow home, beneath the Heart of the Forest. "It's here." She pointed at a patch of bare earth wall.

"But that's empty!" Bram protested.

"There's nothing's there!" Elle said.

"There soon will be," Tempest told them, and as Cora and the others watched in amazement, the elderly Storm Sorceress pressed her hands to the wall and spoke a spell.

"Hidden Map beneath my hands, show me far and distant lands."

Colourful roots, textured branches and tiny flowers of every hue wove themselves together into a complex tapestry picture beneath Tempest's fingers. Cora gasped as they spread and grew to become a gigantic map that filled the wall. The map split into five horizontal strips. Beside each strip a leaf grew, with words etched on it that stated what each particular section showed.

"I created this Root Map long ago," Tempest explained. "So I could keep track of my mother's activities. She rules here." She pointed to a snowy white strip on the map, full of dark skies, sparkling silver stars, winged creatures and a frost-covered forest that stretched on for ever. The strip obviously represented Fairyland. "But she is also the empress of these smaller kingdoms." Tempest indicated two other portions of the map. "The Dream Lands and Noman's Land." At the centre of the Dream Lands was a gigantic tree, labelled the Dreaming Tree. It was so tall its branches reached the heavens, where its flowers and leaves tangled with the clouds and its fruit were moons and planets. Beside the tree was Noman's Land – a barren wasteland dotted with a few clumps of thin forest.

"She only needs one more thing to rule your human world along with all the others she already possesses." Tempest pointed to another kingdom at the top of the map, with a house that looked like Fairykeep Cottage, stood beside the Tambling River. This strip of the map seemed to represent England. "That one thing is the Glimmerglass Crown. It has five magic mirror shards on it that give the wearer complete control over each of the five magic kingdoms. But that crown it is all the way down here, in the fifth and final kingdom…" Tempest pointed to the bottom of the map where the Dead Lands lay, in a long strip beneath everything.

Cora, Bram and Elle leaned forward and peered closely at the bleak and barren landscape beneath her fingers. A black and blue land that looked as ugly as a bruise. A Dead River wound through it. Crossing over that via a Bone Bridge were lines of tearful Lost Souls, wending their way onward to whatever comes next after death. Sitting on a Bone Throne, overseeing them all from a tall, dark tower, was the Dead King, resplendent in ermine robes and a glittering, five-pointed, mirrored crown. His face an angry, dark blur.

"If the Fairy Queen can get that five-pronged crown from the Dead King, then she will be able to use its magic to rule the five kingdoms, including the Dead Lands, and that means she will control not only life, but also death, for everyone for evermore." Tempest shook her head, trying to banish that terrible thought. "With such great power, no one will ever be able to challenge her again."

"To achieve that," Thomas said, "she will have to persuade your brother, by threat, promise, or reward to go and fetch her the crown. It's a risk for her to send him down to the Dead Lands unsupervised, as he will need the crown's powers if he is to defeat her, but it's a chance she'll be willing to take, as she needs the crown's powers too, if she wants to rule for evermore."

"If your brother does manage to return from the Dead Lands with the Dead King's formidable crown," Tempest said, "the Fairy Queen will try to trick him into voluntarily giving it to her. Then," she added, gravely, "she will use it to kill him – and the rest of us."

"But if he does not return," Thomas continued, "it will be no great loss to her. She will have dispensed with the Chosen One, the curse will continue and so will her rule over everyone in the three kingdoms she already possesses."

Cora shivered. It seemed there were multiple ways the Fairy Queen could win against them, but only one slim chance that they could win against her. A slim chance that would involve not only Acton's bravery and cunning in fetching the crown, but their own in facing the Queen.

"Whatever happens," said Thomas, "the fate of all – your brother, you, and us – and the residents of these five lands, will be decided by tonight, sometime on or before the thirteenth stroke of midnight."

Cora gasped in horror to think such terrible things could come to pass before the night was out.

"But the three of you can help stop all of this," Tempest said. "To face the Queen in her Glass Tower and save your brother, you must travel all the way across the map. We are here." She indicated the map's nearest corner. "And you need to get all the way over –" she ran her finger across the endless, pathless, featureless, frozen forest that covered Fairyland, to a clearing in the very furthest corner of the map, where, beneath the jagged Magic Mountain range topped with snow, the towering sharply spiked edifice of the Glass Tower stood – "here."

Cora's heart sank, for the distance looked like a hundred thousand miles. A sickening feeling rose in her throat when she realized the impossibility of the task that lay ahead for them. "How can we possibly make it in time?"

"Put your trust in us," Thomas advised. "And I will take you onwards, to a great Wolfmoot, where help may be at hand."

"What's a Wolfmoot?" Bram asked, intrigued.

"And what help can they offer?" Elle said.

"A Wolfmoot is a gathering of every wolf in Fairyland," Thomas explained. "It's a tradition handed down by the pack that they meet once a year, on the winter solstice, beneath another sacred, magic tree, called the Tree of Life, to celebrate their Wolfishness, and discuss wolf-business. The Seven League Wolves are there this night, so named because they can leap seven leagues in a single bound. We must try to persuade them to help us by carrying you to the Dreaming Tree at the centre of Fairyland."

"There you will find a magical branch that will take you down to the Fairy Queen's Glass Tower in time to save Acton," Tempest said. "You are young and strong, and the Fairy magic we intend to teach you will help you on your journey. With that, and all the skills you have, I really do believe that the four of you have every chance of making it to the Glass Tower, and defeating the Fairy Queen."

"You keep saying 'you'," Cora said. "Aren't you coming with us?"

"I cannot." Tempest shook her head. "It has been years since I left the sanctuary of this home beneath the Heart of the Forest, and I no longer have the strength to make such a perilous journey. Thomas will accompany you as far as the Wolfmoot but after that he will return to my side. He's my only protection from the Fairy Queen if she attacks me now. Her power is strongest on the solstice. She is bound to try to assail me this night. But we will be safe among the tree roots. The three of you, and your brother, carry the hope of all of us, until such time as Fairyland is free. Will you undertake this quest?"

Cora glanced at Bram and Elle, who nodded nervously.

She didn't feel nearly as sure. This wasn't a fairy tale any more. It was a dangerous mission, and if they didn't complete it, Acton was doomed. She gulped that worry away. It was only in the hours since he'd been taken that she'd started to realize how much she missed her little brother: the way he'd listen agog to her stories. The way he daydreamed through life. The way he took in every detail of his surroundings, which meant he stumbled on interesting things, like the key. He loved his family with a purity of heart and a joy so strong it was like standing beneath the streaming cascade of a sparkling waterfall.

"All right," she said. "We'll do it." Though she didn't feel nearly as sure as those words suggested. She took one last look at the map, trying to get their route straight in her head. "We're ready to learn that magic you spoke of now," she told Tempest and Thomas, her voice full of steely determination. After all, they'd need all the help they could muster, if they were to succeed in getting their brother back. "Teach us everything you know."

12

THE QUEEN'S BARGAIN

"So, the boy has finally arrived!" thundered a voice that sounded as sharp as breaking glass. The Fairy Queen rose from her spiked throne on the far side of the long Glass Throne Room and studied Acton from her platform of decaying branches and glass roses above the Fairy rabble.

Acton bit his lip, and stared defiantly back at her. His great-great-grandma.

The Fairy Queen had a knife-sharp nose and pointed ears. Her brittle features were framed by long, straight silver hair. Her cape was sewn from wild flowers and leaves, and her green gauze dress ruffled softly as she laughed.

Her body was surrounded by a halo of white light that pulsed like a flickering lantern. Antlers, twigs, thorns, briars and flapping birds' wings sprouted from her head. She wore a necklace threaded with a single gold oak leaf. Her cloudy black eyes sparkled like distant galaxies, and her gaze felt so powerful, it seemed to Acton as if it was boring into his soul.

She spoke again. "Am I to believe that this cowed and pale youngster, this feeble eleven-year-old quaking in his slippers, shaking in his threadbare nightshirt, shivering fearfully beneath an old dressing gown, this pathetic specimen of humankind – my great-great-grandson, who is up well past his bedtime – is the fabled Chosen One sent to defeat me?" She laughed hysterically. "I think not!"

Hoglet and Auberon and the rest of the Fairy Court joined in her jagged amusement with hearty guffaws. A sudden surge of shame shot through Acton. Their derisive laughter was so cracked and jeering it crashed over him like a wave, and made him feel like he was drowning.

The Fairy Queen raised her hands theatrically to wipe away make-believe tears of laughter. Had there been any real tears they would have frozen to her face. "Look," she said to her hordes, "his minuscule squire Coriel is here in her red coat of arms! How appropriate that he keeps such dreadful company!"

The Fairy Courtiers clucked and tittered, but the Queen got suddenly serious. "Traitorous little bird, you are a most unwelcome guest in my court. It has been many years since we last had contact, since you last darkened my door."

"Too few in my opinion, you rotten harridan," Coriel squeaked from Hoglet's clenched fist.

"How dare you!" the Fairy Queen spat. "Get that treacherous quisling out of my sight, Hoglet. I never want to see her again."

"Yes, Fair Majesty." Hoglet walked to the window and opened his fist.

"Leave now, Coriel, and if you ever dare return," the Fairy Queen warned, "I will turn you to glass."

"You heard Her Royal Frostiness," Hoglet hissed. But Coriel wasn't listening. Instead, she stayed resting on his palm, looking back worriedly at Acton. The little hedgehog man tried to shake the robin from his hand, into the sky. "Begone!" he shouted. "Get out of here."

But Coriel would not leave. Not yet.

She fluttered away from Hoglet and swooped around Acton. "I have to go now, my grebe, for my own safety," she trilled. "Be careful of the Queen. She'll try to trick you into making some sort of bargain. It's what she does. Don't trust her!"

Coriel flapped out the window, and was gone. Acton's

heart sank to have lost his only friend. Still he felt determined to carry on with his plan. Misleading the Queen seemed to him to be his only way out. "Your Majesty, there's been a mistake. I am not the Chosen One," he lied.

"He's the one your magic led us to, Majesty," Auberon carked.

"Maybe her magic was wrong?" purred a suave Courtier with goat horns and cow's ears.

"I beg your pardon!" the Queen snapped icily, turning on him. "What did you say?"

"N-nothing, Fair Majesty," the goat-faced Courtier mumbled. But it was too late; his fate had been sealed. The other Fairies could sense it. They inched away from him until he stood alone.

"How dare you contradict me, Gruntle!" The Queen pointed a pale finger at him, and spoke a spell.

"Magic power, broke and bent, turn Gruntle to an ornament."

The tufted hair growing between the horns on Gruntle's head suddenly stood on end. His skin flickered with crackles of blue energy, as if he had been zapped by lightning. He tried to run, but his feet had already become glass. As he raised one hoofed leg it froze in place, its surface awash with frozen crystals. His body and arms became glass too. The last thing to change was his head.

Finally, Gruntle was frozen in place in a pose of shock, his mouth open in a silent scream, just like the statues Acton had seen earlier.

The Fairy Court chittered nervously. Some of the Courtiers even gave a half-hearted clap, as if the Queen had been putting on a show for everyone.

Or maybe the show was for him, Acton reflected, anxiously. A show of strength. Poor Gruntle! Acton took a nervous step backwards, trying to shuffle away from the Queen and her minions, but she caught him in her gaze once more.

"As you can see, boy," said the Queen, "I am not to be trifled with. Now, let's agree that you *are* the Chosen One, and that you will serve me in a mission. I've had this in mind for you for a long time."

"W-what is it?" Acton's heart jumped to his throat. He was about to refuse outright, when his gaze caught on the brittle Glass Statue.

The Fairy Queen's smile cracked her face like porcelain as she saw him staring at Gruntle. "It's a small thing really," she said, curling her fingers into a fist and floating towards him. "A trifle of a task. I want you to go down to the Dead Lands and steal me the Glimmerglass Crown from the Dead King. I've offered him many gifts in the past in exchange for it, but each time he's refused." Her eyes blazed angrily.

"You, boy, will enter his kingdom and his palace, by cunning or by force, and take the crown.

"Bring that crown back to me, and I promise I will set you free."

As she spoke those last words, her eyes became hypnotic golden pools, sucking Acton in. Draining him of all of his willpower. Dread pierced Acton's belly. His heart beat in his mouth. He tried to formulate some thoughts about the Queen's deal but his head was a muggy mess… He shut his eyes for a second, and pinched himself hard, concentrating on that one point, letting it pull him back to clarity… Surely the Dead King knew everyone who entered his palace? How could he, Acton, a boy with little cunning, and no strength or skills to speak of, possibly enter his realm unseen? The whole idea sounded horribly dangerous. "No," he spat, shaking off the Queen's malignant influence. "I will do no such thing."

The Fairy Queen's face flushed red for a second, but it quickly turned pale again. "Before you settle on that answer," she warned, "you should know that it has consequences, not just for yourself…but for others…your brother and sisters, for example. Would you want them to end up dead along with you, or perhaps frozen for ever in a silent scream, like this one?" She nodded at Gruntle's brittle statue.

Acton shivered, but it didn't make him change his mind. "You don't know anything about my brother and sisters," he whispered.

"Oh, but I do. I know *everything* about them." The Fairy Queen turned to Hoglet and Auberon. "Clear the room. Acton and I need a moment alone."

"You heard Her Exalted Majesty, everyone out!" Hoglet waved his arms at the Fairy Court, flicking his hands like a zealous guard, one with an angry, flapping raven on his shoulders.

The rest of the Courtiers bowed and scraped and stepped away, disappearing through the rippling glass walls, until, along with Acton, only Hoglet and Auberon remained.

"Wait in the corner," the Queen told the unctuous pair, "until I have need of you." They slunk off at once. The Fairy Queen put one clawed hand on Acton's shoulder, raised the other and spoke a spell.

"**Glassy magic, cold and clear, make my crystal ball appear.**"

The floor rippled, like a wave in a pond. Acton shivered as a transparent sphere rose from it, bobbing light as a soap bubble and floating in the air between them.

"I can see anyone and anything in my three realms, and even abroad of those lands, through this," the Queen explained. "All that's required is that one of my glass roses is near, and those grow almost everywhere in Fairyland. Knowing that I could be watching them at any time is what keeps my subjects loyal, and in check. Now look!"

She cupped her hands around the great glass ball and held it up to Acton's face, and he found he could not disobey. As he stared, tiny storm clouds erupted inside the bubbling, bobbing crystal ball, swirling together in wispy clumps, in time with the Queen's spell...

"Enchanted glass, crystal ball. Show me one, and show me all."

Vague images solidified to form a distorted, rippling picture. Acton peered closer.

It was Cora, Bram and Elle, in a homely underground space that looked like a human rabbit warren. A space filled with shelves of spell books and colourful potion jars, which could only mean one thing: they were somewhere in Fairyland too. The three of them were talking to someone, and something stood before them.

"CORA! BRAM! ELLE!" he cried out. He wanted to shout louder, warn them they were being spied on, but his voice was hoarse, and the words dried in his throat.

"They cannot hear you," the Fairy Queen explained. "I have not set the spell to transmit our voices to them, only to listen in on what they say."

The picture crept closer, until Acton could see who his

112

siblings were speaking with: an old lady, and a wolf just like the one he'd glimpsed in the graveyard.

"Your brother and sisters have found my son and daughter, I see," said the Queen,

Acton stared in shock at the old lady and the wolf. Of course! Great-grand-uncle Thomas was the wolf! The old woman was Tempest, the Storm Sorceress and Acton's great-grandma! He had heard so much about them in Mama's stories, but he never thought he'd get to see them, even if it just was in a magical moving image. The sight of their smiling faces was like a ray of sunshine in the darkness.

"I can't believe they're living in the roots of the Heart of the Forest, of all places! How grubby!" The Fairy Queen tutted. "I'd wondered where they'd been hiding to avoid my curse all this time. And here they are, right under my nose, in my own Fairy kingdom! It's remarkable that my spyglass roses never alerted me to their presence before. They must've hidden themselves with glamours and tricks! But now, thanks to the enchanted glass rose your sister picked, I finally have them in my sights. Your siblings too."

What glass rose? Acton felt momentarily confused. Then he caught a glimpse of it pinned to Cora's chest. That was what she'd been hiding at Fairykeep! He wished he could warn her and the others how dangerous the glass rose was, but it was no use. She couldn't see or hear him.

"Soon," the Queen continued, "those three fragile Glass-Belles will have to leave the safety of my children's protection. And when they do, I will turn them to statues, and smash them to smithereens." She took her hand away from the crystal ball and as it popped like a soap bubble, the picture of Cora, Bram, Elle, Tempest and Thomas disappeared.

Acton stared nauseously at the blank space where they'd been. It felt almost as if the Queen had carried out her threat already. "Only *you* can save them from that terrible fate, Acton."

"How?" he asked, in shock.

"Change your mind and take on my mission. Bring me the Glimmerglass Crown from the head of the Dead King. Do that one deed, and your brother and sisters will be free to leave my land and return home, as will you."

Acton felt sick. How could he possibly refuse the Fairy Queen this time, when his siblings' lives were at stake? "How will I know this crown when I see it?" he asked.

"Easy," said the Queen. "It has five enchanted mirror shards on it, one from each of the five magic kingdoms that the wearer of the crown can rule. They sparkle with the power of all eternity. Now," she asked, smiling again graciously, "do we have a deal?"

13

MAGIC LESSONS

"Witches have wands, wizards have staffs, but sorcerers have Talismans," Tempest told Cora, Bram and Elle, as they stood before her in her underground burrow home, hidden beneath the tree roots of Fairyland, in the Greenwood Forest, beside the Tambling River. "Each of you will need a Talisman, if you are to do magic."

"But what are they?" Elle asked.

"Magic tokens that focus your power; like a magnifying glass focuses sunrays," Tempest explained.

"Each must be an object you already own," Thomas added in a growl, scratching his ear with a hind leg, "invested with your heart: a precious thing you always carry."

"So, are those your Talismans?" Cora asked, pointing at the carved boat and bone cloud around Tempest's neck, and the hag stone and the wolf's tooth around Thomas's.

Thomas nodded. "Have you anything similar?"

Cora secretly touched the glass rose. Could that be her Talisman? It felt cold and new, and now didn't seem like the right time to speak of it.

"Our soldiers!" Elle pulled the Green Soldier from her pocket.

"We each have one." Bram took out the Yellow Soldier. Cora then took out the Red Soldier.

Thomas jumped up and shook his mane excitedly. "My pa and da, Marino and Prosper, made those for me when I was a boy." Cora felt a glimmer of hope. That meant Acton had a magical Talisman too: the Blue Soldier...but would he realize that? If they could get to him in time they could let him know.

"I'll strengthen each of your soldier's powers," Tempest said. "Hold them tight, and shut your eyes." Bram and Elle did as they were told, but Cora kept her eyes open a smidge to witness the magic. Tempest's bone cloud and boat Talismans glowed with power, as she stepped round the circle brushing the children's hands in turn.

"Fairy sorcery, magic grand, make these soldiers into Talismans."

"My soldier's humming!" Elle cried.

"So's mine!" Bram cheered.

Tempest touched Cora's hand to complete the spell, and Cora felt her soldier vibrate with power. She peered through her half-closed eyes to see Bram and Elle were hopping with excitement. Thomas lay on the floor, his ears slicked back and his tongue lolling, panting in amusement.

"I cannot send you off without any training," Tempest said. "But we've barely time to practise, so I've picked one spell for each of you from my sense of where your skills lie. Cora's is healing. Bram's is weather. Elle's is a Growing Spell."

"I thought I'd get a Fighting Spell," Bram complained.

"Weather can fight," Thomas said. "It's the strongest thing there is."

"You first, Cora," said Tempest. "Here are the words you must speak to heal a hurt: 'Fix, repair, heal, restore. Be hale and well, just like before.' Practise on the cut on your finger."

Cora touched the place where the Magic Key had bitten her when she and Acton had first found it. She clutched her Talisman tight and felt the tingling hum of it, as if the Red Soldier was fizzing and rumbling in her fist.

"Connect to your Talisman with feelings," Tempest said. "Let the magic stream through you like river water.

The spell is the groove guiding its path. The more you let go and swim with the current, the easier it is for your power to navigate into this world. You can help it by directing your energy outwards as you speak."

Cora tried to imagine the magic flowing, but, as soon as she did, she felt its power start to drain away. Quickly, she said the spell, but the energy fizzled like a wet match, and she failed in her casting. She felt ragged with disappointment. "What am I doing wrong?"

"Too many worrying thoughts," Thomas growled. "Too much distraction. Just breathe, feel what you are feeling, and trust that the magic will come from here." He touched his chest with his snout. "Let your thoughts fall away, and be present with the deep knowing that every creature possesses in their heart. The one knowing that makes the sun rise and set, the moon wax and wane, that makes the desert dry and the ocean wet, the spider weave and the seed grow, the rain fall and the mower mow; then all you need to do is let go, and let the magic flow."

"But how?" Cora grumbled in despair. She still didn't understand.

"Visualize a strong memory associated with your Talisman," Tempest suggested. "Allow that energy to wash over you. Let the flavour of that moment flood your senses. Do not try to grasp those feelings, let them come and stay and let them leave, then listen to the whispers of your heart and believe!"

Cora clasped the Red Soldier in her palm and remembered the day it had been given to her: kissing Papa's stubbly cheek, the hug she'd given Mama, who'd smelled of oil paint and perfume. Papa and the four of them had weathered such storms since then, and now Acton was missing. Cora knew if she was writing this story, she, Bram and Elle would do everything in their power to save their brother. She also knew that, though this might not be a story they were writing with words, they were writing it with their actions, and those actions had to be decisive, hopeful and true.

To her surprise, the tingling hum reappeared in the little figure. The magic of it travelled up her arm into her shoulder and filled her chest with heat and light, buzzing through her whole body as she spoke.

"Fix, repair…"

She panicked. She couldn't remember the rest of the words. Tempest reminded her. "…heal, restore."

That was it! Cora spoke the whole spell:

"Fix, repair, heal, restore. Be hale and well, just like before."

The leaves on the floor whirled around her. She felt the spell depart her fingertips and leap across the cut on her finger.

She watched in amazement as the cut healed. A moment later it was gone, as if it had never been there. Cora rubbed her finger and blinked in shock. She had done it! She had done magic! It was like Thomas and Tempest had said: all she had to do was trust her heart and believe!

"The spell will work for bigger healings too," Thomas growled.

"Time to learn your spells," Tempest said to Bram and Elle.

Cora felt suddenly weary. She sat down in one of Tempest's armchairs, made of woven branches and leaves, and watched as Tempest took Bram to one side of the underground room, and Thomas took Elle to the other.

Thomas's voice rumbled beside Elle, giving a long explanation of the Growing Spell they were about to try. While, on the other side of the room, Tempest put a hand on Bram's back and whispered quiet instructions to him. Bram clutched his Yellow Soldier in one hand and waved the other, casting the Weather Spell.

"Fog haze. Gloom slather. Murk come. Mist gather."

A thin fog floated up from the earth floor, but it melted away as soon as it reached Bram's ankles.

"Try again," Tempest said, encouragingly. And he did.

This time, Cora was amazed to see the fog fill the whole cavernous underground space. Making everything, from the tips of Bram's fingers to the far end of the room, where the root map and the spiral staircase stood, into a hazy unknowable blur.

After a while, Tempest whispered something else in Bram's ear. From the little Cora could hear, it sounded like another spell. Bram nodded and shouted the fresh words out loud:

"Smog and haze dissipate. Gloom go. Mist abate."

The air cleared immediately, and it was as if the gloom that had surrounded them all had never been.

Cora glanced in the other direction to find Elle had started her training with Thomas. Elle was kneeling and had a hand placed on the ground while she muttered a spell full of tearing words:

"Spike barb, bristle, rip, torn. Forest, make a ring of thorns."

She was growing a thorn bush! Branches sprouted up from the cracked earth floor, and wove together to make a spiked ring of barbed thorns around Thomas and Elle.

Typical Elle to get her spell right first time. Nature was her forte.

"You can use this ring of thorns to shield yourself from an enemy's attack," Thomas explained. "If you need to step through them you must say a second spell." And he chanted…

"Bushes made of spikes and stalks. Create a path that we might walk."

Cora watched in amazement as the thorn bushes turned their barbs away at Thomas's command, and opened up to make a safe path for him and Elle to step through.

Since she'd been sitting, Cora was beginning to feel a little better. She'd almost recovered her energy by the time Bram and Elle joined her, looking exhausted.

"Why did I feel so tired after I cast my spell?" Cora asked, through deep breaths, as the wilting Bram and Elle sat down in two chairs of twisted roots beside her.

"The bigger the spell the more energy it uses," Tempest explained. "With practice the three of you can channel that power from the natural world. But as a beginner, and in places where nature is scarce, the energy will be siphoned off from inside yourselves: that's why you feel so empty."

"And why you must be careful using magic." Thomas swept his tail to include everyone in the warning. "It drains you, and if you cast too many spells it can make you unwell." He paused. He was obviously not used to speaking so candidly on the subject, and it seemed as if he didn't know how to say what came next.

Tempest said it for him. "You must beware. If you cast a big or wild enough spell it can use so much power, that it can put you to sleep for ever." Cora shivered. "There's one way to guard against that," Tempest said. "One of your companions must say the Waking Spell to wake you up again."

Bram and Elle leaned forward in their seats, eager to learn more magic.

"There isn't time to practise now," Tempest warned. "But I suggest you commit it to memory, just in case one of you needs it to rouse a brother, or a sister. You must place your hands around the sleeper's head like this." She placed a hand on each side of her own temples and spoke the spell:

"All dreams and nightmares now abate! Rise and shine, come, sleeper, wake!"

Cora tried to commit the Waking Spell to memory, but the entire lesson – doing the magic, and thinking about it – had made her feel so tired, she could barely take this new spell in.

"There's one more thing I must give you." Tempest waved her hand and a pocket watch appeared magically in it. She flipped the watch open and consulted it, before snapping it shut. "Four in the afternoon. The exact opposite of the time in England. Which means your brother's been in Fairyland for four hours. And you only have nine hours left to save him."

Cora couldn't believe they'd been at Tempest's house in Fairyland for so long already. She thought of the terrible danger Acton was in, on the far side of that great, wide kingdom. They needed to rescue him as soon as possible and let him know how much he was loved and missed. "We'd best get a move on," she told the others. "Tempest is right, time is running out!"

"Take this with you on your journey." Tempest handed her the watch. "It always tells the right time here, in Fairyland, and you never need to wind it."

"Thank you." Cora took the watch and shakily flipped it open. The face was carved with intricate leaf patterns and had thirteen numbers, just like the grandmother clock at Fairykeep Cottage. On the inside cover a hand-engraved inscription read:

To my Darling T. Love O x

"Take good care of it," Tempest said. "It was a wedding gift from my late husband Otto Glass, your great-grandfather. It is the last thing I have of his. And it was given with hope and love."

The watch from Mama's stories! The one missing from Fairykeep Cottage! It was an honour for Tempest to entrust them with such a precious thing. Cora flushed with pride.

"Goodbye, my great-grandchildren," Tempest said, hugging and kissing each of them in turn. "It was a pleasure

to meet you. You will always be welcome here in my home."
She grabbed their hands and squeezed them in one last
goodbye. "May the blessings of the trees, mountains,
woodlands, streams, oceans and untamed world be with
you from this moment until for ever. Oh…" She scratched
her head. "One last word of advice: do not eat or drink
anything in Fairyland, no matter how hungry you get. Food
here is very dangerous to humans."

"We can't thank you enough for all you've done for us,"
Bram said.

"We only hope it'll be enough to succeed," Elle added,
anxiously.

"It will," Tempest said.

"And I will be with you for the first part of your way,"
Thomas said. "After that you will be on your own. But do
not worry. You have everything you need to rescue Acton."

"If you believe in yourselves, and the magic and each
other," Tempest said. "And each of you lets your own unique
light shine."

Cora only hoped that was true and that when they
arrived at the Glass Tower, on the other side of Fairyland,
there would still be time to stop the Fairy Queen's evil plan,
and save Acton.

14

ACTON'S ANSWER

Acton bit his lip. If he fetched the Glimmerglass Crown for the Queen it would give her dominion over life and death, and with that she could rule every one of the five magic kingdoms, including England, for evermore! There was no doubt in his mind that she would rule in his homeland with the same icy fist she used in Fairyland and all the others, making everyone suffer, including his family. They couldn't take that. They'd suffered enough.

Another horrible realization dawned on him. Thanks to Cora's glass rose, whatever they did, and wherever they went, the Fairy Queen could see and hear his brother and sisters in her crystal ball. With that advantage and the

Queen's immense power, she'd have no trouble capturing them, or worse, he realized with a lurch of terror, the Queen might turn him, Cora, Bram and Elle to glass; or kill them outright. If he wanted to save them from her clutches, he had to accept her offer. So when he opened his mouth to answer the Fairy Queen this time, the word that came out was not a *no*, as he would've wished, but a *yes*, and the taste of it felt like a jagged bee sting in his throat.

"Excellent!" the Fairy Queen laughed. "There is one more thing I must warn you of. If you do succeed in your mission, be sure not to look back when you leave the Dead Lands, else you'll lose the crown, which I *must* have at all cost, and you will be stuck there for ever, unable to return to Fairyland, which means you will be…"

"Dead," Acton said, finishing her sentence with a shudder.

"I see you understand," the Fairy Queen said.

Goosebumps rose on the back of Acton's neck. How could he do what the Fairy Queen asked? With no magic or strength, he'd have to rely on his wits and knowledge.

And if he didn't survive, he realized with a shiver, he would be leaving Cora, Bram and Elle to face the Fairy Queen alone. He had to bring back the crown and save them and himself.

"Remember your mission," the Queen warned. "Fetch

me the crown, then my curse over your family will be broken, and you four Glass-Belle children will be free. Fail, and I will see to it that you and your three siblings do not live to see another dawn." She raised her arms and spoke a spell.

"**Crow Army, dark and sour, fetch Acton's siblings to my Glass Tower.**"

At once, a great flock of murderous crows flew through the glass walls and circled the Queen in a cloud of beaks, talons, wings, claws and angry caws. Auberon flew up to join them. Screeching loudly he shook his feathers until they turned from black to white, so that he was a unique bird among them: their leader. "You heard our Icy Empress, my troops," he croaked. "We must fly south, find the Chosen One's siblings, and bring them here."

"YES, HIGH COMMANDER! CRAW! CRAW! CRAW!" the crow army screeched, and then swooped after Auberon, disappearing through the walls in a flurry of feathers.

Acton's heart thrummed between his ribs as he watched through the side of the Glass Tower as the white raven led his black-winged battalion off into the sky. "You said no harm would befall them if I did as you asked!" he shouted to the Fairy Queen.

"No harm *will* befall them," the Fairy Queen said. "I'll see that they're well looked after in my cells, but you must keep your side of the deal, Acton. If you don't want their lives to be laid to waste then you must descend to the Dead Lands via the Well Between Worlds, crawl through the Tunnel of Death, row across the Dead River with its ferry keepers, walk the Dead Gardens to the Dead King's dark tower, and sneak to the Throne Room of his palace to steal the Glimmerglass Crown."

The thought of that perilous journey made Acton tremble with fear from head to toe. He couldn't let the Fairy Queen destroy Cora, Bram and Elle. There was no doubt in his mind that if he didn't succeed she would annihilate his siblings. He knew what he had to do: fetch the crown, or die trying. There was something in his dressing-gown pocket. He felt around it. It was the Blue Soldier. He was glad of the little wooden charm. He hoped it would bring him luck on his mission.

"Hoglet!" the Fairy Queen shouted. "Lower my great-great-grandson into the Well Between Worlds. Only allow him back when he has the crown."

"Yes, Majesty," Hoglet said. "Come on, snot-stoat," he griped, waddling over to Acton. "Time to go." Hoglet grabbed at Acton's nightshirt lapels and yanked him across the Throne Room. "This way!"

As they left, Acton glanced one last time over his shoulder at the Queen, who was returning to her glass throne. He only hoped he could make it back to her with the crown in time, and that in giving her her longed-for prize, she might, as she had promised, save his and his siblings' lives.

Hoglet took Acton down the grand floating staircase. When they reached the base of the tower the little hedgehog man stopped and touched the wall with a warty hand and spoke a spell.

"Tower wall, thick and stout, open up and let us out."

A great glass door etched with runes appeared in the wall and swung open to reveal the snowy courtyard outside, surrounded by high, impenetrable glass walls.

A well stood in the centre of the courtyard. Hoglet and Acton crossed towards it. The cold seeped through Acton's slippers, as his feet and Hoglet's trotters made footprints in the snow.

They reached the well. Its hole, sunk in the frozen earth, was surrounded by a circle of glass bricks that rose to the height of Hoglet's hips. A covered arch stretched over the cylindrical hole and hanging beneath it was a metal pulley, attached with a winding handle to a bucket on a rope.

Hoglet grasped the handle and turned it, lowering the bucket onto the walled rim of the well, ready for Acton to climb in. Then he dropped a stone down the well shaft and waited for it to hit the bottom.

Acton waited too.

Both of them were expecting a plop, but it never came.

At least, not within earshot.

Acton's stomach lurched into the soles of his slippers. It must be a long, long, long way down. Alone in there, he might be tipped from the bucket at any moment and fall to his death in the forever darkness below.

"Get in the bucket!" Hoglet commanded. "And hold on tight!" he advised.

Acton gulped and clambered up into the bucket. It was barely big enough for him to sit in and wobbled precariously on the wall of the well. As he squeezed into his seat, Coriel suddenly fluttered down from the sky above. Hoglet was so busy untangling the rope he didn't see her.

"I'm back, my puffin," Coriel whispered. "I couldn't leave you on your own. But I had to wait until you were out of the Fairy Queen's sight to return. Where are we going?"

"Down the Well Between Worlds," Acton told her, quietly. "To fetch the Glimmerglass Crown."

Coriel gave a shiver. But to her credit she didn't flinch. "If you think that's best, Chosen One," was all she said. And she hid at the bottom of the bucket behind Acton's feet so that Hoglet wouldn't see her. Acton's guts spasmed as the little hog man wound the bucket handle round a few times and spoke a spell:

"Rope and bucket, lower slow, take this human boy to the Dead Lands below."

Hoglet let go of the handle, and the bucket with Acton and Coriel tumbled off the wall and into the well, lurching and jolting downwards as the winding handle unspooled the rope, magically lowering them at a steady pace.

Acton felt the air get colder and the sunlight disappeared overhead.

He looked up at the silhouette of Hoglet shimmering in the circle of light at the top of the well, but soon that was gone too. Shrinking to a tiny spot that ws soon engulfed entirely by the growing darkness. A darkness so cold and miserable it made Acton suddenly realize what his father must feel like, alone in his melancholy without reprieve.

The well rope stretched away from him, lengthening and tangling, until it disappeared from view. Acton hoped it wouldn't snap and break, along with his last remaining thin strand of hope. That well rope was all that connected him to the world of the living above, and, if his mama's old stories were anything to go by, he'd need to climb back up it with the crown to return.

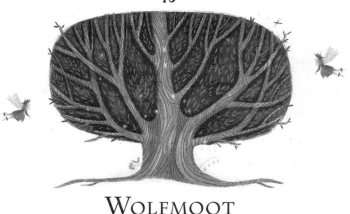

15

WOLFMOOT

When Cora, Bram and Elle climbed the stairs from Tempest's house in the roots of the Heart of the Forest and stepped back into the Greenwood, it was late afternoon, well past four o'clock. The sun had already set, leaving them in a dusky half-light. Behind a distant hill, the full moon was beginning to rise. It seemed that the winter solstice day in Fairyland was just as short as it was in England. In the dark night of this foreign place, it would be even scarier trying to find Acton.

She, Bram and Elle followed Thomas along a snow-covered path through the murksome Greenwood, where frosty spiders' webs, large as dinner plates, sparkled in the crooked trees. Great howls echoed in the distance and shook through Cora like shivers.

"We are nearing the Wolfmoot," Thomas whispered. "As a wolf, I am safer there than you are, but I'm not Wolfborn, so I'm still not exactly one of them."

Cora looked down and noticed that, at the edge of the path, there were hundreds of paw prints scattered in the snow. "When we arrive," Thomas growled, "I'll introduce you to the pack, and try to convince them to hear your case. If I succeed, you must offer them a spellbinding and unique gift that will persuade the Seven League Wolves among them to carry you to the Dreaming Tree."

"What kind of gift could wolves possibly want?" Elle said.

"Whatever we offer," Bram said, gazing anxiously around the dusky, moonlit woods, "it has to be good, or else there's no chance of them taking us across Fairyland."

Cora racked her brains. Suddenly she had an idea. "The gift must be spellbinding, but does it have to be real?" she asked. "Can it be a riddle or a story?"

"A story is best," Thomas advised. "Wolves don't like riddles."

"How about Little Red Riding Hood?" Elle said. "It was one of Mama's favourites."

"I don't think that's a good idea," Bram said, nodding at

Cora's red cloak. "Besides, doesn't the Big Bad Wolf die at the end?"

"We could change the ending to make it less bloody and bitey," Elle replied. "And maybe not call him the Big Bad Wolf!"

"Perhaps a different tale?" Thomas suggested, kindly.

"But what?" Bram asked. "And who's to tell it?"

"Whoever thinks of the best story by the time we are called to speak," Cora answered.

The discussion was over, and just in time. The many lines of paw prints they were following through the drifts arrived at a great snow-covered clearing filled with wolves. Thomas gave a warning howl, and Cora, Bram and Elle found themselves approaching the edge of the Wolfmoot.

Cora's skin prickled with sweat and her heart beat nervously, as the three of them followed Thomas through the sea of wolves. Wolves with beige, grey, brown, white, brindled and tawny coats, with bristly fur and manes, silky whiskers and thick tails. Wolves with missing incisors and scarred noses. Wolves with drooling tongues, and wolves with mangy muzzles and dirty, gnawed paws. They were all staring at her and her brother and sister with their hackles raised, and hungry expressions on their faces. What big eyes they had! What hairy legs! What pointy ears! What long claws! And what sharp, sharp teeth!

"AWHOOOOOOOOOOOOOOOOOOOOOOO COMES TO OUR WOLFMOOOOOOOOOOOOOOT UNINVITED?" howled a raggedy old wolf pacing back and forth on a frosty mound at the far end of the clearing. The full solstice moon rose behind him, big as a giant's dinner plate. He was standing beside another tall majestic oak tree, that Thomas whispered was the Tree of Life. The old wolf's words were peppered with barks and growls, but, thanks to her new-found magic, Cora found she could understand them.

"That must be their alpha," Elle whispered. "The leader of the pack... I wonder if he's a just and fair ruler."

"Those are not the words I'd use to describe him," Thomas replied quietly.

"And we have to appeal to him?" Cora swallowed a lump in her throat.

"Shush, all of you," Thomas advised, softly. He bowed his head. "Lord Silvertooth, Wolves of the Greenwood, my great-grand-nephew and great-grand-nieces are in need of your illustrious and famed hospitality."

The pack yipped at this unexpected turn of events. "NOOOOOOOOOO HELP FOR HOOOOOOMANS!" they howled.

Cora sagged, Bram slumped and Elle stared at her feet. But Thomas was not dissuaded. "I invoke the First Wolf's

Commandment: '*We must aid our kind.*'"

Cora's heart skipped a beat. She knew about the First Wolf from Mama's old fairy stories. One sprang into her mind now, like a leaping growling pup, demanding to be heard. She decided she would tell that tale, if they got a chance to give their gift.

"The First Wolf's commandment applies only to wolf-kind!" Lord Silvertooth yapped. "You are not Wolfborn, Thomas, and neither are these humans."

"Each creature sprung from the earth is part of our pack," Thomas growled. "Help everyone: that is what the First Wolf's words mean."

"I, Faol, am tired of this!" snapped a charcoal-coloured wolf at the front of the crowd.

"Hear the human children out!" barked a dark wolf, who was licking his paws at the back.

"Blaidd is right!" snapped a rough-voiced wolf, who was scratching her jowls with her claws. "I, Cu, say what do we have to lose?"

"We owe Thomas," said Faol. "He's one of us."

Bram and Elle perked up. Cora did too. The pack were prepared to listen!

"Then approach, Thomas," Lord Silvertooth commanded. "Tell us of these strangers in our midst who you have brought to our sacred Wolfmoot."

137

"Sit while I speak with him," Thomas advised quietly. Cora, Bram and Elle sat down cross-legged, waiting. Cora wrinkled her nose. Now that they were in among the pack, the smell was overwhelming; a mix of musk, sweat, dirt and ripe meat. Holding her breath she watched their great-grand-uncle as, with his ears slicked back, he carefully approached Lord Silvertooth on the moonlit mound.

Lord Silvertooth rubbed cheeks and touched noses with Thomas, and Thomas crouched and licked Lord Silvertooth's snout, then the pair put their heads together and spoke quietly. The other wolves watched fascinated, their ears pricked. Occasionally, they'd glance at their guests. "Don't run," Faol growled at Cora. "Or I, Faol, will catch you."

Cora had no intention of running. She knew she'd be brought down in a heartbeat.

Slowly, so as not to frighten any of the wolves, she took out Tempest's pocket watch and checked it. Five-thirty. They'd been in Fairyland for many hours, and were no closer to Acton. She wondered what terrible things might be happening to him at this very moment in the Glass Tower.

The discussion was over. Lord Silvertooth and Thomas faced the pack.

"WOLFMOOOOOOOOOOOOOOOOOOOOOOOOT!"

Thomas howled. "These children have brought you a gift."
A hundred ears pricked with excitement.

"A gift! Let's see it!" yipped a snaggle-toothed wolf.

"Zeev's right!" growled Faol. "Let them share it!"

Thomas leaped through the air, floating over the heads of the many wolves to land at the children's feet. "Now is the time to tell your chosen story," he advised, nudging them each with his nose. "Spin your yarn well, or they'll vote against you, and you won't make it to the Dreaming Tree."

"I've thought of one." Cora gulped nervously. "One of Mama's. May I tell it?"

Bram and Elle nodded, their eyes wide with fear.

"Go ahead," Bram said.

"We're right behind you," Elle added.

Cora stood and faced the pack. "Our gift is an old wolf's tale," she announced.

"We have tales and tails aplenty!" Lord Silvertooth snapped. "It'll have to be a special one to earn our favour." He watched Cora, licking his lips as if considering a tasty meal.

Cora's hands shook. She hid them beneath her red cloak. "It'll be the best story you've ever heard," she claimed, bravely, but Lord Silvertooth's snide comment had made her nervous. She felt as if her knees might buckle. How could she be sure her story was good enough? She began to lose confidence and her mouth dried around the words.

"*SPEAK, STORYTELLER!*" Blaidd commanded.

"*TELL YOUR TALE!*" Cu barked.

"Once upon a time…" Cora said, huskily. She tried to continue then, but her voice dwindled away as the hungry wolves crowded closer. Their eyes blending and blurring in the dusky half-light into one big mass: a many-headed wolf-monster, ready to eat her all up.

"*GET ON WITH IT!*" snarled Zeev.

"*BE QUICK!*" Faol growled.

"*BEFORE HUNGER TAKES US!*" Cu barked.

"*AND WE STEAL A JUICY TREAT!*" Blaidd grouched.

"*IN A RED RIDING HOOD!*" Lord Silvertooth snapped.

"Have you hearts of stone?" Bram pleaded. ""Listen to what my sister has to say!"

"Use those big ears of yours!" Elle implored. "A story is nothing without good listeners."

Cora took a deep breath. Elle and Bram's belief helped her confidence rise again. She couldn't let herself fail, not when their one route to rescue Acton was at stake.

"My story is about why some wolves can leap seven leagues," she explained to the pack. It's called *The First Wolf's Tale*…

"Once upon a time, in the early days of the First Wolf there was only darkness. In that darkness nothing was separate and everything was one and the same. There was no here or there, or space in between, and so the First Wolf could leap everywhere in an instant. The leaps felt so joyful that the First Wolf opened their mouth and gave the longest loudest howl of happiness ever heard.

"'*AWHOOOOOOOOOOOOOOOOOOOOOOOOOOOO OOOOO!*'

"The howl was fulsome enough that the First Wolf cried tears of wonder to hear it. The tears fell until they made an ocean. Since there was nothing to bind it, the ocean filled all the space there was, and the First Wolf had to paddle with their paws to stay afloat.

"As the First Wolf swam, they smelled a shallower place. The scent of the water was fresher there, not quite as salty. The First Wolf was parched from all their leaping, howling and swimming, so they stopped and took a drink.

"Now, the sea may have been less salty then, but it was still *quite* salty. The First Wolf drank gallons, but it did not quench their thirst.

"They drank more and more, until they'd swallowed almost the whole ocean.

"The First Wolf had drunk so much, in so many different places, that they had soon made an archipelago of islands, called the Fair Isles.

"Each isle was full of noise but the First Wolf was not

afraid, for the sounds were sweet and delightful: rushing rivers, babbling brooks, stretching plants and growing trees.

"The First Wolf was so ecstatic they barked a great big spell to make a variety of other vegetation erupt from the ground. Then they howled enough magic to create the First Wolf Pack. The First Wolf Pack joined in the song of the First Wolf, and the baying that they all did together made insects in the air, birds in the sky, and all the varied beasts of the forest.

"With so many plants and creatures in the wood of the world, the Fair Folk finally appeared, arriving of their own accord, materializing from thin air, born into a world that the First Wolf had made. They were magical creatures who'd come to live as one with everything, as nature intended.

"Then humans came, rising up from the sludgy clay around the islands, forming themselves from mud and discarded bones left on the shoreline. The humans ate the plants, hunted the birds, slayed the beasts, and drove the Fairies into hiding in their own domain of Fairyland. But they did not master the wolves. The wolves remained kings and queens of the forest. They had long memories too. Longer than if the tail of every wolf that's ever lived was placed end to end, through all of time."

Cora paused. There was a little more, but that was almost the end of her story. So she felt she should stop for a moment.

"That is our creation story, known only to those who are wolfborn," Lord Silvertooth snarled, interrupting the silence. "How are you familiar with it?"

"Our mama, Maria, told it to us," Cora said. "She heard it from her papa, Bob, who heard it from his mama, Tempest, who heard it from…"

"Me!" Thomas said. "I used to tell my sister wolf stories that I first learned from the grandparents and great-grandparents of every wolf here tonight."

"Very good," said Lord Silvertooth. He looked pleased that wolf mythology had spread so far into the human world. "Continue then, storyteller."

"And so," Cora went on, "every wolf cub remembers the First Wolf, and the First Pack, and what it means to leap across the sky. The First Wolf's magic is not so strong now as in those earliest of days, but in Fairyland there remain some Wolfborn who can sky-leap great distances in a single bound. They're called the Seven League Wolves, and they are wolf-kind's messengers, spreading the wisdom, words and trickery of the First Wolf through the roaming packs of the five kingdoms for evermore."

Their tale was told. Cora licked her dry lips nervously as she finished speaking, and sat down beside Bram and Elle. Thomas slunk close and lay protectively at their side.

Lord Silvertooth and the pack sniffed around the story,

wrinkling their noses as they considered it. Cora couldn't be sure, but she hoped she'd told it well enough to win their votes. She waited with bated breath to see whether the pack considered her old legend of the First Wolf creating the world worthy of a favour. And she hoped, when they finally heard what that favour was to be, the wolves would agree to help the three of them rescue Acton from the clutches of the Fairy Queen.

16

THE WELL BETWEEN WORLDS

Acton and Coriel sat swaying in the jerking bucket, in the creaking, howling, growling, descending shaft of the Well Between Worlds. Acton could no longer see his hands in front of his face. Since the start of this mission for the Fairy Queen, and the start of their descent, the well had become a black morass. He sat in that darkness praying for a plan for how he was going to steal the Glimmerglass Crown. "You shouldn't have come with me, Coriel," he told the little robin, at last. "You don't have to stay. It's scary here. Fly away home."

"Oh no," Coriel twittered. "I won't abandon you again, my puffin. Not now that we're such close friends. Besides,

I've never travelled to the Dead Lands before, it's bound to be an awfully big adventure!"

"If we don't die for real," Acton sighed. "It's so gloomy down here. If only we knew a spell to make some light..."

"I remember one from the olden days, my little dabchick," Coriel chirruped. "From when Tempest was my mistress. It won't work for me because I can't do magic, but you might try it. All you have to do is speak these words and, if you have magic inside you, then a light will appear." She whispered the spell's words to Acton and he said them aloud, in the bravest most magic-filled voice he could muster.

Nothing happened.

He tried again, for a second time.

Nothing happened again.

"Never mind," Coriel clucked. "Perhaps I was wrong."

But Acton felt only despair. He'd never be able to fetch the crown if he couldn't master a simple spell. He slumped down in his seat so hard the bucket almost tipped them out.

"Calm yourself, my cuckoo," Coriel said. "Panic and overthinking won't help. Tell you what," she suggested. "I'll sing something to cheer us up. It's a song I made up for my baby chicks, Tempest and Thomas, when they were young." She opened her mouth and began to trill...

"Sleep, little one, sleep,
the sky is full of sheep,
Night stars are lambs of tenderness,
the ghostly moon their shepherdess."

Acton was shocked to find that he knew her song. He joined in the second verse.

"Sleep, little one, sleep, dream your home is Fairykeep;
A dragon guards the Dreaming Tree,
where the Green Man grows sweet dreams for thee."

"How do you know the words?" Coriel asked in surprise, when they'd finished.

"Mama sang it to us when we were babies," Acton explained.

"She sounds lovely, my meadow pipit. I'm sorry she's gone."

"So am I," Acton said. "Perhaps we'll see her when we reach the Dead Lands. I miss her terribly." He shivered. The loss that he felt for Mama deep inside was as wide as a chasm, and sharp as a knife. But his memory of her was still as fresh as the first day of spring. Did that mean that her soul was still around, lost somewhere in the Dead Lands, suffering under the curse? He thought of all the gifts Mama had given him. The gift of her knowledge and company, and time, and conversation, and listening, and her stories, and poems and songs – and most of all the gift of her love. As well as her

147

real gifts: the solstice and birthday and Christmas presents, like…the Blue Soldier! He felt for it in his pocket, pulled it out and showed it to Coriel.

"Mama gave this to me one Christmas," he explained. "It's precious. I carry it everywhere with me. I've had it so long, it feels like a little piece of my heart. There were four. One for each of us four children. Mama made up stories about them."

As Acton spoke and thought of Mama, the Blue Soldier seemed to hum in his hand. Slowly, it began to pulse with the faintest of blue lights.

"Of course!" Coriel stared at the figure. "How stupid of me! The Blue Soldier is your Talisman!"

"My what?" Acton asked, confused.

"Your Talisman," Coriel repeated. "All sorcerers have one to focus their magic. It's an enchanted object gifted to them by someone they love. Try the Light Spell again, my warbler. Be sure you're holding your Talisman tight and think of a memory of your mama that's full of love. That should bring the magic!"

Acton clutched the Blue Soldier in his hand and thought of the Christmas day Mama and Papa had presented it to him. Of Mama's smile. Of her smell, oil paint and perfume. Of her laugh, like the tinkle of wind chimes. The Soldier began to tingle in his palm. Coriel was right, it was his

Talisman! He remembered one of his last conversations with Mama.

"Did you know *Magi* means wise men?" she'd said. "Most stories say there were three, but there could've been four, or five, or more. It's where the word magic comes from. Before words, people couldn't differentiate between things. Only when the wise scholars from those different kingdoms named each plant, beast and creature did each of those wonders gain their own unique magic.

"Words don't just put power into things, but into stories too. I don't mean fairy tales, I mean the stories we tell ourselves and each other about the fears we have bubbling inside us. My one wish for you, Acton, and for Cora, Bram and Elle, is that the four of you put those fears aside, and use your magic and words of wisdom to write stories for yourselves full of hopes and dreams."

Hopes and dreams, yes! That was what they needed! Acton clutched the Blue Soldier tight and spoke the words of the magic spell Coriel had told him.

"Glow light, make darkness bright."

The Blue Soldier hummed softly in his hand. A tiny spark of magic leaped from Acton's fingertips into the air and flowered into a perfect ball of light that floated above his palm. It was like the soft haze of an oil lamp illuminating the well shaft, except this light was far purer and truer. It fell away in a wide circle around them.

"Nice work, my shelduck!" Coriel cheered. "Your first spell! You are the Chosen One! I never doubted it, not for a second!"

Perhaps he was the Chosen One. Acton let himself believe for a moment that they might make it out of the Well Between Worlds and the Dead Lands in one piece. That feeling didn't last long, for he found that concentrating on the magic drained him. "Why do I feel so tired, Coriel?"

"Every spell feeds off living energy," Coriel warned. "It will be worse the deeper into the Dead Lands we go. Further on there are no other living things. Then the magic will have nothing to feed off but you and me. And it will always feed off the biggest living thing first, which, in this case, is you!"

"This light is using up my energy?" Acton stared at it.

"It is," Coriel replied. "One big spell, or even a small one, which goes on for too long, will drain your energy dry. First you will fall into a deep sleep, then you will shrivel to nothing, and finally you will be as dead as everything else down here."

"What should I do?" Acton asked.

"My advice, little skylark," Coriel said, "is only use magic as a last resort. When we don't need it, put the light out."

"How?" Acton asked.

"If memory serves, my pintail," Coriel said. "You just say

150

'extinguish' to cancel out the Light Spell. It works with most other spells too."

"**Extinguish!**" Acton mumbled, and the light went out.

They sat in silence for a long time, dropping down the midnight-dark well.

Soon Acton began to worry again, about what would happen to them when they reached the bottom. He missed his siblings so much. He hoped Auberon and the Crow Army hadn't captured them and taken them to the Fairy Queen. And he hoped he'd get to see everyone again, when this mission was over. If he was still in one piece, he'd put his arms round his brother and sisters and hug and tickle them until they couldn't stop laughing. Aunt Eliza too, and Kisi. And Papa. He would do everything he could to make Papa truly laugh again.

17

SEVEN LEAGUE WOLVES

On the other side of Fairyland, the Wolfmoot was still taking place. Cora sat cross-legged among the wolves beneath the Tree of Life. Bram and Elle fidgeted to one side of her in the shadowy moonlit grove, and Thomas kept vigil on the other. Cora checked the pocket watch. Seven o'clock.

They only had six hours left to save Acton. She hoped he was safe in the Glass Tower, and that the Fairy Queen had not done anything terrible to him. The decision from the wolves about her story seemed to be taking an awfully long time, so long that the first evening stars had started to come out, and the moon had risen high in the night sky.

Lord Silvertooth paced around the grove speaking to every wolf in turn, to hear their verdict, until, finally, he returned to his mound. "I've consulted the leaders among you: Faol, Cu, Blaidd, Zeev, Ruth, Lupin, Chann, Connor, Gundulf, Shaw, Conri, Fridolf, Tala, Ulf, Kurt, Duko, Dolphus and Lobo. And, between us, a decision has been made. The pack agrees your retelling of our creation myth is a worthy story about the First Wolf. Now what help do you require?"

Cora breathed a sigh of relief. She stood up, along with Bram and Elle, and gave their request. "My brother and sister and I need three Seven League Wolves to carry us to the Dreaming Tree at the centre of Fairyland."

"From there we'll make our own way to the Glass Tower," Bram said. "To help our brother defeat the Fairy Queen."

"And set the whole of Fairyland and its kingdoms free," Elle added.

"Three small pups cannot possibly hope to defeat the Fairy Queen!" sneered a tawny wolf at the back.

"If you help us we can," Cora said.

"The Fairy Queen is wicked," said Lord Silvertooth. "She's made life tough for every one of us. We will offer our best Seven League Wolves to assist you."

"Thank you," Bram said.

Thomas stood. "Who among you is willing to take these

children on your backs and ride with them to the Dreaming Tree?"

Three wolves leaped from the crowd; pack members who'd spoken during the meeting. "Faol, Cu, and Blaidd, at your service," they snapped in unison. "We'll go with you, if you promise to obey our motto: *Roses have thorns, prickly and untrue. Keep no secrets from us, and we'll keep none from you.*"

"We promise," Bram and Elle said at once, together. Cora thought of the glass rose beneath her cloak. If that was a secret it wasn't one she felt she needed to tell these three wolves about. "I promise," she said.

"Run fast and wild, my Seven League Wolves," said Lord Silvertooth. "May your fur be unmatted, your teeth spotless, your noses scent-filled, your paws swift and your whiskers attuned to everything! Children, climb onto their backs. One wolf each." He nudged Cora, Bram and Elle in turn with his nose and they did as he commanded. Cora's wolf, Faol, had charcoal-coloured fur and speckled grey feet. Bram's, Blaidd, was dark as midnight with yellow eyes and a glossy black ruff. Elle's, Cu, was the colour of coal dust, with green eyes and a long, silky, furred tail.

"Goodbye, Thomas," Cora said. "Thank you for your help. We shall miss you."

"I'll miss you too!" Thomas jumped up and licked each of them on their cheek in turn to say goodbye.

154

"Hold on to our ruffs," Faol warned Cora and the others, in a low growl. "And don't let go. The speed of travel will be immense once we are off bounding among the stars, and there will be no stopping, until we reach the Dreaming Tree."

The three Seven League Wolves pawed the ground. The other members of the pack barked and howled encouragement, and then, in the blink of an eye, they set off, vaulting into the air and circling the Tree of Life.

At once, Cora began to feel sick from the speed and agility of Faol as he leaped through the dark. She hugged him tight, burying her head in his scruff, clasping his fur with all her might to keep herself on his back. She could feel his powerful muscles expand and contract beneath her in waves, as they raced across the night sky.

Eventually, she felt brave enough to open her eyes and look down. She squinted, battered by the biting wind. The moonlit grove and the Wolfmoot, and Thomas, and Lord Silvertooth and the circle of wolves were disappearing like a dot in the distance beneath the blur of Faol's furry, galloping foot pads.

Cora, Bram and Elle skimmed over the night-dark Greenwood on the backs of Faol, Cu and Blaidd. A cold wind shook snow from the treetops, ruffled the wolves' fur, tangled Elle's long locks, flicked Cora's cloak and flattened Bram's spiky hair.

Each seven-league leap revealed a new part of the night forest in a blur of midnight-blue branches that wove so close together that Cora could not pick out one tree from another.

But Elle could. She shouted the tree's names to Cora and Bram as they whisked past... Apple, ash, oak, elm, larch, plane, yew, hornbeam, alder, elder, hazel, chestnut, cherry, beech, blackthorn, hawthorn, rowan, willow, and many more that Cora lost in the wind.

A dizzying wealth of nature spread beneath them in the moonlight, with only the occasional snowdrift or frozen river to break up the forest of frosted branches. Cora glimpsed two or three icy streams, running like white and purple veins through the forest, their tributaries stretched on for ever, like frozen fingers towards the edge of darkness, as far as the eye could see.

The three leaping wolves sped higher into the atmosphere, and the children found themselves surrounded by cold grey vapour. Moments later, they burst through to the purest night sky. A full moon shone overhead, throwing their ghostly moon shadows onto patches of rolling cloud below. The night-time cloudscape went on for ever, broken intermittently by a swirl of stars, and the wolves leaped across it, as if they were traversing space and time itself.

"Look!" Bram pointed to a cluster of distant black dots swarming in front of the full moon. "Are those bats?"

Elle shook her head. "Crows," she said, fearfully. "A murder of them."

"The Crow Army," Faol growled.

"Winged henchmen of the Queen," Blaidd snapped.

"Led by her faithful lieutenant, Auberon Raven," Cu howled, pointing with her nose at the white raven up front.

The thousand strong squawking Crow Army reeled closer, in a spiral of beaks and wings, each one screeching a murderous battle cry...

CRRRAAAAWWWWW! CRRRAAAAWWWWW!

The fearsome feathered troops glided towards them, croaking an ominous war song. *"GOUGE AND MAIM, SNAP AND BITE! OUR CROW ARMY'S NEVER LOST A FIGHT!"*

The white-feathered Auberon flapped before the hordes, screeching commands in a deep, throaty voice. "CAPTURE THE CHILDREN! KILL THE WOLVES!"

As the screaming, squawking, clawing, writhing, winged warriors swooped towards them, blotting out the moon like an ink spill, Cora nervously clenched her frozen fingers in Faol's fur and wondered how on earth she, Bram, Elle and the wolves could ever defeat this army of angry crows.

18

THE DEAD LANDS

Coriel flew up in alarm from the edge of the bucket as with a shudder it hit the bottom of the well. Acton stiffened and threw his arms up in the air, attempting to shield himself from the coils of rope as they dropped around him. When everything was finally still, he climbed from the bucket.

The darkness had grown so thick around them that, without his magical light, Acton couldn't even see the end of his nose. Though he could sense a wide opening leading off from the bottom of the well in either direction. A sulphurous breeze blew down both tunnels. It tasted stale, like it had been stuck beneath the earth for ever. Acton shivered. The hairs on the back of his neck prickled. This must be the Tunnel of Death.

He couldn't go on without taking a quick look. He needed some light to help him see which way to go. He had to say the Light Spell once more. A part of him didn't want to, because of what Coriel had told him about doing magic here, but right now he needed to make an exception to that rule. He gripped his Blue Soldier Talisman until it hummed, then spoke the spell. The ball of light appeared at once and hovered above his palm.

"Well done, my puffin," Coriel twittered. "You're getting good!"

Acton's senses had been right; a narrow tunnel led off in both directions. Blackened roots poked through the tunnel's walls, along with the yellowing bones of long dead beasts. How far did the tunnel go? Both paths must lead somewhere, but which direction was the right one? He could easily make the wrong choice…

"Which way?" he asked Coriel.

"Trust your instincts, my pigeon," she twittered. "But don't take too long deciding. You need to douse that light."

Acton considered both passages. Clinging to the wall in one was a small and half-dead thorn bush, barely bigger than his fist. It had no leaves or flowers to speak of. Growing on the border between the living and Dead Lands, it was half-dead itself.

Something deep inside Acton felt sorry for the bush and he had the sudden impulse to save it. An unexpected enchantment flourished in his mind, like a restless seedling. It was almost as if, now he had discovered his magic, more power was flooding to him of its own accord. He touched the bush and spoke his fresh new spell.

"Blackthorn bush, dying and done, remember flowers and leaves, and seek the sun."

White flowers sprouted from the bush's branches and green leaves uncurled from its twigs.

When the spell was finally complete, Acton was exhausted. Perhaps it had been an unnecessary use of his magic to heal the woes of the little plant? But he had always thought that helping others was equally as important as helping oneself. And now, because of his actions, tiny, fresh flowers were blooming in the borderland. The sight of them set a new hope blossoming inside him too, a hope that made a different kind of strength return to him; a strength of the heart. Maybe he could succeed in his mission for the crown after all, though he still didn't know which path to take…

As he stared once more in each direction, a gust of wind blew down the well. It ruffled his hair and, plucking a handful of white petals from the bush, sent them skittering down the length of the right-hand passage and off into the distance. It felt like a sign. Acton had helped the bush and it was showing him the way.

"Thank you," he whispered to the bush as he started out along the right-hand passage, hurrying to ward off the cold. He took a few paces and put his hand on the cold wall to guide them, then he called to his ball of light bobbing above.

"**Extinguish.**"

Pitch black smothered them once more. "I'm scared, Coriel," he whispered.

"I've got good night senses," Coriel twittered. "I'll fly ahead and trill a warning if anything dangerous appears." She fluttered off to return moments later, announcing, "Careful, little goose. The way ahead narrows and the rocks are sharp."

Acton tried to make himself small. As he moved forward, he could feel the passage closing in and the roof lowering. The wall beneath his palm became jagged, as Coriel had said it would. Soon he was crouching and ducking. Then he was crab walking and jiggling his way through narrow openings in the rock. His clothing and fingers snagged a couple of times in sharp crevasses of rock, but on each occasion he managed to carefully free himself without damage.

After a long while, Coriel called out that there was a tunnel mouth ahead. When Acton reached it, he called forth his ball of light once more and looked around. The tunnel led out into a great underground cavern with a broad river running through it. A river so wide Acton couldn't see the far side.

"The Dead River," Coriel announced.

There was no life on the river. No plants, trees, birds, kingfishers, insects or frogs. Instead, death was all around. The ball of light illuminated rippling black, gloopy water, thick as tar, that drifted slowly past, barely making a sound.

A narrow band of rock ran along the river's nearside, making a bank. Acton sent his light soaring high above. Until, in the distance he saw a bridge made of heavy white stone. The arches and great piers that rose from the river to hold up the bridge were carved to look like polished human bone.

"The Bone Bridge," Coriel muttered.

A long line of dead souls, walking flat and silent, had reached the Bone Bridge and were walking across it. But, at the centre of the river, the bridge stopped as if it was unfinished. There at the front of the line, the very first souls were jumping into the air above the river. As they jumped, each one disappeared in a sparkling stream of light that arced into the sky.

"What's happening to them?" Acton asked in awe.

"They are leaving the Dead Lands for whatever comes

next," Coriel said. "The wind and sky will sweep them off into the unknown of the afterlife, a place where everything is one, and where each soul may join with the universe."

"Can anyone come back from that place?" Acton asked.

Coriel shook her head. "That is the final journey of no return that one day we all must make."

"But not today," Acton said. "We mustn't go that way, for we need to reach the Dead King's Palace in one piece." He squinted hard. "I can see no evidence of that palace anywhere near the Bone Bridge, so it must be on a different path."

"Let me take a look for it, my sand martin." Coriel took off from his shoulder. "Put your light out 'til I return. Stay unnoticed and save your energy." Acton did as she asked. As his view was plunged into darkness and his heart into worry, he heard Coriel flutter off.

A long moment passed. So long that Acton began to wonder where Coriel was, as he stood there shivering in the gloom. Perhaps dead-time flowed differently than living? He hugged his dressing gown and nightshirt close, and shuffled anxiously about on the rock. The cold in the ground was so sharp and bleak it was seeping through the soles of his slippers. Images of the many awful things that could've happened to his friend floated through his head. She could've got lost, been spiked by a stalactite or fallen in the Dead River. He was still thinking this, when he heard the beating of her tiny wings flitting towards him through the distant murk.

"Good news, my swift!" Coriel twittered, fluttering round him. "I've found a crossing; a jetty and a ferry that'll take you to the Dead King's Palace, on the Dead River's far side. Nobody seems to be using it...I beg your pardon... I mean, no soul seems to be using it."

A surge of relief flooded Acton's chest. For a moment, he'd thought their mission had failed, but if he could catch that ferry across the river to the Dead King's Palace, he'd be a step closer to finding the Glimmerglass Crown and completing his mission for the Fairy Queen. And perhaps, being a little further into the Dead Lands, he might see Mama again.

It took them a while to sightlessly navigate the rocky riverbank. Eventually, Acton felt something before them. A narrow wooden jetty that sprang out from a stone promontory into the river. He spelled up his ball of light once more and they examined the spot. A small driftwood hut was built on stilts near the middle of the pier. Beyond that, at the end, an old bell hung on a high gallows over the slow, black waters of the river.

The jetty creaked beneath Acton's slippered feet, as he walked towards the hut and bell. The boards were set wide apart. Between them, in the light of his glowing ball, he glimpsed more dead souls. The wispy spirits of selkies and mermaids glided beneath the surface of the river, swimming onwards to their final unknown destination. The screams of those submerged souls grew louder as Acton neared the hut, and the black waters glooped beneath him, slurping like a toothless old man trying to swallow a morsel of fish in a chunky soup. Acton sickened with fear. It was almost as if the river and its inhabitants could feel his aliveness, and didn't like it. A sign carved on what looked like part of an elephant's hip bone hung on the gallows below the bell. Acton put his light up to read it.

RING TO CALL THE FERRY KEEPERS. WHO WILL FERRY YOU TO THE DEAD KING'S PALACE. (Ask not for whom the bell tolls. It tolls for thee.)

Suddenly Acton found himself having second thoughts. He worried what the dead ferry keepers might be like, and what they would do when they found out he was still alive.

What if they asked him to pay a fare, when he had nothing to give? But it seemed this was the only way to get to the palace. He clasped the bell rope and pulled it. A loud

$$B \qquad O \qquad N \qquad G \qquad !$$

echoed across the river. Then all was silence.

Acton decided he would rather wait in the hut for the ferry keepers than out here where he might be seen. He turned to the door. Above it was another sign carved on a piece of driftwood:

We are such stuff as dreams are made on,
And our little life is rounded with a sleep.

He hoped the hut was empty. He knocked three times just to be sure. He was about to turn the handle and go in, when an impatient voice behind the door snapped, "What do you want?"

The voice sounded angry. Coriel shivered and ducked into Acton's dressing-gown pocket, burying her head to hide. Ghostly, light footsteps approached the door, and a light shone through its cracks. Acton thought he'd better put his own light out.

"**Extinguish!**" he muttered.

"What do you want?" the thin male voice repeated.

"I want to cross the Dead River," he called out in reply.

The door swung open to reveal the soul of an old man, with brown eyes, white hair that stuck up in wisps, and a form that was stooped and bent, but, nevertheless, floated inches above the jetty. This soul didn't look like the others Acton had seen in the Dead Lands. It was more present and substantial than those he'd witnessed on the path and bridge, but something about old Brown-eyes seemed more lost than all of those other souls put together.

Brown-eyes wrinkled his see-through face and a vague, blurred expression appeared on it. "Do you have the toll?"

"What toll?" Acton asked.

"Two gold coins," Brown-eyes said. "Your family should've left them on your eyelids after you died. It's tradition."

Acton had certainly never heard of any such tradition. He felt confused by Brown-eye's explanation. "Are you a ferry keeper?"

"'Fraid not," Brown-eyes said sadly.

"How long will they be?" Acton asked.

"Not long." Brown-eyes peered closer at Acton. His pupils widened. "You're alive!" he whispered hoarsely. "Your soul's still in your body! No wonder you haven't the toll for the ferry! What on earth are you doing down here?"

Acton didn't answer.

Brown-eyes turned his head and shifted anxiously about.

His face shimmered vaguely, as if he was contemplating something interesting. "Jolly cold out there for the living," he muttered, smiling a little too broadly. "Why don't you come in?" He pushed open the creaking door to the hut.

"Don't do it!" Coriel whispered from Acton's pocket, but Acton felt fate was guiding his hand and he had to accept the invitation. Especially if he wanted to find out more about the ferry and the Dead King's Palace and all the remaining parts of his mission. And so, with a feeling of trepidation, he stepped into the cool, dry darkness beyond the doorway, following old Brown-eyes into the hut.

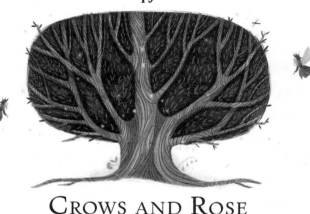

19

CROWS AND ROSE

Cora hugged low on Faol's back. Beside her, Bram and Elle did the same as the Crow Army approached, their wings black against the night sky, the white-feathered Auberon barely visible among their swirling, squawking mass of darkness.

"We cannot win," Faol muttered. "There's too many of them."

"But we can't let them defeat us," Cora urged. "For Acton's sake we need to keep going and hold our nerve."

"HOW?" the three wolves howled in unison.

"Bewilder and disorientate them," Elle suggested.

"Hide and confuse them," Cora said. "So they cannot find us."

"I've just the thing!" Bram clasped his Yellow Soldier and spoke his Weather Spell.

"Fog haze. Gloom slather. Murk come. Mist gather."

At once they were surrounded by a fog so thick Cora could no longer see the crows, moon or stars, let alone Faol beneath her, or Bram and Elle riding Blaidd and Cu at her side.

"Good work, Bram!" snarled Blaidd.

"This way," barked Faol. "If we fly low, we can slip beneath them!"

"Like shadows in the fog!" Cu growled.

Cora and Faol took the lead, swooping downwards.

Blaidd and Cu followed.

The three wolves galloped inches above the inky treetops, their bellies skimming the crowns of the trees that poked through Bram's ever-present murky mist.

Soon they were passing beneath the army of crows. Cora could hear their wing beats and their squawking calls overhead. Then their screeches gradually died away.

"I think we've lost them," she whispered to Faol in relief, just as Auberon dived through the fog.

"ATTACK!" he screamed, and a hundred guttural cawing crows flocked behind him, surrounding and slashing at the wolves and children. Cora shielded her face against the wild forest of flashing feathers, clawing talons and snapping, screaming beaks.

"They're trying to force us from the air!" Cu snapped.

"We must retreat!" Blaidd howled.

"Wolves, to me!" Faol dropped quickly through the bare forest canopy. Bram followed on Blaidd's back and Elle on Cu's. Branches batted Cora. Clouds of snow sprayed her face, almost unseating her, but this was not nearly as bad as the crows.

The three wolves landed in a snowy glade and quickly gathered under the largest tree. Bram's fog was denser here. Its thick tendrils swirled around the pitch-black forest, hiding them. Cora could hear Auberon and his raggedy, black-winged troops squawking angrily overhead.

"Climb from our backs," Faol commanded. "We will form a protective ring."

The three wolves gathered in a fighting stance, baring their teeth. Cora, Bram and Elle crouched between them. Despite their hearts' frantic beating and their breath loud in their ears, they kept quiet. For a moment it seemed as if the crows had lost them in the fog and dark. But then they heard their battle cries nearby...

CRRRAAAAAWWWWW! CRRRAAAAAWWWWW!

The winged army swooped, hacking at the wolves' heads

and feet. Faol, Cu and Blaidd fought as best they could, gnashing their teeth, but the crows got past their defences and soon reached the children.

Cora, Bram and Elle battled the birds with their hands. Cora swatted each swirling black beak that came her way, but the crows were too quick. They sliced at her fingers and tugged at her hair and clothes, trying to pull her away from the protective ring of the wolves and the cover of the tree.

After each attack, the crows would regroup in the fog for a new wave. Soon Cora, Bram and Elle were covered in stinging red cuts on their hands, arms, legs and cheeks.

"We have to try something else!" Blaidd cried desperately. "Cora, Elle, have you any spells?"

Cora could think of nothing. Her Healing Spell was no good in a battle.

But Elle clutched the Green Soldier in her hand and spoke up.

"Spike barb, bristle, rip, torn. Forest, make a ring of thorns."

A wave of branches sprouted from the earth, as they had in the magic lesson, and wove together to make a spiked ring of thorns around the children and the wolves. This time the thorns even grew overhead, stopping the airborne attack.

The crows screamed in frustration, but they couldn't get

172

past the thorn wall. It scratched at them twice as hard as the wolves had and barred their path completely, until they had to turn back.

In the chaos of their retreat Cora heard Auberon screech loudly. "WE'LL NOT GIVE UP! WE'LL BE BACK WITH REINFORCEMENTS TO TAKE YOU TO OUR QUEEN! THERE'S NO ESCAPE!" With that final warning, he and his army disappeared in a flash of feathers into the ashen sky.

The children and the wolves waited until they heard the last croak of the last crow, the last wing beats of Auberon, and the last raven vanish into the distance. Then they stood and hugged each other in relief.

Elle spoke the spell to free them from the ring of thorns.

"Bushes made of spikes and stalks. Make a path that we might walk."

The thorns turned their barbs away at her command, and opened up a safe path for them to step through.

Bram spoke his spell to dissolve the fog:

"Smog and haze dissipate. Gloom go. Mist abate."

The fog drifted away. In its place snowflakes began to pummel them from above, whooshing through the air.

Cora looked around and found they were in a grove of silver trees, covered in frost. Elle was visibly wilting, leaning on Bram's shoulders to rest, but he looked tired too. His face was pale and drained of colour. Performing his magic had sucked all the energy out of him.

The wolves were covered in slashes from the crows. They licked their wounds wearily. Cora felt tired and broken too. She had cast no spells during the battle, but she was covered in cuts and bruises just the same. "Here, let me help you," she said, and clutching her Talisman in one hand and touching Faol, Blaidd and Cu in turn with the other, she cast her Healing Spell.

She had thought, with her weariness, the spell might not come, but then she felt the hum of the Red Soldier in her fist and a crackle of magic gathered beneath her fingertips while she spoke her spell.

"Fix, repair, heal, restore. Be hale and well, just like before."

The wolves' cuts closed up and they licked Cora's face in gratitude. Then Cora spoke the Healing Spell for Bram, Elle and herself.

"We shouldn't hang about, in case the Crow Army returns," Faol growled, when she was done.

"They're bound to have stationed a lookout to circle high above," Elle said. "That's what crows do when they're on the move together."

"In that case, we should walk for the next few miles," Blaidd advised.

"Good idea," Cu said. "Down here, night and the trees will hide us from view."

"And the fresh snowfall will cover our tracks," Bram added.

The six of them set off through the deep snow. It was slow going in the dark, but at least the falling flakes hid their foot and paw prints, as Bram had said they would, and with the inky canopy of trees there was no chance of being seen from above.

"I don't understand how the crows found us in my fog," Bram said, as they walked. "It was so encompassing! We shouldn't have needed the Thorn Spell as well."

"I don't understand it either," Faol said. "Perhaps the Fairy Queen used her crystal ball to see where we were going and informed her army. But there are none of her spyglass roses around here, so she should not have been able to see us."

"Spyglass roses?" Elle repeated. "What are they?"

"They are enchanted glass roses that bloom by both sun and moon, and grow wherever the Fairy Queen's magic plants them," Faol explained. "The Queen created them so she can keep a close eye through their rose petals on those who interest her, like watching through a spyglass."

Queasily, Cora remembered the glass rose pinned to her dress. She had thought it was a gift from Mama, but could it be one of the Fairy Queen's spyglass roses? Had she been tricked by its beauty into bringing the rose on this journey?

Had she allowed the Fairy Queen to spy on her family all this time? Was that how the Crow Army had known where they were even through the fog?

She pulled her cloak aside anxiously and revealed the rose to the others. "I found this in the churchyard yesterday. Is it…?"

Cu snarled at the sight of it and Blaidd let out a low growl.

"Indeed it is a spyglass rose," Faol barked, angrily. "I wish you'd told us of it earlier."

"There's no point in us trying to cover our tracks, when the Fairy Queen and her army can trace our movements through that vile thing," Blaidd snapped. "Take it off at once."

Cora reached for the rose, to pluck it from her chest. As she touched the sharp glass petals, a sudden image flashed into her mind: a pair of scheming, sparkling eyes, black as distant galaxies, watching her with intent. They were set in a pale porcelain face with a nose sharp as a knife, and long silver hair, tangled with wings, antlers and thorns. The Fairy Queen! It had to be!

Cora shivered. It was as if she could feel the Fairy Queen's gaze sending waves of power out through the glass rose, and as if those waves were somehow hooking into her soul. She shut her eyes and closed a hand round the rose, trying to make the images stop. She felt a sudden shiver as she did so, that felt like waking from a dream, and she knew at once that the wolves were right: the Fairy Queen had been using the glass rose to spy on them. In disgust, she ripped it from her dress and threw it down in the snow.

"Now crush it," Faol snarled.

Cora nodded, she put her boot over the rose to squash it, but an image of Mama flashed into her head and she flushed with pain. "It was growing beside Mama's name on her gravestone," she muttered.

"The Fairy Queen has truly marked your family," Blaidd said sadly, "if a spy glass rose was able to grow on your mother's grave."

"But, surely it *can't* be evil?" Cora said. "Not when it's so beautiful…"

"Beauty has nothing to do with goodness," Faol replied. "You cannot tell a thing's character by the way it looks; you must judge it on what it does."

"I don't believe you," Cora told the wolf, angrily. "That's nonsense. And it's the last thing we need to hear right now, quite frankly!" She felt horrible as she said this, like Papa at his most angry.

"It's the truth," Cu growled. "Why would we lie to you?"

Cora shook her head. She didn't know what more to say; she couldn't deny the wolves were right, and yet she couldn't put her foot on the rose either. It was like the little glass flower was calling to her, telling her not to.

"I don't understand why, but I don't think I can do it," she admitted.

"Then we can go no further with you," Blaidd said, "for you agreed to keep no secrets."

"And your lying recklessness about that has endangered us all," Cu growled.

"So we'll risk our lives for you no more," Faol added.

"Cora…" Bram said, nudging her. "Do something."

But Cora was too upset to protest.

"Where will you go?" Elle asked the wolves, sadly.

"We shall return to the safety of our pack," said Faol.

"What about the Dreaming Tree?" Bram pleaded. "You promised to take us there."

"It is a league's walk in that direction," said Blaidd, pointing out of the clearing with his nose. "You will find it in a clearing yonder, directly beneath the white belly of the moon. Follow your feelings," he advised. "The sleepier you get, the closer you are to the tree."

"Don't lie down and rest before you reach the clearing, no matter how tired you are," Blaidd added, "or you will fall into a sleep from which you may never awake."

"That's all the aid we can give," Cu snapped. "But we suggest you crush that rose at once."

"I understand," Cora told him. "Thank you for taking us this far."

"You will be fine from here on your own," Blaidd said. "The Dreaming Tree is not far, not at this hour. But smash that rose, and leave it behind."

"Goodbye," said Elle. "And thank you."

"Fly safely!" Bram called, and the three children watched disheartened as the wolves turned and leaped off to the south.

"Well done, Cora," Bram grumbled when they were finally gone. "You've cost us at least an hour on our trip. And thanks to you, the Fairy Queen knows exactly where we are."

"You should never have picked that rose," Elle said, staring down at it.

"Oh, shut up, both of you," Cora snapped angrily. "How was I to know?" Her toes were freezing and her face felt hot with shame, plus the tears would not stop.

They were right. She was to blame. It was all her fault the wolves had left. Everything was her fault. All the bad things that had happened to them. She looked at the watch.

"Eight-forty-five," she told Bram and Elle, speaking in a crisp and efficient way that she definitely didn't feel inside. "We've barely four-and-a-quarter hours left to save Acton. We'd best get going."

"What about the rose?" Bram folded his arms across his chest.

Cora stared at it, lying on the ground in the snow. She needed a moment. A minute on her own, without the others' constant questions and interruptions. "You go on ahead. I'll crush it, then follow."

Bram nodded, and he and Elle stepped off into the dusky forest.

Cora watched them go with tears streaming down her cheeks.

She lifted her foot and held it over the rose ready to stamp, but a wave of anxiety flooded over her like dirty river water.

It felt like she was about to crush a part of herself. How were they going to save Acton without it? Hadn't it brought her luck? Hadn't it helped her come this far?

She couldn't do it. Couldn't smash a thing of such beauty. She picked it up and, with a quick guilty glance ahead to check Bram and Elle weren't watching, she put it back in her pocket and followed her brother and sister into the dark.

20

LOST SOULS

"Make yourself comfortable," Brown-eyes said, ushering Acton into the driftwood hut and pulling the door to behind them. The old soul's lamp revealed the gloomy interior; a simple shelter that was little more than a roof and four walls, with a bone fireplace, a table and a few hard bone chairs where two more old souls sat. An old man with blue eyes and a woman with green eyes. This pair were whispering to each other behind their wavering see-through hands.

"Still living…" Blue-eyes whispered.

"Soul and body still together…" Green-eyes muttered.

Acton shivered as he took them in. "Thank you for your

hospitality," he said politely to the three old souls. Coriel shifted nervously in his pocket. He pressed a hand gingerly to his chest, warning her to stay hidden. It seemed enough of a shock to these three that Acton was alive, he didn't need them to witness a living bird as well.

"Are you cold?" Brown-eyes put his lamp down on the mantelpiece. "We never get cold. But I can light a fire, if you like. I've some driftwood I collected from the river." He took a tinderbox from the windowsill, crouched by the hearth and struck flint against steel a few times until a spark jumped from the flint to the driftwood in the fireplace. It smouldered feebly and, with no energy to burn, crackled and hissed disappointingly.

"Is this your home?" Acton asked the three of them.

"More of a prison," grumbled Blue-eyes at the table. He had white curly hair and a misty-looking face the colour of a leather satchel. "We're Lost Souls. The Fairy Queen gave us as gifts to the Dead King, when she was trying to bargain with him for the Glimmerglass Crown. I don't know how we came to be in her power after we'd died, though."

"Some curse of hers, probably," added Green-eyes. She had a blurred complexion and long white hair that was pinned up and decorated with a yellow glass tulip.

"Whatever it was, it has made us forget everything," Blue-eyes explained.

"And that means we're doomed to remain in the Dead Lands, in purgatory, until we remember our True Names," added Brown-eyes.

"Only then will we be free to leave this place," Green-eyes said. "And move on to whatever comes next in the afterlife. To be with the newly dead souls on the path, jumping into the sky and becoming one with the universe once more, that's all we want now. But until that happens, we must wait here and work in service of the Dead King."

"I'm sorry." Acton felt an odd sort of kinship with them, stuck in this isolated spot, unsure of who they were, or how to move on.

"Every curse has a splinter of a blessing embedded in it, even this one," said Brown-eyes. "My blessing is that I get to spend an eternity with these two wonderful old souls. Over...however long we've been here...we've become fast friends."

"We're acquainted with other Lost Souls too," Blue-eyes added. "Like the ferry keepers, we think they are under the same curse we are."

"And the Dead King's Portrait Painter, up at the palace," Green-eyes added. "She's very nice, but we all reckon she's under the curse too. The six of us work for the Dead King, but we still have hope of discovering our lost identities, so we can leave this place."

"Meanwhile," Brown-eyes gestured round the hut, "there's plenty to do."

The fire had grown stronger as it burned. Its light made the edges of the room much clearer. Acton could see shelves covered with marvellous objects: little glass sculptures, and metal mechanisms from clocks. "Is this how you fill your hours?" he asked. "Making and repairing things?"

"Oh, there's no time here." Brown-eyes's laugh was like a crackle of static. "I should know, I'm the Dead King's Clockmaker. My job is to cross the Dead River every week and wind the grandfather clock in his Throne Room. Because the Dead Lands have no time, that clock doesn't have any hands, nor any clockwork. There's no pendulum inside it and no winding key, but I pretend to wind it anyway. I mime the movement. That's what the Dead King wants, that's what he likes. It pleases him when people obey his commands. Plus, it seems to bring him some happiness to make-believe he rules a land where time exists. It makes him feel like he could be alive."

Acton shivered. "And what do you two do for the Dead King?" he asked the others.

"I'm his gardener," said Green-eyes. "He gets cross if he sees bare flowerbeds in his garden, but nothing grows here, because nothing's alive. So I sow plants that I carve from old pieces of glass and wood and bone that wash down the river, to trick him into thinking seeds are flourishing."

"And I help this good lady to make and plant the flowers," Blue-eyes mumbled. "I do the finishing on them. I polish them until they gleam, to try and make them as beautiful as I can, and please the Dead King. She and I go over in the boat together every now and then, with the ferry keepers, to plant our creations."

As Acton listened to their stories, deep in his mind he felt a glimmer of recognition. So much of what they were saying sounded like Mama's fairy tales of old. A sudden realization struck him, like a flash of lightning. "I know who you are," he shouted joyfully. "All three of you!"

"Tell us!" Blue-eyes and Green-Eyes implored him excitedly, together.

"Your name is Bob Glass," Acton told Blue eyes. "And this lady," he pointed to Green-eyes, "is your wife, Anna."

Bob and Anna hugged each other in joy, and whirled around the room in a jig of surprised delight. Brown-eyes smiled at his friends in awe. "Who am I?" he asked

"You're Otto Glass," Acton said. "The Clockmaker! Bob is your son. And Anna is your daughter-in-law."

"So we are!" cheered Anna and Bob, and rejoicing, they pulled Otto into their dance. The three of them spun in dizzy, ecstatic happiness and, with each turn they took about the room, their age and blurriness fell away like they were shrugging off heavy layers of tatty, old, moth-eaten clothing that no longer belonged. Their eyes brightened, their skin glowed, their hair grew wilder, and the light of being inside them grew stronger and more intense.

Soon everything about them looked fresh. It wasn't that they were younger, or older even, but more that they had transformed into richer, more authentic reflections of what they'd always been underneath their worries, become distilled to their essence, and truer versions of themselves.

"Thank you," Otto cried elated, hugging and kissing his son and daughter-in-law in glee, all the time grinning wildly at Acton. "Thank you for helping us remember who we are! It is the funniest feeling to forget yourself. It feels like you have lost something from your pocket, and that it has slipped ever so slightly out of reach. You tend to pick at that sensation like a scab, but still you don't recover the memories you once had. They could be nearby, almost within your grasp, or they could be a long way away from you, and if someone asked, you couldn't say which was true!"

He pulled apart from their embrace and smiled at Acton. "Only now, I have my name back! We all do! And I am starting to remember, *everything!* My wife…she was called Tempest! She was beautiful! A Storm Sorceress! She had a twin brother, a wild wolf named Thomas! Where are they now?"

"Alive and well in Fairyland," Acton said. "I saw them in the Fairy Queen's crystal ball." He didn't mention that Tempest and Thomas might be in danger, along with his brother and sisters, if he didn't succeed in fetching the Dead King's Glimmerglass Crown. He didn't want to alarm Otto, Bob and Anna any more than he already had, at least, not yet.

"Tempest and I lived in a house called Fairykeep Cottage!" Otto shouted, excitedly. "There was a Green, Blue, Yellow and Red room, each with their own brightly painted door, and unique weather!"

"Tempest was my mama," Bob said. "She was a herbal healer, who cast spells for the whole village. Anna and I took over Fairykeep Cottage, after she was gone. And after we married, you kept the garden, didn't you, Anna?"

Anna nodded. "And we had two darling daughters, Bob, remember? Maria and Eliza…but who are you?" she asked Acton. "How do you fit into all of this, and how do you know so much about us?"

Acton smiled and tears filled his eyes to hear these stories of his family's past. "My name's Acton Belle. Bob and Anna, you are my grandparents! My mama was your elder daughter, Maria Glass. She married my father, Patrick Belle. But she died last year, and we think her death was connected to the curse."

Acton hadn't wanted to say that last part, but he felt like had to let them know.

"Then why is Maria's soul not here with ours?" Bob asked, sadly.

"I don't know. It's a mystery," Acton admitted. It was something he'd been wondering himself.

"At least you're here," Grandma Anna said. "Though you look quite alive, quite...embodied...so we hope it is only for a flying visit. We met your brother and sisters when they were babies," she added. "Pat and Maria brought them to see us at the cottage, after they were born." She was quite chatty. Acton could suddenly see where Aunt Eliza got that from. "But we never got to meet you in real life!" Anna and Bob put their arms around him and gave him the most enormous hugs and kisses.

When they were done, Acton grinned at Otto, who had been waiting patiently to find out more about how he and Acton were connected. "Your wife, Tempest, is my great-grandma," Acton explained to him, and his brown eyes wrinkled in recognition. "You're my great-grandpa, Otto Glass!"

"I am!" Great-grandpa Otto said, delightedly shaking Acton's hand, and then thinking better of it and bringing him in for a hug too. When that finished, Acton remembered Coriel, who'd been hiding in his pocket this whole time.

"Coriel!" he called out. "Have you fallen asleep? It's safe. Come and see who I've found."

Coriel poked her beak out of his pocket. Her head jerked back in startled surprise when she saw who was before her. "Great Mulleins!" she cried. "Otto, Bob and Anna! How old they look! How pasty and see-through!"

"It's because they're souls, Coriel," Acton explained.

"Of course, my pigeon!" Coriel flew to each of the old souls in turn, and gave them a little peck of a kiss with her beak on their see-through cheeks. She fluttered to Great-grandpa Otto last of all and somehow, by some magic trick of the Dead Lands, managed to alight on his arm, despite his insubstantial nature. Great-grandpa Otto reached out and stroked her feathers with his thin fingers.

"Hello, Coriel," he cooed. "You were Tempest's best friend."

Coriel chirruped hello back.

"She remembers me!" Great-grandpa Otto said, petting Coriel under her chin. "She always adored me! Can you understand her, Acton, as Tempest did?"

Acton nodded.

"But what are you both doing here?" Grandma Anna asked.

"We're on a mission to fetch the Dead King's Glimmerglass Crown for the Fairy Queen," Acton explained. "If we don't

189

succeed, my brother and sisters, and perhaps Tempest and Thomas, and even the whole of Fairyland will be in danger."

"How awful," Grandpa Bob said.

"If there's any way we can help," Great-grandpa Otto added.

Acton shook his head. "Thank you," he said. "But I think I must do this on my own." He was about to say more, but he was interrupted by a rhythmic splashing outside.

"That's the ferry keepers," Great-grandpa Otto said. "The Blind Rower and the Seeing Navigator. They are answering the toll of the bell. They will take you across the Dead River to the Dead King's Palace."

"They may even be able to give you some advice on how to face the Dead King and win the crown," Grandma Anna said.

"But be careful how you approach that subject," Grandpa Bob advised. "They're not fond of strangers, or the living."

"You mustn't keep them waiting," Great-grandpa Otto said. "They don't like that. And you must think of something you can give in payment, as you have no coins."

Acton shivered. What could he possibly give to the two ferry keepers? A story perhaps?

"I wish I had time to get to know you properly," Acton told his grandparents and great-grandpa, as they showed him out of their hut and walked him to the end of the jetty.

He lit his magic ball. It bobbed above him, throwing a ring of sparkling light onto their happy faces. Coriel circled joyfully around them.

"We wish so too," said Grandpa Bob. "But I suppose it is time for us to move on to whatever comes next."

"And I must complete my mission," Acton said.

"Be careful in the Dead King's Palace," Grandma Anna said. "There are many dangers there. The Dead King's Portrait Painter will help you. She is a friend of ours, and a good soul."

"If anyone asks," said Grandpa Otto, hugging Acton one last time, "tell them you're the Clockmaker's Apprentice come to wind the Dead King's grandfather clock. That should get you to the Throne Room and the end of your mission without too many questions."

"Thank you," Acton said.

"No, thank *you*!" Otto replied. "You have saved us."

One by one the three old souls stroked Coriel's head. Then they kissed and hugged Acton farewell. As they held him in their arms, Acton felt a soft warmth surround him. It was a feeling of such deep bliss of belonging that it seemed as if he was not only being hugged by the three of them, but by all his ancestors. When his grandparents and his great-grandpa finally let him go, Acton felt as light as wind and as right as rain. He watched in a daze as the three old people held hands, and said their names.

"Robert."

"Anna."

"Otto."

When they'd finished, they shot up into the sky together in a stream of bright light, twinkling with magic and waving to Acton and Coriel as they streaked by across the black sky.

Acton watched as their light gradually faded away. He was glad Grandpa Bob wouldn't have to make flowers for the Dead King any more, and that Grandma Anna wouldn't have to plant them in the Dead Garden. He was happy too that Great-grandpa Otto wouldn't have to wind the clock with no time in the Dead Palace. But he was sad to see them go and scared to be left without them, as he stood on the pier knowing that there was still so much of his mission ahead, that he and Coriel would have to face alone.

The sculling of the boat grew louder in the distance. "Keep your wits about you, my fulmar," Coriel advised, jumping down into his pocket once more, so the ferry keeper wouldn't see her. "Play your cards close to your nest. Remember your cover story."

Acton nodded. First he was the Chosen One, now he was the Clockmaker's Apprentice. He wondered if he would ever get to be a son again, to Papa, or a little brother to Cora, Bram and Elle. He missed them more than ever.

As he stared anxiously into the murky distance a rowing

boat appeared through the black fog, gliding across the tarry water. A lantern hung from its prow, and two figures in black cowls sat at its stern. The Blind Rower and the Seeing Navigator. He shivered at the sight of them. They were finally here to take him across the Dead River, one step closer to the Dead King's Palace and hopefully finding the Glimmerglass Crown.

21

NOMAN'S LAND

Cora slouched along behind the others as they marched across a bare, snowy, moonlit landscape. The forest had ended a few minutes ago, and their surroundings had become a flat, barren, frozen wasteland. She checked her watch. Nine-thirty. Another forty-five minutes gone, and it felt like they were no closer to Acton!

Bram and Elle were far ahead. Cora let the space between them grow. Why didn't they look behind to see where she was, or wait for her to catch up with them? How were the three of them even going to rescue their brother if they couldn't stick together? Did they even care about her? If they didn't, then she decided she wouldn't care about them either.

She let the distance between them grow wider, until her brother and sister were so far off and so small that only their very edges glinted with moonlight, and they looked no bigger than the Red Soldier in her pocket. Or the key Acton had found, she thought angrily, or...the glass rose.

Was that really spying for the Fairy Queen, like the wolves had said? Cora still didn't quite believe it. She had an urge to look at the rose once more. Check it again. She pulled it from her pocket and stared mournfully at it. A teardrop fell from her cheek and splattered onto its icy, frozen petals, making a ripple of magic. Suddenly she saw, not her reflection, but another. Her heart leapt to her throat as she recognized it... those hard black eyes, the silver hair tangled with horns and thorns, the cracked porcelain smile...she was once again looking upon the glamorous face of the Fairy Queen.

"Come!" the Queen whispered, in a voice like breaking glass, then she raised a hand and beckoned.

Cora felt a fuzz fill her mind. She blinked blearily and tipped her head towards the rose. She felt, no wished, she could fall into its centre and escape all this. She just had to do as the Queen commanded.

"WHAT ARE YOU DOING!" Bram grabbed her, and tugged her away from the Queen's image.

"DON'T!" Elle shouted in her ear, snatching the rose and throwing it down on the frozen ground.

The Fairy Queen's eyes shone with anger beneath the rippling petals, turning the rose from white to red. "Come to me!" she called, before Bram's big-booted foot stamped on the rose, crushing it to shards in the snow.

Cora blinked.

The spell was broken.

She snuck a guilty glance at the other two, through eyes hot with tears.

They said nothing, just turned and kept on walking, and she had no choice but to wipe the stinging shame from her cheeks and follow.

A scrub of shadowy black woodland appeared, and, as the three of them stepped through it, a new sound accosted their ears.

At first Cora thought it was a bubbling brook, but then she recognized the chatter of cheerful voices. They filled the night air, floating in dribs and drabs on the cold breeze.

They were far enough away that it was hard to distinguish the words. But near enough that Cora could guess which side of the darkened wood they echoed from.

Soon they saw glimmers of light between the tree trunks, flickering at chest height like some sort of spell. For a second Cora thought it might be the Fairy Queen playing tricks again, but this felt different. There wasn't the same anxiety in the magic.

"Whoever they are out there," she said, "maybe they'll help us!"

The three of them carefully approached the sound and light, but the direction they were coming from kept changing. First it seemed to be to one side of them, then the other, then up ahead, then far behind.

Cora, Bram and Elle began running frantically towards the fizz of sounds and lights in the dark – they didn't want it to get away. They stumbled this way and that, but each time they turned in a new direction, the magical sounds and lights shifted.

Soon the three children were dizzy and lost, deep in the dense wood. Cold, coated in snow and breathing heavily, they lurched into a clearing, where a great long wooden table with thick oak legs stood. It was laid with stacks of plates, a regiment of silver cutlery, and rows of tall glass goblets, clay vases filled with holly branches and tall, brass candelabras. Rows of empty, polished mahogany chairs with curved and spoked backs stood along the length of the table on either side. Each empty place seemed to be waiting for a guest, one of the many, whose voices and lights they'd seen and heard dotting the woods. But they had yet to appear. A white tent with golden tent poles arched over everything, keeping the snow at bay. As the children stood staring at these place settings, the guests started to arrive, crunching through the moonlit snow.

Cora recognized their types from the descriptions in Mama's stories: they were goblins, kobolds, boggarts, gnomes, pixies and naiads. Some had spines like porcupines, others snouts like pigs or eyebrows of ivy, some had thick fur, a few had deer horns, a handful had hair made of brambles. And each wore a winter coat made of cobwebs, with scarves, hats and gloves made of moss to ward against the cold of the night.

Cora, Bram and Elle hid behind a tree trunk and watched the strange company squawk, chirrup, cheer, clap, dance and leap across the clearing to take their seats.

When everyone was finally settled, a Fairy at the head of the table spoke.

"For what we are about to receive, I offer maledictions to the Fairy Queen. May every affliction on the Fair Isle and our dear Noman's Land prick at her glass heart. May the streams, rivers and oceans swallow her whole, then run dry. May the mountains, cliffs and rocks grind her to dust. May the woods, trees and plants grow on her grave. May her stalactites and stalagmites melt, may her Glass Tower fall. And may we finally be free of her icy grip, so that new life can sprout in our land once again."

The motley company cheered and clapped and banged their knives and forks on the table in agreement. Cora felt relieved. These Fairies were against the Queen too. Perhaps they'd be on her and her brother's and sister's side?

"Please," she said, stepping forward into the ring of flickering candlelight, to reveal herself. "We're lost."

The Fairies shrieked and scraped their chairs back at the sight of her. Bram and Elle waved nervously for her to duck back into the dark, but Cora dragged the pair of them up beside her, and continued speaking. All eyes at the table were on her, but their cold gaze barely dented her confidence, not after her grand speech and story to the Wolfmoot.

"Can you help us reach the Dreaming Tree?" she asked. "We've been walking for ages, but we can't seem to find it."

"Noman will help you, young humans!" said a Fairy gentleman in the nearest seat.

"Are you sure he should, Sir Woodruff Sneezewort?" asked a Fairy lady opposite him, who would've looked rather grand if her clothes had not been patched with twigs and mud. "They look positively waif-like…wind-tousled and wild. And they appear to be covered in raven and crow poop!"

"And the coarse hair of moulting wolves," said another Fairy fellow on the far side of the lady, who wore a wig made of grass that sprouted grey mushrooms and a beauty spot on his upper lip that was quite obviously a resting ladybird. "But, Lady Primrose Cowslip, if these wastrels demand our help, Noman should give it."

"Here, here, Sir Argus Firebrat!" said Lady Primrose Cowslip clapping delicately. "Do you young humans know Noman's Song?"

Cora, Bram and Elle shook their heads. "Who's Noman?" Bram asked.

"Noman is an island," said Sir Woodruff Sneezewort, "entirely of himself."

"Noman is the ruler of this land," added Lady Primrose Cowslip. "It's named after him."

"Noman is a storyteller, a poet and a singer," said Sir Argus Firebrat, cheerily. "We sing his song every evening at dinner, and make up new words each time. Since you're here, you must help us."

"We sing a verse," said Lady Primrose Cowslip, "and you sing an answer."

"So it goes on, until we – and each of you – have sung a part," said Sir Woodruff Sneezewort.

"If Noman deems the song worthy," said Sir Argus Firebrat, "then you may sit and partake with us, and he will answer your question."

"How's that sound?" asked Lady Primrose Cowslip.

"What do you think?" Cora asked Bram and Elle.

"It sounds like a riddle," said Elle.

"It *sounds* like a trick," said Bram.

"Perhaps the song'll be like one of Mama's?" Cora suggested.

Elle ruminated on this. "It's our only chance to get back on the right path and find Acton."

"Then let's do it," Bram suggested nervously.

"We agree to sing your song," Cora told the Fairies.

The Fairies cheered and snapped their twiggy fingers in crackling rhythm, and the flames of their candles seemed to leap and dance to the beat, as with a grating mixture of high and low voices, the incongruous group began to sing…

"Welcome to Noman's Land. Green as the moss.
Stay and look round for the memories you've lost."

They waved at Cora. It was her turn to join in. Her heart beat faster than their clapping hands and snapping fingers, and her thoughts fluttered with possibilities, like a moth round a candle flame. She was in such a daze, she could conjure no new words to mind. The Fairies' raucous, wild, drumming rhythms echoed in her ears. Finally, she took a deep breath and tried to slow her thoughts and a rhyme came to her:

"Search as you might, fear is melted away,
like the sun thaws the frost on a cold winter's day."

The Fairies cheered her success, and countered with a gloomy couplet:

"Life is washed out of mind on the Dead Land's dark river.
Dreams burn to dust in the present's bleak glimmer."

Bram sang a brilliant playful answer:

"Everything that you see, everything that you are,
Sparkles like the hope of the first evening star."

A confused Elle sang her part straight after Bram's:

"There's only this moment, that much you'll agree,
So dance and be merry! Rejoice and be free!"

The Fairies whooped with joy and astonishment at their contributions and sang a last more ominous verse:

"Noman makes his home in the now and the never,
You have no other choice you will be here for ever!"

"Bravo!" Noman shouted from the head of the table, when they'd finished. The Fairies around him banged their fists merrily on the tabletop, making the glass and chinaware and flaming candles jump in the air, and land back down again.

"What beautiful voices you have!" said Sir Argus Firebrat.

"What poet's hearts, and storyteller's souls!" added Lady Primrose Cowslip.

"Come, sit! Join us!" trilled Sir Woodruff Sneezewort.

Cora felt as if she hadn't rested her feet in hours. She slumped down with relief in an empty chair at the table, which was laden with silver cutlery and sparkling, gold-rimmed plates.

Bram and Elle sat down in two free spaces beside her.

"About our question…" Cora said.

"Noman thinks you should eat first," said Sir Woodruff Sneezewort. "You must be absolutely famished after all your terrible travails, so have some repast! Supper time is almost past!"

Cora blinked as great dishes magically appeared among the plates. Golden platters filled with the most appetizing meal she'd ever seen. There was cold chicken, cold tongue, cold ham, cold beef, pickled gherkins, salad, rolls, cress sandwiches, potted meat, ginger beer, lemonade, soda waters, iced tea, fresh strawberries, sugared buns, jellies, plum cake.

"Noman says 'enjoy!'" Sir Argus Firebrat whispered, nodding at their distant leader, far off at the head of the table.

Cora's stomach rumbled. She hadn't eaten in many hours, not since last night's supper at Fairykeep Cottage with Aunt Eliza and Kisi. She wasn't even sure how long ago that was. She would've checked the time again, but Papa had always told her it was rude to look at your watch at the dinner table. At any rate it would have to be after ten by now, which was way past the end of supper time back home, and they did need to keep their strength up if they were to free Acton and face the Fairy Queen.

But even as Cora had this persuasive thought, which hardly seemed to be her own, she suddenly remembered that they weren't supposed to accept Fairy food and, just in time, for Bram was already reaching for a cold beef sandwich. She slapped his hand away. "Remember the last thing Tempest said to us," she hissed. "No eating!"

"She probably didn't mean freshly prepared, delicious-looking food like this," Bram wheedled. "Only foraged stuff, picked from the forest."

"Poisonous fungus, and the like," Elle suggested. "This'll be fine, won't it, Bramble?"

Bram nodded. Cora wasn't so sure, but she felt hungrier than ever. Everything smelled so flavoursome! She licked her lips. Saliva gathered in the corners of her mouth. Finally she gave in and nodded to Bram and Elle. The Fairies watched with what seemed like far too much interest as the three of them gorged themselves on the succulent meal.

The more Cora ate the more she wanted. Everything tasted so amazing, and she stuffed her face as if she might never eat again. But no matter how much of the irresistible fare she swallowed, she never felt full. None of the luscious treats seemed to sate her gnawing hunger. She kept going, so did Bram and Elle, but, as they continued to feast, Cora felt herself slowly unmooring from reality. A funny new sound started ringing in her ears. A kind of…

Buzzzzz! Buzzzzz! Buzzzzz!

Gradually, Cora began to notice flies everywhere. They were on everything. Hopping over the food. Jumping round the plates. Crawling over drinking goblets. Flitting in and out of the Fairies' open, smirking mouths. The meal had started to rot and decompose. It was festering faster than Cora could swallow it. Soon the whole banquet looked mouldy and rancid, and it stank to high heaven of putrefying decay. The stench was so strong it made Cora want to gag.

She stopped eating at once. Her eyes watered and nauseous bile bubbled in her throat. When she glanced at Bram and Elle they were still gobbling down the grotesque, septic filth, along with the Fairies. Or had the Fairies been eating? Cora looked down at their plates, full of slop, and realized she hadn't seen a single one of them lift a fork or finger to take a single bite.

Dizzily, she tried to push her chair back from the table, but found she could not stand. "The food's toxic," she slurred.

Bram and Elle put down their forks and tried to leave too, but neither could.

"Don't go," said Lady Primrose Cowslip. "You sang Noman's Song so sweetly."

"Noman needs fresh faces," said Sir Argus Firebrat.

"And new mouths to eat his delectable treats!" said Sir Woodruff Sneezewort.

Cora bit her lip. She could feel her chin beginning to drop. She tried to shake her head to rid herself of her sleepiness, but it was no use. The rotten tripe she'd so willingly eaten was having a soporific effect. It filled her brain and belly with a heavy, woollen feeling, dragging her down in its knotted sickly grip. Out of the corner of her drooping eyelids she could make out her brother and sister. They were slumping forward in their seats, their eyes slowly closing. Cora was beginning to forget their names. What were they called again?

Bran…?

Bran-elle?

Branwell…?

…Br-ellis…?

…Emily…?

…sounded wrong…

…she'd didn't recall…

…her own name either. Was it…

…Charlotte…?

…Curer…?   …the words tangled…

…like spindle threads…

…in her sewing box…

…and drifted away…

"Don't sleep at dinner, Jane dear," she mumbled. "It's terribly rude in mixed company. I'll open the window to let in some fresh Eyre…" She pinched herself, but no sense would come. She needed the Waking Spell. How did it go?

"If we shadows have offended,"

…no, that wasn't right…

"think but this and all is mended."

Too late! Cora's head plopped into a vibrant green, mouldy jelly full of frogspawn, which caught her like a soft pillow as she tumbled into a deep sleep right then and there at the table.

22

FERRY KEEPERS

Acton stood outside the little hut, on the jetty's end, over the Dead River. His magic orb of light floated overhead. Coriel fidgeted in his dressing-gown pocket, as he watched the two dead ferry keepers, in their hoods and long black robes, approach in their boat. A lantern hissed and flickered at the boat's prow, smearing a weak light on the river, and the oars made horrible sucking sounds each time the Blind Rower thrust them into the water.

"Ahoy there!" Acton called, remembering Grandma Anna's advice about being nice to the ferry keepers. "The three Lost Souls in the hut wanted me to send their regards. They couldn't be here themselves, but I…" His voice dwindled away nervously.

"Starboard a fraction," the Seeing Navigator growled, ignoring Acton and talking to the Blind Rower, who was bringing the boat in beside the rickety old pier.

"Who is doing all that chattering?" the Blind Rower asked.

"A lively looking alive boy," said the Seeing Navigator, staring inquisitively at Acton.

Acton shivered and stared back. The Seeing Navigator's face was not as unpleasant looking as his gruff voice had led Acton to believe, instead he had friendly green eyes, and an old, wrinkled smile. His white hair was streaked with a few strands of red.

"One of the living," the Rower muttered. "Never had that before." He rubbed his pale, lined face, while his eyes, blind and milky-white, stared past Acton. A few strands of blonde hair grew on his head, curling around his ears. Both ferry keepers were far more normal looking than Acton had been expecting, and, somehow, that had a calming effect over him.

"What's that bright light yonder?" the Rower asked.

"The boy has a moon," the Navigator replied.

"A moon, eh?" The Rower laughed. "Must be a powerful sorcerer to own a moon."

Acton's globe was nowhere near as bright as the moon,

but perhaps they'd forgotten what that looked like. "It's a magic orb," he explained, extinguishing it. He didn't want it to distract them. Keeping the light going was draining his energy anyway.

"What brings you to our crossing?" the Rower asked.

"I'm the Clockmaker's Apprentice," Acton said, remembering the story Great-grandpa Otto had advised him to tell. "I'm going to wind the grandfather clock in the Dead King's Palace, while the *Clockmaker* is…indisposed."

"If you want us to ferry you across to the Dead King's Palace on the far side," the Navigator said, "then we must agree a toll. The payment is two gold coins, given when we reach the midpoint of the river. We never ask for them until the midpoint, because we never know if we'll make it that far."

"Those that haven't found the fare by then," the Rower added, "are thrown overboard, and washed down to the Dead Sea."

"But I'm not dead!" Acton protested. "And I don't have two gold coins. Nobody told me there was a fare, or that I would be sacrificed to the Dead River if I couldn't pay it. How can you be so mean and unfair?"

"They're not our rules," the Rower said. "They're set by the Dead King. Those that want to see him must pay the crossing fee. We cannot disobey that command."

"If he doesn't get his coins from us at the end of the day," the Navigator explained, "and if the souls who've crossed don't tally with the coins given, then we are the ones who suffer."

"For ever," the Rower added.

"Can't you make an exception in my case?" Acton said.

"No exceptions." The Navigator shook his head. "It's more than our job's worth."

"Unless..." The Rower smiled knowingly at the Navigator. "We took another form of payment."

"Like what?" Acton asked, with a shiver.

"If you can guess our True Names by the time we reach the centre of the river," the Rower said. "Then we'll accept them as your fare."

"But if I guess your True Names," Acton said, "you'll shoot up into the sky and disappear, and I'll have to row the last stretch to the far bank myself. And if you're gone, then how will I call the boat from the other side to take me back when I want to go home?"

"No need to worry about that," the Rower said.

"Why not?" Acton asked.

"Because no one ever comes back from Dead King's Palace," the Navigator said. "At least, not this way," he added, sadly.

"I see," said Acton with a shiver. "But what if I *can't* guess your True Names by the time we reach the middle of the river?"

"Then, like we told you before," the Navigator said, "you'll suffer the same fate as all other non-payees."

"To be thrown overboard," the rower reiterated. "As the Dead King decrees. So are you taking the deal, or what?"

Acton thought about it… He didn't like the terms, but if he didn't agree to them then he couldn't venture further into the Dead Lands to fetch the crown and complete his mission. But if the Rower and the Navigator didn't know their True Names, how was he to discover them?

"Coming aboard, then, lad?" the Navigator asked, and, in answer, Acton climbed into the boat and took a seat. When he was finally settled, the Navigator untied the mooring rope and the Rower sculled away from the pier. Acton stared as it disappeared into the fog, knowing now for certain that there was no way back in that direction.

The air out on the Dead River was bracing and chilly. Coriel fidgeted secretly in Acton's pocket, making the only warmth on the cold waters, and the black sky stretched off infinitely as far as the eye could see. "What's out there?" Acton asked, pointing downstream, as the Rower rowed ever onwards, directed softly by the Navigator.

"The Dead Sea, like we told you," the Navigator said. "Where the melancholy souls go. The ones who've given up completely and despair of everything so much that they do not want to move on to the bright light of what comes next."

For some reason this made Acton think of Papa, and he felt overwhelmed with sadness.

The Navigator eyed him suspiciously. "You're not actually the Clockmaker's Apprentice at all, are you?"

Acton shook his head.

"So what brings you to our crossing?" the Rower asked. "Be honest," he advised. "You're on our boat, and there's no turning back."

Acton thought of their earlier threats to throw him in the river if he didn't help them, and decided he'd better answer truthfully. "I've come to steal the Dead King's crown."

"Oh?" said the Navigator. "Why take on such a foolish mission?"

"I made a bargain with the Fairy Queen," he replied. Coriel pecked anxiously at his chest, warning him to say no more, but Acton ignored her. "If I can get her the Glimmerglass Crown, she has promised to send me and my siblings safely home to England.

"Never make a deal with a Fairy, lad," the Rower advised. "They'll steal the coat off your back, the coin in your pocket and the wits in your head, and, finally, if they can, and just for fun, they'll take your heart and soul."

"You won't be able to steal the crown," the Navigator said. "You'll have to challenge the Dead King for it. He'll wager for your soul, so try to make a good bargain on your side."

Acton didn't like the sound of that.

"The Dead King is fond of chess," the Rower advised. "He learned it from a Swedish knight, centuries ago."

"I'm no good at chess," Acton lamented.

"Then you'll have to challenge him to another game," the Navigator said. "Do you know any riddles?"

"A few," said Acton.

"Be sure to pick one he's not heard of," the Rower said. "You'll have to be very clever to stop him winning."

The Navigator nodded in agreement. "The Dead King's been around since the dawn of time. He knows the answer to most things. And if he doesn't know the answer, he will use his magic and his cunning to cheat. We ourselves have tried many tricks to get free from his service, but we've never succeeded."

The pair of ferry keepers went silent for a moment. The navigator took a pair of items out of his pocket. One was a small piece of bone, and the other, Acton was shocked to see, was a flint sharpened to a point. The navigator chipped away with the flint at the bone as if he was sharpening them both.

"Is that flint to defend against river spirits?" Acton asked.

"It's a whittler." The Navigator held up the bone. "This is what I'm whittling."

"He used to be a woodcarver," the Rower explained.

"That much I remember," the Navigator said.

Acton nodded. He could see the shape of a person hidden in the bone's rough carving. It would take a little more whittling for the Navigator to bring it out, but it was there distinctly, beneath the surface, like a soul hidden inside a body.

"What's it going to be?" Acton asked.

"A soldier," the Navigator explained. "I make them for the younger children crossing over. Sometimes they're scared of what comes next, so I give them one of my home-made toys to help them feel better."

"A soldier," Acton repeated. It was an odd thing for him to be carving.

"We're almost at the centre of the river now," the Navigator announced, putting the flint back in his pocket, but keeping the carved bone in his hand. "Time for you to try and guess our True Names."

"I cannot," Acton admitted sadly. "I don't know them." He looked at the pair sitting side by side, and as he studied the Navigator, still holding the bone figure of the soldier, he suddenly knew.

"I've got it!" Acton told the ferry keepers. "But there's one way to be sure." He took his Talisman from his pocket, and showed it to the Navigator. "Do you recognize this?"

"The Blue Soldier!" the Navigator said, excitedly, and as he said those words it was as if his face came into focus. "I whittled him long ago! For my son…from the wood of the Fairy Tree…planted in the Tambling churchyard. I don't remember my son's name, or mine, but there were four soldiers altogether, Red, Yellow, Green and Blue. Here, look…" He took the soldier from Acton and turned it over to reveal the M. and P. carved there. "This is my initial, on the base." He pointed at the M, before handing the Blue soldier to the Rower.

"And mine!" said the Rower, tracing the groove of the P. with his fingers. "I painted this soldier for our son, back when I could see… I think his name was Thomas, but I don't remember my name, or yours, my dear navigator."

"You're Prosper!" Acton said, excitedly. "And you," he pointed at the Navigator, "are Marino. And, according to my mama's old stories, when you were alive the pair of you were together, just as you are now!"

"So we were, and so we are!" The two ferry keepers' souls smiled at each other, and as they did they lost their pale ravaged look and became more human. Prosper's greying curls grew thick and wild and blonde on his head and his white eyes became blue again and filled with joy. Marino's cheeks became rosier, his hair a proper red, and his green eyes flickered with happiness.

Acton was almost as shocked by their sudden transformation as he had been the first time, with the others in the hut. Words tumbled out of him ecstatically. "You were the adoptive parents of my great-grandma Tempest, and my great-grand-uncle Thomas... I'm your great-great-grandson, Acton Belle! He tapped his chest happily. "A pleasure to meet you. And this... This is Coriel! Tempest's robin!" He shook his dressing gown. "Come out, Coriel. Come and see Prosper and Marino!"

"Really!" Coriel twittered, swooping from Acton's pocket. "It's really them! You guessed right? How marvellous, little puffin." She soared up excitedly in the air and circled the ferry boat, staring at the two ferry keepers.

"Coriel!" Prosper called, holding out his hand. Coriel landed on his arm and pecked him a little kiss on his palm. Prosper threw up his hands and released Coriel into the air and she fluttered over to Marino and kissed his ear, then she flew back to Acton's shoulder.

"I remember my daughter Tempest!" Prosper said, excitedly. "She would row out on the river with me, and

Coriel would join us, just like this, And when I started to lose my sight, Tempest and Coriel, and my son, Thomas, and you, my darling Marino," he added, smiling adoringly at Marino, "would help me on the boat."

"Of course we would, my love," Marino said.

"The four of you lived at Fairykeep Cottage together," Acton said. "Coriel too!"

"I was the ferry keeper on the Tambling River that ran behind our house," Prosper said.

"And I carved wooden toys for the children of Tambling Village, and for our own children... But where are Thomas and Tempest now?"

"They're alive in Fairyland," Acton said. "I saw them in the Fairy Queen's crystal ball. All these years and they have managed to avoid the tendrils of her curse. I hope, if I can end that curse for ever, I might get to meet them."

"I believe you will do both those things!" said Marino.

"We don't doubt it!" Prosper added. "After all, look how far you've come. It takes great bravery for the living to cross this far into the Dead Lands. We'll row the pair of you to the far side of the Dead River, and see you on your way."

The four of them rowed on together. Not as strangers, but as family. Coriel sat on the prow with the lamp.

"I miss the gabbling joy of a real river," Prosper announced as he rowed. "And the sea. The living ocean, up there. The smell of its warm salt on the wind's breath, its deep blue, stretching off as far as the eye could see."

"Perhaps in the great beyond, or whatever comes after this," Marino suggested, at the other oar, "there will be an ocean for us to swim in."

"There is always water!" Prosper said. "Where there is water there is life! We can say our True Names together. There'll be no more rowing or navigating for us, we can move on as one to the peace, tranquillity and love of whatever's next. All thanks to our great-great-grandson!"

"All thanks to Acton!" Marino agreed.

The two of them smiled at him as they finally arrived at the far side of the river.

Another wooden pier jutted out of the water. Marino tossed the rope over a mooring post and brought them alongside it, and Acton and Coriel got out of the boat.

"Goodbye, Acton." Marino hugged him.

"And good luck!" Prosper kissed his forehead. "Give our regards to the Dead King's Portrait Painter. She's up there by herself, in his palace. It'll be lonely for her without the rest of us to talk to, but she's a good soul, I'm sure she'll help you in your quest for the crown."

"Thank you again for our True Names," Marino said. Then the pair took each other's hands and looked into each other's eyes, and said their names at the same time.

"Prosper."

"Marino."

And like Otto, Anna and Bob before them, they shot up together into the sky, sparkling like shooting stars and disappearing on to the peace of whatever came next.

Acton stared up at the Dead Sky, watching the light they had made slowly fade away. He was glad that his great-great-grandpas no longer had to row Death's ferry boat together. And he knew they were not gone, not really. For he could feel the memory of them and the warmth of their company burning in his heart. A last flicker of their light reflected off the side of the ferry boat, and Acton saw its name written there, mirrored in the black waters. It was only one word –

Nixie

– but it made him smile, because that was the name Prosper and Marino had given their boat when they'd been alive. She even had a scratch down her starboard side, like in Cora's story, where she'd scraped a hidden river rock.

As far as Acton could tell, she was the same boat, her name revealed once more, now that her ferrymen had found themselves and their own True Names.

He supposed that he could leave *Nixie* tied up, so that he could find her for his return journey, but Prosper and

Marino had told him that he wouldn't be coming back this way, and he had a strong feeling they were right.

You can never step in the same river twice, Mama used to say. And this was a river he had no desire to revisit.

Everything had changed, and if he truly wanted to find the Glimmerglass Crown, then he'd have to find another path out of the Dead Lands.

He untied the little boat from the dock and let her float off downstream, so she would be free to drift out to the Dead Sea and the peace of wherever that ocean would take her.

When she was finally gone, like Prosper, Marino, Otto, Anna and Robert before her, he turned and, with a queasy feeling in his belly, set off walking through the Dead King's Gardens, towards the Dead Palace.

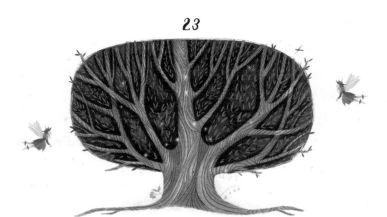

23

THE TROLL

Cora dreamed of nothing. She woke some time later in a night-shrouded wintery clearing in the woods, face down in the frost-rimmed grass. Her bones had frozen and a chill ran through her like damp up a wall. A horrible leaden feeling filled her belly; the kind you get after going to sleep on an unpleasant meal. She clapped her hands to ward off the cold and sat up.

The rancid banquet had disappeared, so had the Fairies, along with the table laden with candlesticks, china and cutlery, and the warm tent. Only Bram remained, dozing in the night shadows at her side. The frost had melted beneath his body, and his breath blew from his mouth like clouds…

But Elle…where was she?

As her eyes became accustomed to the dark, Cora peered anxiously into the blackness, searching for her sister. Her shivers turned to fear as she realized Elle was nowhere to be seen. How could she disappear like that? Where on earth was she? Had Noman taken her? Or Auberon and the Crow Army? Or the Fairy Queen?

Nerves buzzed through Cora as she tried to order her muddled thoughts. She needed to wake Bram and, together, they had to find Elle, because the three of them needed to reach the Dreaming Tree to rescue Acton. She checked her watch. So much time had passed since she'd last looked, many hours had slipped away. It was now one minute past eleven.

There was no more time to lose. She shook Bram. But could not rouse him. The drowsiness lay so heavily over him it was like he was sleeping beneath a slab of stone. Then she remembered Tempest's Waking Spell. She clasped the Red Soldier in her fist and felt it hum, and touched Bram's temples as she spoke the spell:

"All dreams and nightmares now abate! Rise and shine, come, sleeper, wake!"

Bram sat up with a yawn and looked around. "Where's Elle?"

"Missing," Cora told him.

Bram staggered anxiously to his feet and wandered around, shocked at the sight of the dark, empty clearing. His eyes were red from the cold. "She could be anywhere, Cor. How do we find her?"

An idea pricked through Cora's panic. "We'll make a new spell. A Finding Spell!" She touched her chest. "Remember how Tempest and Thomas, and even Aunt Eliza said magic comes from the heart, in here?" She pressed a hand to her chest. "If we keep Elle in our hearts as we create the spell and truly believe we can find her, then it's bound to work! Then, as we're focusing on her, we need to make rhyming couplets that tell the magic what to do."

They both thought hard about Elle. Cora remembered everything she'd learned from her sister about nature, flowers and trees. How Elle loved insects, animals, and all living things.

"I think it's working," Bram said. "But what about the words, where should we start with those?"

"Say the first line that comes into your head," Cora suggested. "I'll say the second."

Bram clutched the Yellow Soldier, thought for a moment, and said:

"Magic gleam and magic glister."

Cora held the Red Soldier, felt its hum, and said a second line:

"Go find Elle, our younger sister."

The pair of them put the whole spell together:

"Magic gleam and magic glister. Go find Elle, our younger sister."

Cora felt her fingers crackle as soon as they finished the spell. She glanced over at Bram. His hair was stood on end, as if he'd had a static shock. She was about to say something more to him, when sparks leaped from each of their hands, like flint striking steel.

The glowing sparks circled in the air, then zipped through the dark woods, their glare reflecting off the snow. Cora and Bram raced after them.

Cora's whole body felt ragged with fear as she ran. She floundered and stumbled in her panic to keep up. They didn't want to lose the sparks in the dark! They hurried onwards. They had to keep going. They couldn't afford to stop. The sparks had zigzagged off into the distance, and whizzed on further, before circling around a great hulking mound of rock that looked like part of a fallen mountain.

As Cora and Bram watched, a rocky outcrop on the edge of the mound suddenly moved and became a great raised arm with a hand on the end, whose five slab-sized fingers were clenched in a craggy fist. The fist batted away the sparks of the Finding Spell, and Cora realized with horror that the small mountain was actually a troll. Its massive face looked like a boulder that had been left out on a hilltop in the rain. Its skin was as pockmarked as chipped rock and its hair green as moss. The troll stomped its feet, shaking snow from the canopies of the nearby trees. It yanked on a long dog-lead like rope that it seemed to have been sitting on. Cora was shocked to see that tied to the rope's far end was...

Elle!

"'URRY UP!" the troll growled. Elle pressed her hands over her ears as its voice boomed across the forest, shaking snow from the trees, and shivering through Cora and Bram down to the very foundations of their feet.

The troll was walking quite fast. Its great slab-like legs rubbed together grinding loose dirt, moss and chips of stone and strewing them in its path. Cora and Bram managed to keep up with it by running along, following this scattered trail. It was holding something in its other hand. At first Cora thought it was a large glass marble but, as they got closer, it glinted in the light from the sparks, and she realized that the troll was using it to see through the night. It was a glass eye.

"YOU'RE DAWDLIN'!" the troll screamed at Elle, screwing up its red-capped fungus nose in disgust. Then it began to sing, in a voice that was cacophonous enough to knock the birds stone dead from the sky...

"MY NAME IS GRIPEWATER!

SO LOCK UP YOUR DAUGHTERS!
OR I'LL EAT THEM FOR A MIDNIGHT SNACK,
AND MAKE THEIR BONES GO CRACK!"

"He's going to eat her!" Bram whispered, in terror.

"We have to cut her rope!" Cora said, thinking of the key in her pocket with its sharp teeth.

Under cover of all the noise Gripewater was making, they tried to sneak alongside him in the dark. He had reached a sheer cliff face. Elle let out a fearful scream as Gripewater dragged her into a cave. Cora and Bram crept up to the cave mouth, and peered in. At the far end of the cave was a crackling fire. Mammoth bones, bear skulls and tiger ribcages littered the cave's interior, poking half-buried from the ground like white tree roots. The dancing flames made their shadows loom large on the walls.

"SIDDOWN!" Gripewater said, throwing Elle into the inkiest corner. She watched him miserably as he piled more branches and bones up on the fire. As its flames leaped higher, he began singing cheerfully once again, his voice bouncing off every nook and cranny of rock in an echoing, discordant chorus.

"A HANDFUL OF SPHAGNUM MOSS,
A POCKETFUL OF RYE.
ONE TASTY HOOMAN GIRL,
BAKED IN A PIE."

"What are we going to do?" Bram muttered.

Cora shivered. She had no idea. She put her fingers to her lips to warn Bram to keep quiet, and beckoned him into the furthest, blackest corner of the cave.

They hid behind a giant rock, then skirted behind a humongous gnawed ribcage and a skull the size of a small boat.

With each move they made they got a little closer to the spot where Elle was tied up. But they still had to pass a wide-open space in front of Gripewater, and the light of his roaring fire, to reach her.

"Cast your Fog Spell," Cora whispered to Bram. "Gripewater hasn't a chimney. He'll think it's fire smoke filling the cave."

Bram nodded, and whispered the spell:

"Fog haze. Gloom slather. Murk come. Mist gather."

He must've still been tired, because the spell didn't work quite as well as it had before.

Still there was enough of Bram's fog to float up from the floor and join the smoke from Gripewater's fire. Together the fog and smoke filled the cave with a murky, eye-stinging smog that smothered everything like a blanket.

In the blur of it, Cora and Bram were able to sneak right up to where Elle sat. Her eyes lit up with relief as she saw them. *Hurry!* she mouthed. She leaned towards them, pulling her arms away from her body to show Cora and Bram that they were trussed behind her back.

Bram reached for her bonds. He tried to untie the knots in the rope but they were pulled tight. "You've small fingers, Cor," he whispered. "You try."

Cora shook her head and instead felt in her pocket for the key, but at that moment Gripewater muttered:

"Extinguish!"

And the smog disappeared, leaving them completely exposed in the firelight.

"'ERE YOU BE!" he shouted, thrusting his glass eye in their direction. Quick as a flash, he grabbed Cora with one of his great hulking hands and Bram with the other.

Cora found herself pressed against his muddy, rocky chest. His sharp stone edges cut her face, and grazed her skin. She was crushed so tightly in his arms, it felt as if all of the air had been squeezed out of her, and she wondered in terrified horror, whether she would ever breathe again.

24

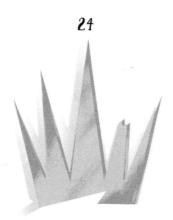

THE DEAD KING'S PALACE

"Here's more of Anna and Bob's carved plants and flowers!" Coriel twittered, swooping inches above the beautiful blooms that were half-buried in the cold, hard ground of the Dead King's flower beds.

Acton crouched low on his haunches, trying to keep a low profile as they crept through the Dead Garden. A dark knot of anxiety pierced him and chilly fear spread through his senses.

Up ahead a shining, black windowless needle of a tower, made from polished rock, cut through the landscape. It had to be the Dead Palace. It was sharper even than the point of the Fairy Queen's glass tower and ended in a crystal-black pinnacle that pierced the dull charcoal of the Dead Sky.

"Remember your ruse," Coriel twittered as they approached the tower's base. "You're the Clockmaker's Apprentice, here to wind the grandfather clock."

Acton nodded. He had a funny feeling he was destined to meet one last lost soul inside the tower: the Dead King's Portrait Painter. Every soul Acton had met in the Dead Lands so far had been family, which meant the last soul had to be family too. And he could think of only one other person that could be... Someone who smelled of perfume and paint, whose portrait had hung in Fairykeep Cottage, until it disappeared. Mama.

His heart soared at the thought of seeing Mama again. How delighted she would be to learn her True Name and recover her soul. He was petrified of entering the Dead King's Palace, but the notion that he *might*, no, he corrected himself, *would*, meet Mama, the idea of feeling her warm embrace again, and seeing her smile once more, buoyed him as he climbed the three steps to the tower's front door.

He gulped. He was about to try the door handle, when the door swung open of its own accord, to reveal a hallway dark as a banshee's mouth that stank of death and stagnant decay. Bile rose in Acton's throat. But there was no turning back. He had to go on!

As he and Coriel crept into the Dead King's Palace
Acton hunched his shoulders, tucked his body in tight, and
clenched his fists steeling himself for whatever was to come.

He'd barely taken more than a few paces down the
echoing stone passageway when the door swung closed
behind him with a…

clunk!

…leaving them alone in the pitch-black nothingness.
Then the door locked itself with a…

click!

He was about to ask Coriel whether she thought he
should magic up his ball of light, but he stopped himself.
He could feel someone watching them in the dark.

Small footsteps pattered up ahead, as fast as his suddenly
pounding heart was beating.

"Who's there?" he called. "What do you want?"

His voice echoed back at him, bouncing in from all
directions.

"I might ask you the same question," came a clear quiet
reply through the darkness.

Acton gulped back a gnawing fear and remembered
Otto's advice.

"I'm the Clockmaker's Apprentice. Here to wind the
Dead King's grandfather clock."

"Are you indeed?" A glowing oil lamp appeared, revealing

a young girl about Acton's age. "And I'm the Dead King's Portrait Painter." Despair smashed into Acton. He'd been so sure the last cursed Lost Soul was going to be his mama, but this was the soul of a young girl.

He stumbled towards her, gawping at her face. Her hair was white as gossamer thistledown and her eyes looked pale and wan. Something about her triggered a memory. "You're the Nameless Girl, from the mirror in my dream!"

"And you're the Chosen One," the Nameless Girl replied, breathless with excitement, as she saw him properly, up close. "I thought you'd never come. You're here to try and steal the Dead King's Glimmerglass Crown; I foresaw that much. Did you bring my True Name, as you promised?"

Acton could only shake his head sadly. He didn't know who she was, or how to help her. He felt powerless in that knowledge, and so sad and guilty he could barely look her in the eye. He felt as if he'd failed the first part of his mission; he could only hope he wouldn't fail what else was to come.

25

GRIPEWATER'S GLASS EYE

"I KNEW YOU WAS FOLLERING!" Gripewater crowed, throwing a skein of rope around Cora and Bram and pulling it tight, before pushing them onto the hard earth floor, beside Elle. "I SAW YOUR FINDIN' SPELL!" His gigantic shadow flickered in the firelight on the wall, as he juggled his glass eye between his hands in delight.

"TRIED TO SNEAK INTO MY CAVE, DIDN'TCHA? TO RESCUE THIS OTHER HOOMAN CHILD. BUT I SNATCHED YOU! CLEVER, CLEVER ME! THE THREE OF YOU'LL MAKE A TASTY MIDNIGHT FEAST!" He stoked his flames some more, and sang another verse of his song.

"GOOD OLD GRIPEWATER,
WITH HIS SHINING EYE.
ATE THREE TASTY CHILDREN,
BAKED IN A PIE!"

Cora shivered. She was lying on something lumpy in the pocket of her red cloak. If only she could get to the key in there, she could use its sharp teeth to cut her bonds, then she could grab her Talisman while Gripewater wasn't looking, and cast a spell to free the others.

Cora sat up. As subtly as she could, she moved her right foot, trying to drag her cloak up the side of her body in the shadowy darkness, towards her hands behind her back.

It was slow going. She'd need to play for time if she was going to manage to get a hand in her pocket. "Gripewater!" she called. "Let's make a bargain… I can tell you a story, and if you like it, maybe you won't cook and eat us?"

"NO BARGAINS!" Gripewater snapped. "TELL YOUR STORY. I'LL DECIDE HOW MANY OF YOU NEEDS EATING."

Cora nodded. While she scrunched as much of her cloak up behind her back as she could, trying to reach her fingers into the pocket, she began to speak. Bram and Elle saw what she was doing and willed her on with their eyes. "This is a story our mama used to tell us," Cora said. "It is called *The Troll's Tale.*

"Once upon a time there was a troll who lived under a bridge, which three billy goats needed to cross. The goats were named Gruff, Tuff and Ruff. When they came to the edge of the river, they discovered that if they wanted to cross the bridge, they'd have to pay a toll…"

"BORING!" Gripewater interrupted. "I HATE YOUR HORRIBLE STORY! TROLLS DON'T HAVE TAILS! NO SUCH THING AS A TROLL TOLL! AND WE DON'T LIVE UNDER BRIDGES!"

Cora had managed to shuffle one finger into her pocket and untangle the key from her hanky, now she was trying to hook the tip of her finger round the key's ring. But she needed more time. "Let's play a game," she suggested.

"WHAT GAME?" Gripewater asked.

"Riddles?" Bram said. "Trolls love riddles." He could see Cora was close to hooking out the key, and was helping, in any way he could, to distract Gripewater.

"MUMMY TOLD ME NOT TO PLAY WITH MY FOOD," Gripewater growled.

"But you don't always listen to your mother, do you, Gripewater?" Elle asked.

"Who's to say she knows best?" Bram added.

"NOT ME!" Gripewater bellowed. "I *LIKE* TO PLAY! TASTES BETTER!"

"So about our riddle game," Cora said. "What are the

rules?" She had finally grappled her hand round the key and was using its teeth to saw at the rope about her wrists.

"I ASK THREE," Gripewater snapped. "YOU ASK ONE. IF I GETS YOURS WRONG, YOU WIN. BUT IF I GETS YOURS RIGHT, OR IF YOU GETS *ANY* OF MINE WRONG, YOU LOSE!"

"That doesn't sound fair," Elle said.

"WHO SAID ANYTHING 'BOUT FAIR?" asked Gripewater. "I'M GIVING YOU A CHANCE, AIN'T I?"

"What about prizes?" Bram said, changing the subject again. "A riddle game without prizes is stupid."

"What'll your prize be if you win, Gripewater?" Elle asked.

"I'LL EAT YOU UP AS A NIGHT-TIME SNACK!" Gripewater spat. "THEN YOU DON'T GET TO MOAN ABOUT IT AFTERWARDS."

"And if we win," Cora said, sawing with the teeth of the key at the rope bonds round her hands, "you release the three of us, we get to keep our lives." She knew her terms wouldn't make a difference. If she didn't cut the rope quickly enough Gripewater was going to eat them anyway, but any time wasted in chatter was helpful.

"AGREED! LET'S BEGIN. RIDDLE ONE…" Gripewater coughed and recited:

"THE MORE I TAKE THE MORE I LEAVE BEHIND. WHAT AM I?"

Cora and Bram and Elle whispered to each other. None of them knew the answer, but they could probably guess it, eventually.

"Hmm…" Cora said.

"What on earth…?" Bram added.

"I wonder…" Elle ruminated.

Cora had almost cut through the strands round her wrists. The rope came loose and fell away. But she couldn't move just yet, she needed Bram and Elle to be free so they could face Gripewater together. She secretly handed the key to her brother.

Bram bit his lip and began sawing at his rope. He could've sworn he'd heard the troll's riddle before. He was certain he had the answer. It was somewhere in the back of his mind, only, at this moment, it seemed to be hiding from him. He shuffled his feet and hacked anxiously at his bonds.

"THAT'S LONG ENOUGH!" Gripewater marched around the cave, leaving footprints the size of tombstones in the mud. "ANSWER!"

Then, just like that, Bram knew what the answer was…

"Footsteps!"

"UNFAIR!" Gripewater bellowed. "YOUR FEET GAVE IT AWAY. SO DID MY STEPS. RIDDLE TWO:

I'M TALL WHEN I'M YOUNG AND SHORT WHEN I'M OLD. WHAT AM I?"

Again Cora, Bram and Elle tried to waste time. Elle looked round the cave for clues, while Cora glanced surreptitiously at Bram to see how he was doing. He'd nearly sawn through his bonds, but not quite. He needed a moment more.

"TIME'S UP!" screamed Gripewater, juggling his glass eye menacingly.

Elle spotted a stubby candle burning on a nearby stone shelf, its light was barely visible against the bright glow of the fire. "The answer's a candle!"

"TOO EASY!" Gripewater shouted. "RIDDLE THREE!"

Bram had finished sawing, and quietly handed the key to Elle. Elle began cutting her bonds, but she'd been trussed tighter than the others. Luckily, Gripewater was so angry he hadn't noticed what they were doing. He stomped up and down reciting his third riddle.

"I'M A PART OF A BIRD THAT'S NOT IN THE SKY. I CAN SWIM IN THE OCEAN, YET I REMAIN DRY. WHAT AM I?"

Bram and Elle hadn't a clue. They shrugged and Cora saw their shadows shift on the cave walls. "I've got the answer!" she told Gripewater. "*A shadow!*"

"YOU KNEW IT, YOU CHEAT!" Gripewater screamed. "ASK ME YOURS! AND MAKE IT GOOD!"

Elle had nearly finished sawing through her bonds.

"Listen carefully, Gripewater," Bram said. "This is our riddle.

"*Four glass bells there were, opposite in every way.*
Each one appeared in a different year, on a different day.
Each rang true and clear and fast,
and their chimes grew stronger as time did pass.
Tough knocks they took, but were not worn.
Bright and cheerful they were, and each glassborn.
I've finished my riddle, there's no more to say,
But now can you tell me who were they?"

"BELLS IN THE GLASS TOWER'S BELFRY," guessed Gripewater.

"Wrong!" Bram said.

"FAIRY BELLS AND BLUEBELLS THE QUEEN HAS TURNED TO GLASS!" the troll shouted forcefully. His brow furrowed. He seemed determined to get it right.

"Wrong!" Cora said. "And—"

"A DRINKING GLASS TURNED UPSIDE DOWN THAT LOOKS LIKE A GLASS BELL!" the troll interrupted.

"Wrong again!" Elle said. "That's three wrong answers. You should really only have had one guess. Three is cheating. And you shouldn't interrupt people when they're speaking, it's bad mann—"

"WELL, WHAT'S THE RIGHT ANSWER THEN?" growled Gripewater.

"The three of us and our brother!" Bram crowed. "We are the four Glass-Belles!" He almost pointed in triumph, but stopped himself just in time.

Cora breathed a sigh of relief. The troll hadn't realized they were free. "Our mother's surname was Glass," she explained to Gripewater.

"...and our father's surname is Belle!" Elle finished, shaking her bonds from her wrists and secretly handing the key back to Cora.

"ASK AN EASIER ONE!" Gripewater moaned. He seemed to have forgotten they were only supposed to get one go. Grasping the key tight made Cora think of one of Mama's riddles:

I'm not a diamond, but I'm put on a ring. When my teeth bite, a lock's opening.

"DON'T KNOW! DON'T CARE!" Gripewater growled, gripping his glass eye. The fire roared and he poked it with a stick. "BORING RIDDLES! ROASTING TIME!"

"Don't you want to know the answer?" Cora said. "It's a...KEY!" She jumped up and spiked Gripewater's hand with the Magic Key. The key bit Gripewater so hard he screamed and dropped his glass eye, which rolled away in the dark. Now he couldn't see at all. He stepped back blindly in the flickering firelight, and tripped over a rock.

Cora felt the ground shake as he hit the floor. The eye

rolled to a stop at her feet. She was about to stamp on it, but as her foot touched the glass an image flashed in the eye's centre: a pale face, hard as porcelain. "*I see you!*" the Fairy Queen whispered from within the eye. It was all Cora could do in that moment to tap it with her toes, so that it rolled away into the inkiest corner of the cave.

She, Bram and Elle stood up as Gripewater crawled about in the dusty darkness, searching for the lost eye. Cora quickly folded the key in her handkerchief and the three of them fled into the woods, leaving Gripewater patting the earth with his big rocky fingers, and wailing.

When they had recovered and walked off far enough into the night that they could no longer hear the troll's moans, Cora brushed a tear from her cheeks.

"What did you see in the eye?" Elle asked.

"Nothing," Cora said.

"Liar," Bram said. "We saw you flinch."

Cora didn't want to tell the others what she had seen. She was terrified that the Fairy Queen was still spying on them, and knew every move they made, and to say that out loud would feel like admitting defeat. She looked at the pocket watch instead.

"Twelve o'clock!" she announced in shock.

"Only one hour left to save Acton!" Elle gasped.

"How are we going to get to the Dreaming Tree, let alone the Fairy Palace, before thirteen o'clock?" Bram moaned.

None of them knew, but they had to keep trying, or else Acton would be lost to the Queen for ever. They stumbled onward in the dark, through the dense vegetation, and came at last to a gap in the forest, which the stars and full moon hung above.

There, beneath the moon's white belly, almost as if it was waiting for them, was the most enormous tree Cora had ever seen.

"The Dreaming Tree!" Elle said. "It has to be. We've finally made it to the centre of Fairyland."

The Dreaming Tree was taller than the Heart of the Forest and Tree of Life combined. It was so large that its branches stretched through the ether, reaching into the heavens to hold up the stars.

Despite the winter weather, each branch was covered in leaves, buds, blossoms and fruits that were as round and large as the planets. Four stags were nibbling at the bushes around the base of the tree, and, on its far side, something was snoring softly in the starlit night.

They walked round to where the snoring was coming from and found a little dragon the size of a cat with long tufted ears, and green scales like a fish. It lay curled up and sleeping among the tree's branches. Balls of smoke wafted from its nostrils with every loud snore it made. And each of the balls formed a phantom scene, like the wispy shape of a dream, before dispersing into the sky above.

"What was it Tempest and Thomas told us to do next, Bramble?" Elle asked.

"Climb into the branches," Bram said, walking away from the sleeping dragon, so he wouldn't wake it, and grasping the lowest branch to haul himself up. "We need to find the magic branch to take us to Acton, in the Glass Tower. It's up here somewhere."

Cora and Elle climbed into the Dreaming Tree after him. As Cora hauled herself into the branches, she scraped her knee on the frozen bark. She bit her lip to stop herself crying out. She didn't want to wake the sleeping dragon, in case it tried to stop them.

The three of them clambered into the crook of the trunk, among the midnight-blue dreaming leaves.

Many thousands of branches were spread out around them. An infinity of choices, with no way of knowing which was the one they needed to take.

"What do you think, Cor?" Elle asked. "Which way is it? Which branch will take us to Acton?"

Cora had no idea. Even worse, she realized, was that there was no way of knowing.

"I can't tell," she admitted, and her heart plunged queasily inside her. "I really have no idea what I'm doing, and…we're nearly out of time."

Cora had been trying to keep that desperate thought at bay since she'd seen the image of the Fairy Queen in the troll's glass eye, but the terrible truth of it engulfed her like a wave as she spoke it out loud. She slumped against the tree trunk in despair. "I think we've probably lost."

"Surely not?" Elle asked, taking her hand.

"We've still got a chance," Bram said, squeezing in beside her.

"But don't you see?" Cora waved angrily at the never-ending choice of branches. "It's a hopeless cause! There's no chance we can check every path in the time we have left."

She brushed her eyes. Tears were falling faster than she could wipe them away, so she let them come. She cried for herself and Bram and Elle, stuck here as the evening set in, stuck in the branches of this stupid, useless, nightmare of a tree, and still so far away from rescuing their brother.

And she cried because she knew that this time there was no way she could fix things. Soon Bram and Elle were crying too. Tears fell from all their cheeks, dropping onto their feet, then seeping into the ancient tree trunk. None of them noticed, that where their tears fell in the moonlight, little green shoots of hope began to sprout on the Dreaming Tree.

26

THE NAMELESS GIRL

"I'm sorry," Acton told the Nameless Girl. "I'm not the Clockmaker's Apprentice. I'm not the Chosen One either…at least I don't believe I am – not any more. And I don't know how I'll steal the crown if that's not the case. Plus, I don't know your True Name."

"I don't know it either, little lapwing," Coriel twittered, fluttering at Acton's side.

"But if you're not the Chosen One, or the Clockmaker's Apprentice, then who are you?" the Nameless Girl asked.

"Acton Belle," Acton said. "Just plain Acton Belle. And this is my friend Coriel."

"Well, at least you still know that much," the Nameless

Girl said. "The Dead Lands make those who come here forget themselves. But yours are nice names."

"Mama gave me mine," Acton explained.

"I don't remember my mama," the Nameless Girl said, sadly. "Is yours nice, Acton?"

"She was the best," Acton said. "She told me fairy tales and sang songs to my brother and sisters and me, and gave us precious gifts. She was an artist, like you. She drew and painted all kinds of beautiful things…nature and people and scenes from her imagination… Her illustrations were how a story would look, if you painted it just as you saw it in your mind's eye. And the fairy tales she told were like that too. But now she's gone," he added sadly. "She died." He wouldn't normally be so open with strangers, but the Nameless Girl had a kind face. He raised a hand to brush the tears from his cheek.

"I'm sorry," the Nameless Girl said. "I wish I could give you some news of your mama, but her soul hasn't come this way through the Dead Lands. Not since I've been here. How long that is exactly, I'm not sure, but I've painted a thousand portraits of the Dead King. It's a lonely sort of existence, but occasionally I have company: five other cursed Lost Souls, who've forgotten themselves. We don't meet often, but they're my friends."

"They send their love," Acton said, "but I'm afraid they're gone."

"What do you mean?" she asked, shocked.

"I knew their True Names because they were members of my family," Acton explained. "When they said their names, they shot up in the air like fireworks, just as the souls on the Bone Bridge had, and moved on to whatever comes next."

"Perhaps I'm one of your family too?" the Nameless Girl suggested, hopefully.

"I wondered that," Acton said. "And I wanted you to be. But if you are, I don't know you."

"Oh dear," said the Nameless Girl.

Acton felt awful. He really did want her to be free like the other souls. He wanted it for her more than he'd ever wanted anything, but that wasn't down to him. He didn't know who she was and there was nothing he could do to change that.

"I've an idea," he said. "If you help me steal the Glimmerglass Crown, I'll take you back to Fairyland. My brother and sisters are there, and if the five of us and Coriel can defeat the Fairy Queen, then we'll be free, you included."

"I can't leave the Dead Lands and go to the lands of the living," the Nameless Girl murmured. "No one can, once they're dead. Us souls in the Dead Lands can only move onwards to whatever comes next, we can never move back. It's like that saying the living have: *you can never step in the same river twice*, especially when it's the Dead River."

She smiled as if she'd made a joke, though it wasn't really funny in Acton's opinion, just sad. "But, since you came to visit me, as I asked when we talked through the mirror," the Nameless Girl continued, "and because you've been so nice, and you're the first living person I've met for as long as I can remember, I'll show you to the Dead King's Throne Room, and help you all I can to try and steal the crown." She held her lamp high and beckoned them onwards. Coriel swooped along after her and, with some trepidation, Acton too followed.

It was a long walk, following behind the Nameless Girl and her raised lantern, and all through it, Acton worried about what he would do when he reached the Throne Room.

He had got this far on brains alone, but he still had no idea how he was going to defeat the Dead King and win the crown. Even if he succeeded, how would he get the crown back to Fairyland? And how could he use its powers to save his brother and sisters from the Fairy Queen and her evil curse? He was so worried, he'd barely looked where they were going. When he raised his head again, he saw they were in a seemingly endless gallery full of framed pictures so gigantic it looked like you could step into them. Each featured a horrifying-looking faceless man in the foreground.

The faceless man wore different outfits from different eras in every picture. In one, he was laughing uproariously as a great library behind him burned in a fire and turned to ash and smoke. In a second, he was stood before a tall ancient tower, his arms thrown joyfully in the air as people and stones toppled from the heavens. In a third, he was on a clifftop with an evil smile on his face, as a giant flood washed the world away beneath him. In a fourth, he floated above a great erupting volcano that was smothering an ancient city in red hot lava.

Acton shivered. "The Dead King!" he whispered. It had to be! For each painting was filled with death. It was like the man was taking ownership of those terrible disasters. If he had that much power, how was Acton going to defeat him?

"He wanted me to paint him at the site of all the greatest tragedies in history," the Nameless Girl whispered, "because he was responsible for each of them. There's a certain cosiness in a crisis that folks like the Dead King enjoy. That's why he wanted the images – to remind him of that feeling. I was older when I painted most of them. And I had to use my imagination, of course, since, thank goodness, I wasn't there with him when he caused those horrifying events."

"How could you be older?" Acton asked. The girl's remark had confused him so much that for a second it made him forget the ghastly painted images, and his gnawing anxiety.

"My soul started off older when I first came here," the Nameless Girl explained as they walked on. "But I've been growing younger with each picture I paint. That's how it is here in the tower. Outside, in the wider Dead Lands, every soul experiences their death the normal way round, but in the Dead King's Palace, everything is a bit backwards."

Acton tried to understand how this knowledge might help him in his battle with the Dead King, but he couldn't imagine a way that it might.

They came at last to a polished black basalt staircase, and climbed it to an upper hallway filled with rows of shimmering, ebony doors set in black papered walls. Each door was a different shape and dimension, some were small as a mouse hole, some tall and thin as a broom handle, some wide as a carriage and each so skewed and wonky that they seemed the wrong shape for the hall. Finally, they arrived at a set of double doors made of charred hardwood, which were so tall and wide they looked big enough to allow all the sorrows of the world to slip through side by side.

"This is the Dead King's Throne Room," the Nameless Girl said.

"Is the Dead King in there now?" Acton asked, with a shiver.

"He is," the Nameless Girl said. "And if you want the crown from his head, you'll have to win a game of wits against him. You must bow when you enter and address the King as 'Your Royal Deadness' when you speak to him, and never turn your back. He'll sneak up on you, and no one likes to be surprised by Death."

Acton's head swam. It was a lot to take in. He thought for a moment about turning and running, but it was far too late for that now. This was his mission and his brother and sisters needed him to succeed, though the more he heard about the Dead King, the more he felt that his destiny could not be to escape from this palace with his life. Suddenly, he desperately craved some reassurance that everything was going to be all right.

"I think I'd better make myself scarce again, my grouse," Coriel said, swooping into Acton's pocket. "If there's an advantage to me secreting myself, we should take it." She nuzzled against his chest beside his heart, and her warmth gave him a dose of courage he sorely needed.

Before she pushed the door open, the Nameless Girl turned to him. "I've brought you this far, but I must request one last favour."

Acton knew what it was going to be. "You want me to ask the Dead King for your True Name as well as for the crown."

"My hunch is the Dead King will be happy to offer that

deal because he thinks you can't win." The Nameless Girl looked Acton in the eye. "But I do. I feel something in you, Acton. Something I've not seen in a long time."

"What's that?" Acton asked, with a shiver.

"Hope," the Nameless Girl said. "Even a small spark stands a chance against the Dead King. Do you promise to keep it alive, no matter what happens in there?"

"I do," Acton said. He took the trust the Nameless Girl had put in him and felt it bloom inside his being. And he hoped that, along with her belief in him, it would be enough to see him through the trials to come.

"You're finally ready," the Nameless Girl said, pushing open the doors with a creak. And so, with one new-found friend at his side and another in his pocket, Acton stepped into the Dead Throne Room to face the Dead King and ask him for his Glimmerglass Crown.

THE DREAMING TREE

Cora, Bram and Elle wiped their eyes and looked around. Things didn't seem half as bad to Cora now that they'd had a short rest and a proper cry. Sometimes crying was a release. Whereas ignoring your emotions left you tied up in knots.

The enormous Dreaming Tree's thousands of limbs stretched around them in the night like a giant, many-armed hug. Suddenly a light arrived in the darkness. A little glowing magic lantern made of leaves. It was carried by a man dressed all in green with twigs, ivy and branches sprouting from his hair and woven through his beard. He peered out of a hole in the canopy above them and called down.

"Children! There you are! I've been expecting you!"

"Who are you?" Bram asked, in shock. "How can you have been expecting us? How would you even know we were going to be here?"

"I'll tell you that, if you tell me who I am," the man said, his face shining green in the lantern light.

"Please," Elle begged, brushing away the last of her tears. "No more games, or riddles. We're in terrible trouble."

"Ah, yes," the man said. "Acton, your brother, is suffering under the long-tangled tendrils of the curse. He has been inveigled into a mission for the Fairy Queen, and you've less than an hour to save him."

"How do you know all that?" Cora asked.

"I know everything," the man said. "I am the knowledge of the forest and the trees and the sky, and the wisdom of the land and the growing. I am always here. That's why Thomas sent you to me."

Then Cora realized who the man was. "You're the Green Man!"

"Of course!" said Elle. "*A dragon guards the Dreaming Tree!*"

"*Where the Green Man grows sweet dreams for thee!*" Bram finished. "Our mama sang that nursery rhyme to us when we were little and couldn't get to sleep. That's your dragon, snoozing in the dreaming branches!"

"It is my dragon, and I am indeed the Green Man!" said the cheery, ivy-clad fellow. "Some know me as the King of Life, or Lord of the Greenwood, others as Herne the Hunter, when I wear my horned crown. But it sounds like Azouf, my dragon, is napping on the job." He frowned. "The cost of travelling into my Dreaming Tree is a story. Are you willing to pay that price?"

"We are," Cora agreed hastily. Though, unfortunately, she couldn't think of an appropriate tale right now, and they didn't have much time left.

The Green Man reached down through the gap in the leaves with his free hand, and suddenly it was as if he was in the tree's lowest branches with them. His fingers were near enough to grab theirs.

Cora held out her hand first to the Green Man and he pulled her upwards. As she was propelled towards him, she felt as if seeds and flowers were filling her heart, growing inside her. Bram was next, and then Elle, who had been inquisitively examining the unique bark of the tree and the dense foliage, in the flickering light of the Green Man's lantern.

"Let me show you to the branch you'll need to find your brother," the Green Man said. "It is a little way's walk from here, up and down and all around the tree."

"Don't you want the story you requested first?" Cora

asked. "I can't think of one, but I'm sure a tale will come to me, if I say the magic words: *Once Upon a Time...*"

The Green Man laughed. "I didn't mean *you* had to tell *me* a story! I meant *I* would tell *you* one." He ushered them towards a tangle of steps formed from branches and climbing plants that twisted round the Dreaming Tree's trunk like a spiral staircase.

"Jasmine and honeysuckle," said Elle fingering their leaves. "But they shouldn't be blooming at this time of year."

"Everything is always in bloom in the Dream Lands," the Green Man said. "But the Dream Flowers bloom most beautiful of all. At the top of this staircase, in the topmost branches of the tree, is where you'll find them; growing close to the stars. I will take you to them, and their magic will in turn take you to your brother. But in the meantime, all you have to do is climb the stairs with me and listen. Are you good listeners?"

Cora, Bram and Elle nodded. "Excellent!" the Green Man said. "A story is nothing without those!" Holding his lantern up high before him, he led them up the staircase around the trunk of the Dreaming Tree. "My story is called: *The Dreaming Tree's Tale.*

"Long, long ago, before the start of time, there was only blackness. But that blackness was full of goodness and nutrients, like well-mulched soil. Deep in its depths was a

Seed of Hope, destined to grow into everything the universe had been dreaming of.

"Soon after that start, a great wild beast called the First Wolf leaped across the sky and howled enough tears of joy and sadness to water the whole wide world. Those tears seeped into the black emptiness and found the buried Seed of Hope. This restless seed, curled deep underground, drank those teardrops and sprouted into a seedling, that grew just as much from hope as it did from sadness; all those emotions made it stronger.

"The Seedling of Hope grew from the black earth into the black air and produced two bright buds. The two bright buds burst into two flowers that sparkled with light and life. The first flower shone fiery orange, as warm as a hug. The second was soft and yellow as candle wax, and warm as a kiss. The first flower broke from the seedling and floated off into the daytime sky to become the sun. The second broke from the seedling and floated off into the night sky to become the moon, and what was left of the seedling grew into a tall, strong Dreaming Tree whose branches tangled into every corner of the universe.

"In the summer of the Dreaming Tree's first blooming, a hundred-million-billion bright shining blossoms, called Dream Flowers, opened and became stars. In the years that followed the Dream Flowers blossomed into a million-billion other things: planets, plants, people, animals, fairies, wolves, sorcerers, children. Every bird, beast and plant that grew from their dream seeds lived according to their light, flowered for a short season, and faded away to become a memory of the past, as everything does in the end.

"For, one day, in a million-billion-trillion years, even the stars, that once were a part of the Dreaming Tree, will fade and die. As will the very first blossoms that grew – the moon and the sun.

"But do not worry, for when a new spring comes to the universe, the Dreaming Tree will grow new buds, and put forth new shoots to become new celestial bodies.

"Those fresh young stars will shine a radiant light on the growing galaxies. A light that contains both joy and sadness. A light that will be bright enough to warm and revitalize even the coldest, dying heart, and all hope in the universe shall be renewed."

"What a beautiful tale." Cora smiled and wiped away a tear. Hearing it had made her happy and sad at the same time, and, somehow, that restored her self-belief. To lose everything was devastating, but the knowledge that renewal came from such great loss kindled a spirited fire inside her that lightened her soul until it felt like she was floating on air.

The four of them were in the uppermost crown of the

tree now, and could see the whole starlit world of Fairyland stretched out before them.

"This way," said the Green Man, as they climbed from the top of the wooden twiggy spiral staircase, along a winding path.

It was not like climbing up a normal tree, where you hug the trunk and look for hand- and footholds to lever yourself up. But the branches of the Dreaming Tree were so big and wide that they were more like undulating wooden roads in the sky. The crinkled leaves above became silver night-clouds. Constellations of stars sprouted in the gaps between them, like they were growing from the tree.

The children climbed on, and saw tiny sparkling planets tangled in faraway branches of the tree. Soon shooting stars were streaming all around them, falling like midnight blossoms, or winter snowflakes.

Cora felt suddenly as if she was in the Green Man's story and not in anything resembling the world she knew. It made her think of Acton, and one of the last times she'd seen him, crouching beneath the branches of the Fairy Tree, in the churchyard beside Fairykeep's garden, with his robin and the Magic Key.

"The Dreaming Tree stretches on for ever," the Green Man said. "Through life and death and everything in between. Each branch spans space and time, knotting into other limbs and trunks, until all are one. In a few steps, we'll find the branch that will take you down to your brother."

This was it then. Soon they would be with Acton once more. It was a thought that should've filled Cora with joy, but it only made her more fearful of what they might discover when they saw him again.

A cluster of brightly glowing buds grew above their heads, like low-hanging fruit.

"Dream Flowers." the Green Man said.

He hooked his lantern onto a twiggy branch, before picking one radiant bloom for each of them. "Close your eyes and swallow their blossom and a lucid dream will grow inside you. Then you'll visit Acton in the Dead Lands. The Dreaming Tree's roots reach deep under the earth. They will take you to him."

"What do you mean?" Cora asked, shocked.

"We thought Acton was in the Glass Tower," Bram said.

"That's where we were going," Elle added.

"He was in the Glass Tower when you began your quest," the Green Man explained. "Now he is in the Dead Lands. But do not worry, he is not dead himself, merely visiting. Soon he will face the Dead King and ask him for the Glimmerglass Crown and the right to return to the land of the living. He will need your help, if he's to succeed in that mission."

The Green Man paused and looked at Cora, Bram and Elle. "Tonight is the midwinter solstice," he said, "when the Fair Folk ride, and those that look for hope must put their fears aside. On this night Fairyland and the Dead Lands are closest to each other. The Dream Flowers will detach your dream-selves from your bodies and send you in your dreams to the Dead Lands, where Acton is. Do not die in that land, and do not look back when you leave, or else you'll never wake up."

Cora felt a sick jolt of fear. She took a deep breath and tamped it down. If this was the path they had to take, then they must take it. "We'll do it," she said. She checked Tempest's pocket watch. Twelve-eighteen. "We only have forty-two minutes left. How on earth will we be able to get to the Glass Tower afterwards as well?"

"There is no time in the Dead Lands," the Green Man said. "If you can successfully return, your visit will have lasted no longer than the blink of an eye. When you've found Acton down there, and helped him in his mission, you must say Tempest's Waking Spell to bring your dream selves back to your bodies. Then you will wake whole once more, and only moments will have passed."

"But Acton won't be able to wake with us," Cora said anxiously. "Because he's not dreaming. What is the point of us going on a dream-quest to find our brother in the

Dead Lands if we cannot bring him back with us?"

"If you help him complete his mission to fetch the Glimmerglass Crown," the Green Man said, "that will mean he can come back of his own accord. As the Chosen One, only he can take the crown. If he achieves that, he will be able to return to Fairyland with it, and you will meet him in the Glass Tower. And if the four of you can defeat the Fairy Queen when you get there, you will have come a long way since the start of your journey this midwinter night. Now sit down on the branch here, and lean your back against the trunk of the tree. That way you will be supported when you fall asleep."

Cora shivered at the thought of these new dangers. The further into this adventure they got, the harder it seemed, but Cora knew she would stop at nothing to save Acton, undo the curse and bring hope and life back to her family. She took a Dream Flower from the Green Man. Bram and Elle did the same. As the Green Man had suggested, the three of them sat down carefully, making themselves comfortable on the branch, and leaning back against the trunk of the Dreaming Tree.

Cora put her hand on the Dreaming Tree as she leaned against it. In that moment, she could've sworn she felt the sap of the tree shifting about beneath the surface of the bark, travelling to every place and time there ever was.

She glanced at Bram and Elle, who had sat down beside her. The flowers glowed in their hands, illuminating their faces with a bright white light that made them look even more pale and anxious.

"Ready?" Bram asked, raising a shaky hand and placing his Dream Flower in his mouth, where it glowed inside him.

"As I'll ever be," Elle said. Her breath sounded heavy and ragged, but after a moment she placed her flower in her mouth too.

Cora placed the third Dream Flower on her tongue and took her hand away, nervously balling it into a fist. The petals tasted soft and warm, like a mouthful of fiery honey that lit up her throat. She gulped and felt the flower's power warm her belly and hum through her body.

"It's like swallowing a ray of moonlight," said Elle.

"Or a liquid gold shining star," said Bram.

"Or sunshine," Cora agreed. She shut her eyes and took a deep breath. Acton needed them, and if she, Bram and Elle wanted to save him, they'd have to do as the Green Man suggested and fall into a deep and dangerous midwinter-night's dream.

28

DEADTIME STORIES

Acton stared in awe at the grandeur of the Dead King's Throne Room. The walls were made of carved, polished panels of ebony, that were covered in runes and symbols of death. Down the centre of the room, tall ivory columns held up a roof made of crossed bones. The fragments of ceiling that peered between them were black as the night and covered in sparkling glass stars.

With a sickening chill, Acton looked around for the Dead King, on his throne. He couldn't see the King anywhere, but his eye was drawn to something strange hidden behind one of the columns… A little wooden desk.

"What's that doing here?" he asked the Nameless Girl.

"It's my drawing desk," she explained. "I use it for sketching out my ideas, before I paint one of the big pictures for the Dead King."

Acton approached the desk and saw that it had the same inkstand, the same sheaf of paper, the same hourglass, and the same little hand mirror as the desk in Fairykeep Cottage. "I don't understand," he said.

"The mirror is magic," the Nameless Girl replied. "Just like the Glimmerglass Crown. I used it to contact you."

"No, I don't mean that," Acton said. "I mean the desk looks like an exact copy of the one my mama used to own."

"Sometimes the Dead King's Palace does that," the Nameless Girl said. "You see things you remember from life. That's probably why my desk here looks like your mother's in the living world."

"Have you ever seen anything you remember from your life?" Acton asked, but the Nameless Girl shook her head. He wanted to ask her more, but just then a shadow appeared across the centre of the room that hadn't been there before.

In it sat the Dead King, on a Throne of Bones. A chill ran through Acton at the sight of him. The Dead King's eyes were crystal clear black holes, his face pale and blurry. His cape, which looked sewn from pure darkness, ruffled softly in a non-existent wind.

On his head was the Glimmerglass Crown. Its five magic mirror shards, sharp as knives, glittered like jewels. Each shard glinted with life and light from one of the five magic kingdoms. The crown seemed to reflect not only the Dead Throne Room, but a million other places and times from the five unique lands of its origin. The visions of light it created and sent sparkling about the room were so beautiful they made Acton's heart quiver.

"Who..." said the Dead King, leaning back on his throne to stare at Acton with a gaze that glinted bright as glass on a silty riverbed, "...is this?" His words sounded like cliffs tumbling into the sea.

"This, Your Royal Deadness, Duke of Death, Emperor of the Afterlife," said the Nameless Girl, curtseying deeply, "is the Chosen One, a brave and brilliant child named Acton Belle. He came from Fairyland to challenge you for your Glimmerglass Crown."

"Why do you want my crown?" asked the Dead King with an intense stare.

"I want to take it back to Fairyland..." Acton's words dried up under the King's gaze, but Coriel fidgeted nervously in his pocket, bringing him back. "I made a deal with the Fairy Queen that I'd come here on a mission to fetch your crown for her. If I succeed, then she'll let me and my siblings go home to England."

The Dead King's frame shook with silent laughter. The crown seemed to twist and writhe on his head. "You struck a bad bargain there, my boy. My crown is worth far more than that. It lets the wearer control the five kingdoms, and life and death. Its magic is so valuable that I would never consider giving it away. But since you're here, and since there is absolutely no chance of you taking it from me, or me giving it to you, why don't we humour each other with a little game?

"You will ask me one riddle and I will ask you one in return. If I get the answer to your riddle wrong and you get mine right, you win and take the crown. But if I get the answer to your riddle right, and you get the answer to mine wrong, then you lose, and your body and soul are mine for ever. Then you'll work for me until the end of time, doing the many arduous jobs you so generously freed the Lost Souls who were my other servants from."

"What if we both guess right, and it's a draw?" Acton asked.

"Then I get to keep the crown and you get to walk away from the Dead Lands unscathed," the Dead King said. "That is, until you're an old man, and it's finally time for us to meet again."

Acton thought about this. His fate, if he lost, was an eternity of rowing, planting, and pretending to wind the grandfather clock. It didn't seem like he had much of a chance, but the Nameless Girl believed there was a sliver of hope in him, and in that sliver of hope Acton saw a slim chance of success. He looked the Dead King square in the eye. "You know so many riddles that the odds are heavily weighted in your favour, so if I win I should get something more on my side of the bargain."

"Like what?" the Dead King asked.

"I'd like this Nameless Girl's True Name, as well as the crown, Your Royal Deadness."

The Dead King's laugh was like a thousand falling tombstones. "I do not give out True Names. I'll bet the crown only. That is all." He paused, and if he'd been a living person, Acton would've supposed he was taking a breath. But he didn't breathe. It was disconcerting to say the least. "So," the King said at last, "do we have a deal?"

Acton shivered. He'd failed to get the Nameless Girl's True Name as part of the bargain, and he didn't like the Dead King's offer, but what choice did he have? He needed to get the crown if he was to save his brother and his sisters and free himself.

"We do," he agreed.

"Then decide on your riddle," the Dead King said. "But, before you do, I must warn you, I never lose. Not in a million years. You'll soon see that I've heard every riddle there is."

Acton tried to think of something fresh…

"Choose carefully!" Coriel whispered from his dressing-gown pocket.

He wished he could, but nothing was coming to him. His mind was blank with fear. Cora would've known the best riddle to give a dead king, or Elle, or Bramble... Bram's riddle – that was it! The one he had told them in the coach on the way to Fairykeep Cottage! He'd made it up, from his head, so the Dead King couldn't possibly know it. How did it go again...?

"Time's up," said the Dead King. "Have you chosen your riddle, Chosen One?"

"I have," Acton replied.

"Tell it then," the Dead King said.

Acton took a deep pause, then he began.

"Today, as I went down to the Dead Lands, I met an old troubadour with a lute in his hands. Dancing behind him were sixteen brown bears, twelve moles and one vole, and a brace of grey hares. Prancing with them were thirteen black cats, and fifty white mice in the tallest tall hats. Waltzing about them were eighteen young brides, and eighteen young bridegrooms with tears in their eyes. Each traveller waved, with a paw or a hand, but how many were going down to the Dead Lands?"

The Dead King began counting on his blurred, bony fingers, muttering to himself. Acton felt a twinge of elation. The Dead King had fallen into the trap and was trying to add up the people in the riddle, but that wasn't the right way to find the answer.

The Dead King was mumbling now. Acton thought he was probably trying to go over the numbers in his mind, and check he'd got his calculations right. Finally, he gave his answer: "One-hundred-and-thirty-one souls, including yours."

"You're wrong!" Acton cheered. "The answer is *one*." He laughed in hysterical relief. "Me! I'm the only one heading to the Dead Lands. Everyone else is heading away from them."

"I think not, my boy," the Dead King cackled. "I was right and you were wrong."

"You don't understand the riddle!" Acton cried, affronted. He couldn't see how the Dead King wasn't getting it. "It's as I explained: only *I* am on the road to the Dead Lands. Everyone else is travelling in the opposite direction."

"It's *you* who doesn't understand." The Dead King shook his head in mock sadness. "Don't you know how death works? There is no 'away' from death. No 'opposite direction'."

"What do you mean?" Acton asked, aghast.

"All who are born are heading towards the Dead Lands," the Dead King explained. "Whether they think they are or not. There is no birth without death, no living without dying, you cannot have one without the other. Those fellow travellers in your riddle only *think* they're taking a different road that leads away from here. They too are walking towards me. Everyone's path, long or short leads to death eventually. That's the way life is, Acton, the way it's always been, and the way it always will be. The important thing is not *which* direction you choose to take, but that you look around and enjoy the scenery on *your* trip, because it's the one life you get.

"So now you know the correct answer, and it's this: every one of the one-hundred-and-thirty souls you met on your path will come here in the end, just as you have."

Acton felt the truth of what the Dead King had said sink in. He'd lost and now he'd stay here for ever, never see Cora, Bram, Elle, Papa or Aunt Eliza again. He began to cry.

Coriel jumped from his pocket, and fluttered about the room.

"A living robin!" the Dead King exclaimed in surprise.

"Don't be sad, my turnstone," Coriel chirruped. "You're not alone. I'm with you. Just as I have been this whole journey."

The Dead King eyed Coriel greedily. The five spikes of the crown flashed like five sharp shards of lightning upon his head. "It's my turn to ask *my* riddle. But I'm afraid the best you can hope for is a draw. Whatever happens now you cannot win the crown. If you get the answer right, then you leave with nothing, but if you get it wrong your body and soul are mine."

Acton's heart sank. There was no chance left to win, just degrees of loss.

"I'll tell you what," the Dead King said. "This game has been a lot of fun, and, as a result, I'm feeling very generous. So let's make things interesting, and go double or quits."

Acton didn't know what that meant. He must've looked confused, for the Dead King took the trouble to explain.

"I will offer you one more chance to win. If you get the answer right, despite the fact that it's officially a draw, I will give you the crown *and* you and your bird can leave the Dead Lands freely. But if you get the answer to my riddle wrong, I get not only your body and soul, but the body and soul of your little bird there." He licked his cracked lips greedily, with a snakelike forked tongue as if he planned to eat Coriel up.

Acton felt sick. If he lost this time he'd be giving up Coriel as well. He shook his head. He couldn't do that to his friend. She didn't deserve such a fate. He was about to refuse, when Coriel flew to his side and whispered to him. "You must take this new deal, my dove. Whatever it is he's going to ask us, I'm sure we can guess the right answer together."

Acton nodded. "Fine," he said to the Dead King. Then he thought of something else. "But, since you're getting something extra on your side of the wager if I lose, I should get something extra on my side if I guess your riddle correctly."

"I can offer you anything," the Dead King said. "Money, power and riches beyond your wildest dreams, or a life as long and slow as a river."

"I don't want any of that," Acton said, his heart quickening. He'd been hoping the Dead King would agree to his demand for an extra term. "I want what you wouldn't give me the first time round: the Nameless Girl's True Name."

"Fine," said the Dead King. "In that case, that shall also be your riddle. *What is the Nameless Girl's True Name?* Guess correctly, and you and your robin can have the crown and your liberty, and she is free to go and move on to the expansive joy of whatever comes next. But get it wrong and…" He ran a single bone finger like a knife across his throat. "Get the picture? Good! We start now!"

Acton looked desperately about the Throne Room. He needed time to work this one out. His eyes alighted on the hourglass on the desk. If it was truly like his mama's at Fairykeep Cottage, if it worked the same way as that one, then its sands would last an hour, like Aunt Eliza had said. It was his only chance.

"Before we make our guess," he said, thinking on his feet, "Coriel and I want to speak with the Nameless Girl privately, alone. You must leave for as long as the sands fall through that hourglass, Your Royal Deadness. Only return when they are done, then I shall make my guess."

The Dead King considered this request. "All right," he agreed, finally. "There's no time in the Dead Lands, not really. But for you, Acton, in this one case, for the sake of prolonging our little game, which has been most diverting, I shall make an exception." He descended from his Bone Throne, tapped the hourglass with one emaciated finger, and spoke a spell:

"Sands of Time flow once more. Until I return through the Throne Room doors."

Immediately the sands began falling through the hourglass, but they did not trickle from the top glass bulb to the bottom one, as they would normally, with gravity. Instead, they went backwards, rising from the dune-like pile in the bottom bulb to tumble magically upwards into the top one. "These magic, flowing sands do not represent real time in the real world," the Dead King explained. "Just a pool of Dead Time I have created, so we may continue our game."

"And how long will that Dead Time last?" Acton asked.

"As long as it does," the Dead King replied, stepping towards the doors.

"That's not fair," Acton called after him.

"Nothing in Life or Death ever is." The doors opened for the Dead King with a…

WHOOSH!

Then shut behind him with an almighty…

CRASH!

And Acton found himself alone in the Throne Room with the Nameless Girl and Coriel. He glanced anxiously at Mama's hourglass to see how much time he'd got, and was shocked to see that a large pile of sand was already forming in the top bulb.

He didn't have long before the Dead King returned and demanded an answer. Acton wanted to succeed more than anything, so that the Nameless Girl could be free, and so that he would be able to take the crown back to Fairyland and see his siblings safe and well.

He'd have to be careful with his answer, because the Dead King was sure not to play fair. He and Coriel and the Nameless Girl would have to be smart if they wanted to win. And they had to win. How else would he get back to Fairyland and see his family again? And how could he possibly face being sentenced to an eternity all alone in the Dead Lands?

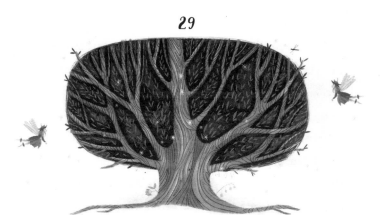

29

MIDWINTER NIGHT'S DREAM

In her dream Cora wore the exact same clothes she'd been wearing while she was awake; her purple dress and red cloak and her stout boots. She was standing in the same spot she had been in a moment ago, only everything seemed a little more shimmery than before. Instinctively, she checked the cloak's pocket. Just like in real life, she still had the Red Soldier and the key, wrapped in her handkerchief. Cora wondered if the objects had become dream-versions of themselves, as she had, counterparts to real things. It was too much of a headache to think about, and that was before she glanced down and saw her body slumped asleep beside her brother's and sister's against the Dreaming Tree's trunk.

"Good grief!" she muttered in shock.

"We're dreaming together!" Bram exclaimed. He was floating beside his sisters, his feet not quite on the branch.

"So we are!" Cora exclaimed, as she realized she was bobbing above the branch like Bram.

"A family dream!" Elle exclaimed. She was drifting a few inches in the air too.

"Follow your path." The Green Man pointed along a branch of the Dreaming Tree that was growing in their dream. He seemed to be able to see their Dream Forms too. "It will take you where you want to go."

They set off along the dreaming branch, that got lower and lower and further and further from the tree's trunk. Soon it became a root that thrust itself down into a deep dark rabbit hole in the ground.

As Cora and the others followed the root downwards, the route became more and more vertical, until there was nothing beneath them. For a second Cora wondered if the rules of reality might not apply in this dream. And maybe they wouldn't have done, but that anxious unsure thought was enough for gravity to take hold and pull them...

down

       down

              down

...into the dark of the Dead Lands below, where they

tumbled through a black sky towards a tower made of polished volcanic rock, that was as tall and thin and sharp as a giant needle poking a hole in everything.

OOOF!

They fell through the tower's roof...

and slowed to a stop, hovering inches above a polished black marble floor.

Cora pushed at the floor with her fingers. Bram and Elle did the same, and the three of them somehow stumbled to their feet. They were in the grand upstairs hallway of the black tower, standing before a door that was so wide Cora thought all the sorrows of the world could fit through it. Cora could hear her brother's voice, soft and muffled, on the other side of the door. The powerful Dream Flowers had brought them right to him!

She tried the door handle but it was locked. Then she remembered she had the Magic Key. She still wasn't sure if it was real or just part of her dream, but when she put her hand in her pocket, there it was. Would a dream key work on a dream door? ...Only one way to find out. She took the key out, still wrapped in its dream handkerchief, and turned it in the lock.

Click!

The door swung wide with a...

Creak!

to reveal a massive dark Throne Room. In its centre was their brother. He was clutching the Blue Soldier in his hand.

"Acton!" Elle called, joyfully, running over to throw her arms around him,

"We finally found you!" Bram said, joining the hug with a grin. "You're still alive!"

"Thank goodness!" Acton cried. He was alert and upright and his chest swelled with joy at the sight of them.

Relief flooded Cora. She put her arms around her little brother, and hugged him tight. Acton slumped in her arms. A little red robin fluttered agitatedly around him. She'd seen the robin in the graveyard; it was the one Thomas had said was called Coriel. Plus, a strange girl was stood at Acton's side.

"Are you all right?" Cora asked her brother. "Who is your friend?"

"Not really," Acton replied. "This is the Nameless Girl. She's forgotten her True Name, and she needs our help to find it."

Cora looked a little closer at the girl. She was pale, with an almost see-through white face, gossamer hair and sad green eyes. "Are you… dead?" Cora asked.

"Are you?" the girl replied.

The Nameless Girl was right, Acton realized queasily. His brother and sisters had appeared here suddenly, they were see-through and a little insubstantial, like the Nameless Girl and they hadn't come to the Dead King's palace in the same way as him. Did that mean they were…? He was afraid to ask…but he had to. He gulped back a fresh flash of fear, staring at them in shock. "Are *you* dead?" he asked.

"We're in a dream," Cora explained. "The Green Man sent us on a dream-quest to find you. He gave us Dream Flowers from the Dreaming Tree to transport our sleeping selves here." Even as she told him, she saw how impossible it was to understand. She barely understood it herself. She was beginning to realize that sometimes words cannot explain the unexplainable.

"We came to help you win the crown," Bram said.

"What do you need?" Elle asked.

"There's no time to tell you everything," Acton said. "But to win the crown I must solve a riddle. This is the Dead King's Throne Room. He'll be back any minute to ask for the Nameless Girl's True Name. If Coriel and I guess it correctly, then I get the crown and our freedom, and the Nameless Girl is free too. But if I fail, she'll remain a prisoner, and the Dead King gets my body and soul and Coriel's too, for ever!"

"That's awful!" Cora exclaimed.

"Worse, little noctule!" Coriel twittered, landing atop the hourglass. "We've only got until these sands run from

281

the bottom to the top of this hourglass to decide our guess!"
She hopped nervously up and down on the hourglass,
inadvertently making a bigger stream of sand spill upwards
through it.

They each considered the sort of name the Nameless
Girl might have. It needed to sound like it belonged. Bram
and Elle scrunched up their faces, thinking hard.

Acton scratched his chin. He'd got nothing. Trying to
think felt overwhelming. He was sure there was an answer
that fitted lurking somewhere in the back of his mind. He
shivered and checked the hourglass. Half the sand had risen
to the top already, and more was spiralling upwards as he
watched. Soon their pool of Dead Time would be up. Coriel
hopped about anxiously on the desk.

Cora glanced at a grandfather clock in the corner, as she
pondered the dilemma. The clock had no hands and did not
tick. Anxiety coiled inside her, tight as a spring, but this was
not the moment to panic, only to think. She turned to the
Nameless Girl. "What do you know about yourself? Is there
any detail that you recall from your life that'll give us a clue
to your name and who you are?"

"Nothing," the Nameless Girl said, sadly. "All I can guess
is that I must've been a painter when I was alive, because
that's what I am down here. Oh, and one other thing, I told
Acton this too… I don't think I was a girl when I came here.

I think I was a grown woman."

"How can you be sure of that?" Elle asked.

"Because I was much older when I first arrived," the Nameless Girl explained. "I've been getting younger ever since, every time I paint. But that's not so unusual in the Dead King's Palace. He makes everything a little backwards...a bit the opposite of what it should be." She scratched her nose. "When I first became a servant of the Dead King he told me if I could guess my own name in one go he'd set me free. I asked him for a clue but he just laughed and said, '*Ellebssalgairam.*' I didn't know what he meant by that. It sounded like gibberish."

"It could be a foreign language?" Bram suggested. "Death knows all the languages."

Cora shook her head. "No, it's some sort of anagram."

"I thought as much too," the Nameless Girl said. "But I couldn't guess the answer and the Dead King cackled and told me I'd blown my one chance to be free." She bowed her head, sadly. "That is, until he offered Acton a second chance to guess my name, just now." She smiled. "Maybe we won't guess right, but I'm glad we met. You've all been so courageous to come here."

"I don't feel courageous," Cora said. "Just full of fear and anxiety."

"True Courage is not the bravery of doing something

you feel confident about," the Nameless Girl said. "True Courage is to feel fearful, but choose to take a risk anyway. All four of you have done that. And your company's made me feel happier than I have in a long while."

"Of course!" Acton slapped his forehead. "How could I have been so stupid! What you just said about courage, our mama used to tell us that all the time. In fact, all your sayings are her sayings. And you told me souls here sometimes see objects from their past lives, when we first saw Mama's desk. The Dead King's clue…it's not an anagram, it's a backwards name, like the ones Papa used to call all of us… Didn't you say that everything was a little backwards here? So it *is* your name, only it's not *one* name backwards, but your *whole* name backwards… *Elleb-ssalg-airam* spells: Maria Glass-Belle: that's your True Name!"

"And we know who your family are!" Elle added, tearfully.

"It's us!" Bram said.

"MAMA!" the four of them said in unison.

As they spoke, Maria aged before their eyes, transforming from a child, to a teenager, to a young woman, to a grown-up. And as she grew her appearance altered, her face became rounder and more lined, and her shape became fuller, her hair got longer and turned auburn and fell loose across her shoulders. She gasped in delight at all these differences, and her hands moved around, patting herself all over in astonishment. "Cora! Bram! Elle! Acton!" she cried in surprise. "It's me! You found me! I'm changing!" Her voice dropped a few notes, and got softer and deeper as she spoke. "I am becoming the person I was in life, when you knew me!" Now her soul looked exactly as she had when she was their mama. "Dear ones!" she cheered. "Lights of my life! Oh, how I've missed you!" And she gathered her four children up in her arms and hugged them so tight Acton could almost smell a ghostly scent of her perfume and paint.

"We missed you too, Mama," Elle said, tearfully. "So much."

"You cannot stay too long, my treasures." Mama glanced at the hourglass. "Only a quarter of the sand remains. We've wasted so much time on the Dead King's silly game. I wish you didn't all have to go, but if the King finds you three in his Throne Room, with Acton, Coriel and me, then he'll deny Acton his guess, and we will forfeit the game."

"I wish the Fairy Queen's curse hadn't affected you, Mama," Bram said.

"She's the one who deserves this fate," Elle added.

"I wish we didn't have to lose you again like this," Cora said, kissing Mama's cheek. "It's not fair that we get to go back to Fairyland, and the living, but you have to stay here."

"I wish I didn't have to lose you all either, my loves," Mama said. "But at least now that we've discovered my name, I *won't* have to stay in the Dead Lands for ever. Thanks to you four, I will no longer be a prisoner in the Dead King's Palace." She smiled. "Finally I am free to move on to the great joy of whatever comes next. But I will never forget our life together as a family. How beautifully and brightly it burned, like a star. I loved every minute of it." She kissed Cora's cheek and Bram and Elle's. "I'm so glad I got to meet you again, even if it was in this dark place! What strange blessings there are in life and death!"

"I don't see it like that," Cora said.

"You won't right now, my love," Mama said. "It takes many years to see things in a different light. But the truth is, it's not always what happens to you that matters, but how you react to it. That doesn't mean you can't be sad, or angry, or happy – or feel whatever it is you're feeling, when you lose something or someone – it just means you have the power to change those feelings and to use them to grow."

"Come with us now, Mama," Elle said, wiping away a tear. "Back to the Dreaming Tree. You too, Acton."

"We can live at Fairykeep Cottage with you." Bram brushed at his red cheeks.

"My darling Bramble," Mama said, ruffling his hair. "You've always been the sensible one, and you know as well as I do that the dead cannot come back with the living."

"And *I* cannot wake up from *your* dream," Acton said. "I have to find another way out."

"Then how will we see you again? And Mama?" Elle asked.

"My dear ElleBelle," Mama replied. "You can visit me again, anytime in your dreams, as you've done tonight. We make ourselves in dreams. Create each new day and decide how we want to live it. That's what life is: the world seeing itself through our dreams." She smiled at Cora, Bram and Elle. "I love you all," she said. "But now you must wake."

"The Waking Spell has slipped my mind," Cora said anxiously.

"Then I'll say it," Mama said.

"Don't you need a Talisman? Elle asked.

"You are my Talismans, all of you," Mama replied, taking their hands.

"Wait! Before we go…" Cora stared anxiously at her brother, who they were about to leave behind with Mama. "Acton, I must give you this! It's supposed to be with you." She pushed the key into his hand. "It worked to get us into the Throne Room, so, somehow, it should work to get you out."

Acton clasped the key in his fist and watched as Cora took Bram and Elle's hands. Mama held his brother and sisters' hands lightly between her own. Kissing Bram, Elle and Cora's foreheads with a light brush of her lips, she said:

"All dreams and nightmares now abate! Rise and shine, come sleepers, wake!"

"Goodbye, Cora, Bram, Elle!" Mama called, letting them slip from her grip.

"Goodbye, Mama, we love you," Bram and Elle said, waving together.

"I love you, Mama." Cora smiled at her, and felt a great light fill her body, as she rose…

up

up

up

…back into the branches of the Dreaming Tree and the waking world of Fairyland.

TRUE NAME

Standing in the Dead King's Throne Room, Acton blinked away a tear. He felt overwhelmed with sadness to see his brother and sisters go again. But he hoped that soon, very soon, he would see them once more. All he had to do was give Mama's True Name to the Dead King.

Mama stroked his back softly. "Everything will be fine, my darling. I promise."

Coriel watched them from her perch on the edge of the hourglass. "Not many grains left now, my rock doves!" she chirruped. "Barely minutes of Dead Time to go."

"I must write to Pat!" Mama rushed to the writing desk and took up the pen, dipped it in the ink and scribbled as quickly as she could. Only a scattering of sand remained in the bottom bulb of the hourglass.

"Do something, my osprey," Coriel called to Acton. "Cast a spell to make your mama write faster!"

Acton thought hard, but nothing was coming. "Please," he begged the universe, "help me." Finally, words came to him and he spoke them, clutching the humming Blue Soldier.

"Magic pen in Mama's hands, make her words flow fast as shifting sands."

Mama's pen flew speedily across the paper. When she was reached the bottom of the page, she signed the single sheet with her True Name. Then Acton called,

"Extinguish!"

and the spell stopped.

Mama folded her letter and sealed it with wax from the red candle. "This is for your papa," she said, handing it to Acton. "Give it to him, when you get home."

"*If* I get home," Acton said, putting the letter in his pocket."

"No," Mama replied. "I said *when*, and I mean *when*. I believe in you, Acton."

The last few grains of sand in the hourglass were finally trickling upwards. The Dead Time had almost run out.

"The Dead King'll return soon, turtle doves," Coriel advised.

"We'll give him your True Name, Mama," Acton said, happily. "Then we'll be free, and I'll get the crown."

Mama wasn't smiling. "That won't work, my love."

"Why not?" Acton asked.

"Death never loses a wager," Mama explained. "He's already made up his mind to take your and Coriel's bodies and souls and keep the crown and me here, no matter what."

"Then how do we win?" Acton asked.

"Cheat," Mama replied. "What happened when the other five cursed Lost Souls said their True Names?"

"They whooshed into the sky like fireworks," Acton said. "Like the souls on the Bone Bridge. And they went together, because they were holding hands."

"I have a plan," Mama said. "It won't hold the Dead King long, but it should be long enough for you to use the Magic Key your brother and sisters gave you to get back to Fairyland, with Coriel and the crown. Now, listen carefully, both of you…" Then quickly, and quietly, Mama told Acton and Coriel what they needed to do.

As the last grain of sand rose, magically skittering through the hourglass, the door to the Throne Room swung open and the Dead King stepped through it, still wearing the glinting crown. "Dead Time has stopped, and I have returned," he announced. "Now do you have the answer to my wager?"

"We do," Acton replied. Mama stood beside him, holding his hand to give him courage. Coriel was perched on the corner of the desk. "But I'll let my mama tell you her True Name…"

As he was speaking he nodded to Coriel to put the plan in motion. She flew round the Dead King's head in a circle to make him dizzy and distract him. While the Dead King wasn't looking, Acton jumped up and knocked the Glimmerglass Crown from his head. It tumbled to the floor, and Mama let go of Acton's hand and lunged at the King, throwing her arms around him and shouting, "MARIA GLASS-BELLE!"

She and the Dead King exploded in a bright white light, swooshing up through the roof of the room together. Acton brushed away a tear and snatched up the Glimmerglass Crown. He wouldn't have long until the Dead King freed himself from Mama's grasp.

"Hurry, my swift!" Coriel twittered, circling round him. "Use the key your sister gave you to open a magical doorway."

"Where?" Acton asked.

"In the clock, of course!" Coriel said.

And then Acton remembered the grandfather clock in

the corner. Quickly, he dashed over the white bone floor of the Throne Room and put the key in the clock's lock.

"Cast the Opening Spell!" Coriel cried, impatiently.

"I can't remember it, Coriel!" Acton realized with shock that he'd been in the Dead Lands so long his memory was starting to slip away.

"It starts with Magic Key, I do implore," Coriel trilled. "Quick! Quick!"

Of course! Acton spoke the spell.

"Magic Key, I do implore, open up a Fairy door."

He turned the key in the lock and opened the clock-face door. Inside the pulsing interior a sparkling, silver web was growing from the keyhole. Its threads twined together to become a doorway in the air. Through it, Acton saw Fairy Queen's Glass Throne Room. That was the last place he wanted to go back to with the crown. It would put him in the eye of another storm!

Coriel flew through the gap and hovered in the icy air on the far side, bobbing and weaving about like a hummingbird in the space between worlds. "Quick, my little redstart!" she called. "We don't have much time. The spell only opens the doorway for a short while."

It looked like Acton had no choice. He had to jump between worlds, back into Fairyland and the Fairy Queen's Glass Tower, and her Throne Room, and through all that he had to take the crown with him. If he didn't do so he wouldn't escape the Dead Lands at all, but, as soon as he got there the Fairy Queen would use her powers to take the crown from him, and use it to conquer the last of the five kingdoms. And yet, there was still one way he could stop her.

He held up the crown and, in one brave, brief motion, slicing with the sharp teeth of the Magic Key, he cut off one of the five shards and put it in his pocket. He hoped, above all, that this small act of sabotage would make a difference. That by breaking the crown he had fractured a part of its connection to the five realms, which meant the Queen would not be able to control its power, or those five kingdoms, when she took it from him and tried to use it for that purpose.

Now he was ready. He held on tight to the rest of the crown, with its four full shards and one broken one, and steeled himself to jump through the doorway. But as he did, a crack opened on the far side of the Throne Room, and the Dead King stepped through it.

The Dead King's feet hovered inches off the ground. Light pulsed from his pupils as if they were aflame. Acton felt caught by them. He thrashed about, trying to break free of the King's dead gaze, but it was no use. He was too weak. He couldn't go on. The Dead King's eyes held him in their grip, and the angry monarch floated towards him, casting a spell:

"**Bind and tie, hold him near. Let him not just disappear.**"

Acton reached a hand towards the King, but Coriel pecked frantically at his forehead, to wake him from the trance. The pecks shocked Acton into breaking his gaze, and that in turn quashed the King's spell.

"GIVE BACK WHAT'S MINE!" the King roared angrily, loud as an avalanche, and his clawed fingers lunged, sharp and quick.

But Acton was quicker. He grabbed Coriel and the crown and jumped into the clock, through the magical glinting doorway that led back into Fairyland. Clutching Coriel and the broken crown close to his chest, as he tumbled...

down

down

down

into the space in between all worlds, the space that led back to Fairyland. And, as he fell, the grandfather clock's doorway slammed in his wake, leaving the Dead King and the Dead Lands far behind.

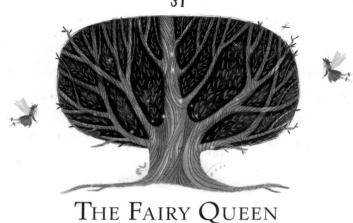

31

THE FAIRY QUEEN

ora opened her eyes in a jolt of shock. Her heart beat heavy and hard, like she was waking from a nightmare, and she had to take deep breaths to calm herself. She hoped Acton and Mama would be all right. That Mama would find peace, and Acton would get the Glimmerglass Crown, and return to Fairyland with it, along with Coriel. It was up to her, Bram and Elle now, to get to that tower, and save Acton from the Fairy Queen's trickery.

She rubbed her eyes and found, to her surprise, that she was still leaning against the trunk of the Dreaming Tree. Its lumps and bumps pushed into the small of her back, as if it had been trying to wake her. Bram and Elle yawned sleepily beside her and the three of them clambered to their feet.

"You're back from your dream-quest, dear children!" The Green Man was once again holding his lantern made of leaves. "You'll be pleased to know that your brother has succeeded in his mission in the Dead Lands. I see all, and he is on his way back to the Fairy Queen's tower with the crown. That is where you must meet him."

"Are you coming with us?" Elle asked.

"I cannot," the Green Man said, handing his lantern to Elle. "I must stay in the Dreaming Tree, but this path will take you to the ground and deposit you in front of the Glass Tower." He shook a leafy branch of the Dreaming Tree and, as if by magic, a path appeared so suddenly at their side, it made Cora jump.

Beyond the branch's last fronds, Cora could see the razor-sharp shape of the Fairy Queen's Glass Tower erupting from the snowy earth like some impossibly large ice stalagmite into the sky. The tower shot up past the high glass walls that ringed it, before thrusting up past the peaks of the distant Magic Mountains, to end in a crystal-clear pinnacle high in the stars that hung in the night sky. Up there, the tower's jagged broken spire looked like the point of a knife slicing through the heavens. Its very tip seemed to pierce the belly of the solstice moon, like it was cutting through a ball of butter.

"Thank you, sir." Bram reached out to shake the Green Man's hand.

"No goodbyes," the Green Man said. "Hurry now, all of you, to your brother. He is still in the most terrible danger!"

"But you said he succeeded in his mission to get the crown for the Fairy Queen," Elle said. "Won't she free him when he gives it to her. That was their deal after all!"

"Never make a deal with the Fairy Queen," the Green Man said. "I would've thought all of you knew that much! Now get going. It's almost thirteen o'clock, and you only have until then to save Acton from her!"

Cora checked her pocket watch. He was right. It was twelve-eighteen, no time had passed in the Dead Land at all, but that still left only forty-two minutes to rescue Acton, else he'd be under the Queen's curse for ever.

Quickly as they could, she, Bram and Elle raced along the new branch. Elle took pole position with the lantern. She was steaming ahead so fast that the tree barely had time to grow beneath her feet. It seemed to Cora that the path ended a few strides ahead of her, in a stubby clump of leaves, but each time Elle's running feet approached that point, the branch grew longer before them, stretching further off into the sky.

The ever-growing branch dropped beneath the moon and raced past the Magic Mountains, where Cora heard a thundering clatter and glimpsed giants stalking in the snowy peaks, smashing glaciers with their bare fists.

At last the branch touched down way out in front of them. Towards its twiggy end, wooden fingers clasped tight to snowy ground. Elle, Bram and Cora stepped across the arched bridge of those roots and found themselves before a glass wall that surrounded a Glass Tower, which was filled with glowing lights.

Cora looked up at the sheer sides of the tower and of the wall; the smoothness of it betrayed no doors. Only the halo of Elle's green lantern and their round worried reflections were visible in its shiny surface, their frowning faces wondering what to do next.

"I know!" Cora put her hand in her pocket checking for the Magic Key, but it was gone, only her Red Soldier remained. Then she remembered: she'd given the key to Acton in their dream. The real key must have somehow been transferred to him at the same time.

As she was thinking this the glass wall swung open. Behind it were two figures. The first a spiny man with a conker-shell helmet on his head, who looked a bit like an armoured hedgehog the size of a child. His left hand clutched a blue frosty glass lantern bright as their own. Perched on his right hand was a white bird – horror of horrors – it was Auberon, the white raven who'd attacked them in the woods.

"You're finally here, little Glass-Belles!" Auberon cawed, taking flight and gliding around the spiny man's head, cackling loudly through his scythe-sharp beak. "Auberon Raven, General of the Crow Army, at your service. We've met before – when you and your wolf friends escaped my air-force battalion."

"Hoglet Hoghedge at your service!" The little hog man's voice was deep and booming and his spines looked sharp as pikes. "I offer spiny blessings and welcome you to the Fairy Queen's Palace, in the Glass Tower. May your spikes be sharp, your claws ever clean. Please, come in! Her Majesty the Fairy Queen has been awaiting your arrival for some time." He sidled round behind them blocking off their escape route, so that Cora, Bram and Elle were obliged to follow him and Auberon through the open door.

Hoglet ushered them across a great glass courtyard where a glass well was sunk into the ground. Auberon glided through a flapping fog of dark, screaming birds that made a cloud of angry beaks, wings, claws and feathers; his Crow Army was circling the well.

"If you'll all please come with me," Hoglet said, pushing open a door in the tower, "I'll take you to our Queen."

Inside the tower's base, he motioned for Cora, Bram and Elle to follow him up a set of floating glass stairs. Auberon flapped his wings lazily behind them. In any other circumstance, Cora, Bram and Elle might have looked around the glinting interior of the tower with awe, but right now they were just worried about Acton.

Cora checked her pocket watch as they climbed towards a hole that materialized magically in the ceiling. Twelve-thirty-two. Only twenty-eight minutes left to save Acton.

She hoped her brother had returned from the Dead Lands by now with the crown, and that he had made it in one piece. She still had no idea how the four of them could use their magic, or even the crown, to subdue the Fairy Queen. Perhaps they should've made a plan earlier, but now there wasn't time.

"We're almost at the Throne Room," Hoglet grunted. Cora shivered in fear.

"You'll have no chance against our mistress," Auberon carked, fluttering his wing feathers and leaping around on Hoglet's shoulder. "She'll make ornaments of you, as she does with all her enemies." Bram and Elle shivered, and Cora's nerves tangled inside her like string. There was no turning back. They'd come this far. They had to save Acton.

"Here we are," Hoglet growled as they arrived at two great glass doors etched with ferns and flowers. "Beyond these is the Glass Throne Room of the Fairy Queen," he announced, opening the doors, and, before Cora could protest, he and Auberon pushed her, Bram and Elle inside, slamming the doors shut behind them.

Cora and her siblings stared anxiously around the gleaming Glass Throne Room. It was long, thin and practically empty of people and things. At the far end was a magnificent throne that looked to be made of a hundred frozen stalagmites. On that throne sat the Fairy Queen. She looked pale and brittle, as she had when Cora had seen her reflection in the glass rose. The antlers, twigs, thorns, briars and wings that sprouted from her head flapped and writhed and snapped. She leaned forward on her seat, her cloudy, black eyes glistening with delight as she stared into a gigantic glowing crystal ball, that floated before her. Its pulsing blue light illuminating the room. A figure was in the crystal ball, falling. It was falling through the empty space between worlds, clutching a crown. Cora recognized this figure at once, it was…

"ACTON!" she called.

"He can't hear you!" The Fairy Queen laughed, clapping her hands together.

"Extinguish!"

she cried and the crystal ball disappeared, popping like a soap bubble.

"So," the Queen sneered. "The other three Glass-Belles have finally arrived to save their brother."

Cora brushed away a tear. Tension bristled through her body, cracking through her bones. "WHAT'VE YOU DONE WITH HIM?" she shouted at the Queen. "WHY'S HE NOT BACK YET?"

"My dear girl," the Fairy Queen laughed. "Please don't panic. We all just saw him crossing the space between worlds in my crystal ball. He is almost back here with my crown, which is lucky for your sake."

She had barely finished speaking when a doorway opened in the ceiling and Coriel swooped through. She was followed by Acton, who plummeted through the doorway and tumbled downwards from the ceiling so fast it took Cora's breath away.

He was clutching the Glimmerglass Crown in his fist, and he slammed into the floor of the Glass Throne Room with a thumping...

CRASH!

The collision didn't wake him. He flipped onto his side with his eyes still shut, groaning and flailing his arms and kicking his legs, as if he was still falling through the space between worlds in his sleep. Cora let out a sigh, relieved he hadn't broken any bones when he hit the floor. "WAKE UP!" she shouted at him.

"Yes, please wake, my little meadow pipit!" Coriel cried, alighting on Acton's shoulder and flapping her wings.

Almost immediately, at Coriel's command, as if someone had pulled a string in his heart, Acton sat up and blinked himself back to consciousness. He looked jittery as a wooden puppet come to life! He hugged the Glimmerglass Crown to his chest, groaning in pain, and rubbed his eyes with his free hand. None of his bones felt broken and he didn't feel hurt by his fall. He looked up to see his brother and sisters running towards him. Coriel glided excitedly over to greet them, soaring high as Acton's heart, which felt overwhelmed with relief that the three of them had made it to the palace in time to fight the Fairy Queen together.

"Acton!" Cora called to him, but he was in such a daze it seemed as if he could barely hear her.

He took a deep breath as she ran towards him. Bram and Elle were at her side, white with fear, speeding across the long, thin Throne Room as fast as their legs would carry them. They almost overtook Cora, but she got to her brother first. She fell to her knees beside Acton and pulled him into a hug, and Elle and Bram joined her.

Coriel swooped around them. "That's it!" she cried, delightedly. "The Chosen One is tired, you must protect him!"

And Cora, who was full to the brim with both love and fear vowed she, Bram and Elle would save their brother from the Fairy Queen.

32

THE GLIMMERGLASS CROWN

Acton let himself sink into his siblings' warm embrace. He felt so tired. More tired than he'd ever been in his entire life. The Blue Soldier was in his pocket. The Glimmerglass Crown was in his hand. And he'd saved Mama from the Dead King. But crossing the Dead Lands had emptied the fight from him.

"Get up, little puffins!" Coriel cried, circling the children's heads, soaring as high as Acton's heart. But Acton's legs were jelly and he could not stand.

"Help me up," he pleaded to his siblings.

As they pulled him to his feet, he slipped something secretly into Cora's pocket. "Take care of this for me," he whispered urgently to her, "I haven't the strength any more." Cora nodded, a tear glistening in her eye. "And…" Acton handed Elle the key and Bram the crown. "Keep these safe from the Queen."

But the Fairy Queen was suddenly at their side. She had floated along the icy floor with supernatural speed, her arms raised in front of her, her twiggy fingers, stretching out for the crown and the key, seeming to grow ever longer as they reached for them.

She plucked the crown from Bram's shaking fingers and the key from Elle's, before they could stop her. "Mine at last!" the Queen cried. "I have triumphed!"

She was right, Acton realized. He could only pray he'd weakened the crown by snapping off the fifth shard and hiding it in Cora's pocket. It was the last shred of hope he had left, but it vanished as the Queen raised the crown and placed it on her head.

At once, the four mirrored glimmerglass shards fused together with the antlers, twigs, thorns, briars and flapping birds' wings in the Queen's hair. Tangling and growing into her skull and melding with her head. When that was done the Queen raised a hand, pointed it at Cora, Bram and Elle, and spoke a spell:

"Cease, desist, begone, beware. Sling three Glass-Belle children over there."

Cora, Bram and Elle skidded backwards across the great glass hallway, and landed with a thump against the doors.

Acton winced in pain, as the Queen grasped his shoulder in her clawed grip, and muttered a second spell:

"**Magic power, broke and bent, turn Acton into an ornament.**"

As she finished, he felt his body shimmer and change. And in that moment it seemed altogether as if he might just…

disappear.

33

THE LAST CHALLENGE

Cora shivered. Her muscles ached from being thrown across the Throne Room, and her heart stung from glimpsing Acton again. On the far side of the room his whole being was fading like a ghost. Coriel circled him, tweeting anxiously, as he disappeared.

Cora clambered shakily to her feet. Bram and Elle groaned and stood up beside her.

"The Chosen One is gone," the Fairy Queen crowed. "None can stop me now I have the crown and with its five shards, I have the ultimate power over life and death in the five kingdoms!"

Coriel swooped across the vast hall and landed on Cora's

shoulder, pecking secretly at her ear. "Your brother's been turned into an ornament, my puffin, but you must still fight the Queen. It's the only way to get him back."

"How can I" – Cora brushed the tears from her eyes – "when she has the crown?"

"Not the whole of it, my kestrel," the little robin whispered in her ear. "There are only four shards on the crown, one of them is missing. Acton snapped it off before he came back from the Dead Lands."

Cora counted the shards of the Glimmerglass Crown. It was hard to see them among the tangle of twigs, antlers and birds' wings that sprouted through the Queen's hair, but Coriel was right, there were only four shards. Cora could just about see the snapped point at the crown's base where the fifth shard had been cut off.

The Queen was spell-casting again:

"Glimmerglass Crown upon my head, let me rule the five kingdoms until all are dead. Grant to me this my one desire, or else each realm will be bathed in fire."

Nothing happened, which seemed to surprise her. "Why isn't it working?" she screamed, angrily. Until now, everything had gone according to her plan. "Something's wrong," she muttered. "Something's missing."

That something, the fifth shard, jaggedly throbbed with magic. Cora put her hand in her pocket and touched it in relief. Without it, the crown was broken and the Fairy Queen's plan couldn't work. If Cora could keep the fifth shard hidden then all would be well, but the Fairy Queen had realized a shard was missing, and it seemed she also knew where it was.

"You!" she spat at Cora. "He passed it to you!" Her eyes became pools of melting spinning gold. "Give it to me now," the Queen whispered, in a voice like cracking icebergs. She opened her palm and held it out, so that Cora might place the shard in it.

Cora felt her mind fill with fuzz, felt the Queen's command hook in to her soul, trying to force her hand. She blinked blearily, and shook her head in disgust.

"NO!" she cried. "I will not do as you ask. And don't you dare try to use your hypnotic powers on me. I won't fall for those tricks twice. Not after the glass rose."

The whirling pools in the Fairy Queen's eyes vanished. "In that case," she said, looking rather disgruntled, "we will negotiate terms, instead. If you give me the fifth shard of your own free will, I promise to bring your brother back. And if you don't, you will all suffer the same fate as him."

"Do as she says, Cora," Elle pleaded.

"Give her the shard," Bram begged.

"Don't, my rock dove," Coriel twittered.

Coriel was right, Cora realized. She knew enough now to

understand that no deal the Fairy Queen made willingly would be honest or fair. To get Acton back, and still keep the whole crown from her grasp, they would have to force her hand. She shook her head again.

"Still she will not do my bidding." The Fairy Queen sneered at Cora. "Perhaps one lost sibling is not enough to persuade her I mean business? Perhaps this stubborn little great-great-granddaughter of mine needs to lose them all, in order to realize that *she* is the one playing with fire." She pointed a bony finger at Bram and Elle and spoke her spell again.

"Magic power, broke and bent, turn Bram and Elle into ornaments."

"What's happening?" Elle cried, fading away.

"We're disappearing!" Bram said, as he slowly vanished.

"Give back my siblings," Cora demanded. "Give back Acton, Bram and Elle."

"We'll play a game for them," said the Queen. "I'll bet your siblings' lives and you wager your fifth shard of the crown."

Cora gasped in disbelief. "No."

"No, you will, or no, you won't?" the Queen asked. "Because if you don't agree to play, then the time runs down without you, and your brothers and sister are already mine and lost to you for ever. But perhaps you should hear the rules of my game before you decide if you want to play?"

Cora shook her head. She was on the brink of tears.

"Your brothers and sister are in the spire of the Glass Tower," the Fairy Queen said. "It is filled with valuable trinkets from my collection. Acton, Elle and Bram have been transformed and are hidden among them. I'll give you three chances to find them, and change them back. You have until thirteen o'clock. After that, time's up. You forfeit the game, I win the fifth shard, and get to keep you and your siblings here for ever. The four of you will *never* return home. Those are my rules. Now, do you want to play my game, or not?"

"Normally I'd advise not, my marsh harrier," Coriel whispered from Cora's shoulder. "But in this case it seems you have no alternative."

Coriel was right. Cora needed her family back if she was to defeat the Fairy Queen. "Your game's not fair," she told the Queen. "But I suppose I have to play."

"I'm glad to see you finally understand how things work around here." The Queen walked towards a small doorway that had appeared in the glass wall of the Throne Room, and beckoned for Cora to follow.

They stepped through to a narrower part near the tip of the glass tower that seemed to rise for ever to a point far above them. Blue lights pulsed in glass sconces on the walls.

Cora glanced at her pocket watch and realized anxiously that she had only fifteen minutes left until thirteen o'clock. Fifteen minutes left to save Bram, Elle and Acton. The Queen watched her amused, like she was watching the last struggling throws of life in an ant she had just squashed.

Cora was so scared that she stared around at nothing for two whole minutes. The tower was empty. There were doors set in the walls far above, in the topmost reaches of the tower, but there was no staircase to reach them. "Are they in those rooms?" she asked. "How do I get to them?"

"No clues!" the Fairy Queen laughed.

"Try the Stair Spell, my sanderling," Coriel twittered, whispering the magic words in her ear. Cora clutched her Red Soldier Talisman, and repeated them:

"Glassy magic, cold and clear, make the floating steps appear."

A spiral of glass steps floated down the curved sides of the tower. Cora glanced down once more at Tempest's watch. Eleven minutes to thirteen o'clock. She ran up the floating glass staircase. The Fairy Queen floated beside her, wringing her hands in glee at Cora's panic.

As she raced up the steps, Cora tried to think. Would the Queen have turned her brothers and sister to glass? Probably not, because that would make it too easy for Cora to recognize them. The Fairy Queen didn't want that, which meant she'd probably turned them into something else instead. The Fairy Queen liked tricks and riddles, perhaps she would've turned Cora's siblings into things that would denote who they were? Cora couldn't work out what those might be, and with time running out, her brain was racing too fast to think straight, and her lungs were out of breath from climbing these steps, which seemed to go on for ever.

She told herself she had to hurry and look in each room. She hoped that when she saw the objects that were her siblings, something about them would call to her and she'd know it was them. Elle's object was probably something natural, or to do with music, or painting...gosh Elle was complicated! Acton's object was probably something to do with magic and fairy tales, that's what he liked best – but still that could be anything! Bram's object was probably something to do with battles, like a model cannon, or another wooden soldier, like the red one in her hand.

Perhaps everyone's ornament would be the same colour as their wooden soldiers? Would that be a logical clue? No time to think. She had to keep running!

She wheezed onwards. Rushing up thirty-nine more steps. The ticking watch in her hand said there were only ten minutes left. The tower was narrowing as they got nearer to its tip. Coriel swooped to one side of her, between her shoulder and the tower's edge, offering words of encouragement.

"Hurry, my little turnstone, there's still time!"

"Not much of it! " the Fairy Queen scoffed, gliding up the airy centre of the tower, at Cora's other side. Cora was running quite fast, but the floating Queen kept pace without even moving her legs. She seemed to be everywhere all at once. "The minutes are ticking away," the Queen jeered, happily. "The jig is almost up!"

Cora tumbled off the top of the flight of glass stairs onto a landing and threw open the door. The room was filled with carved wooden children's toys all painted in beautiful colours. They looked as if they'd been whittled and painted by the same people who'd made the four wooden soldiers, and Tempest's Talisman of the three figures in a boat.

Cora picked up the nearest toy – a tiny carved horse, painted green like Elle's soldier. The letters M. and P. were carved on its base. "These are Marino's carvings," Cora whispered to Coriel, as the bird fluttered at her side. "Prosper painted them."

"They were talented toymakers, my linnet," Coriel chirruped.

"Are you ready to make a guess?" the Fairy Queen asked, from the doorway.

Cora looked around at all the wooden figures. The soldiers and animals. Elle did like animals. Could she be this one? The green paint looked too old and chipped.

It would be a newer one than that, one that didn't look quite like the others, if it was magicked by the Queen rather than carved by Marino. She whirled around the room. What was Elle's favourite animal…a zebra?

There was a little wooden zebra. It was freshly painted with black-and-white stripes, but that didn't have to mean anything, it could be a magic trick. Cora picked the zebra up and examined it. She couldn't see Marino's M.F. mark on it anywhere, which meant he hadn't made it. This had to be it. It had to be Elle.

"How do I make my first guess?" she asked, holding up the zebra.

"Say your spell with your sister's name in it," the Fairy Queen replied.

The Queen had said *sister*. Not sibling! It was a clue. She must *know* this was Elle!

Cora clasped her Red Soldier Talisman and quickly said her spell:

"Fix, repair, heal, restore. Turn Elle back to how she was before."

Nothing happened.

"Oh dear," said the Fairy Queen, with mock sadness. "You guessed wrong. You only have two guesses left. Not enough to save all three, which means one is fated to remain here for ever. If you find them now, you'll have to choose which to keep and which to lose!" She laughed ecstatically at her own evil. "A horrible choice to make. Perhaps you'd rather give the shard to me now, and just go free yourself, instead?"

Cora shook her head. The Fairy Queen was trying to play tricks on her, to confuse her and make her doubt herself. But somehow she was sure she could still win and save them all. She couldn't let fear cloud her mind. Couldn't let herself be distracted. There was nothing else in this room that made her think of her siblings. She closed the door and ran up the next flight of floating glass stairs as quickly as she could.

The tower was so narrow now, it was bending sideways, and so was she. There were only nineteen more steps in this set, and the pocket watch in her hand told her she had only four minutes left. Out of the window she glimpsed the solstice moon, high in the sky.

"Look at that glorious full moon," the Queen sang, gliding beside her. "In a few minutes it will reach its zenith. Then the thirteenth hour and the winter solstice will be over for ever, the shard will be mine, and your time will be up!"

Cora felt her heart drop into her shoes. "Shut up!" she told the Queen. "I'm thinking."

She stumbled onto the second landing and threw open

the second door. The room was a long, thin bare gallery. One small framed picture hung at its far end. "Mama's missing painting!" Cora cried. "The one from the wall at Fairykeep Cottage!"

"A prize part of my Glass Collection," the Queen jeered from the doorway.

Cora ignored her. She ran up to the picture. It had been painted a couple of years earlier, when they were younger. It showed the four of them with Mama and Papa, before all the terrible things that had happened. In the picture, each of their faces looked so full of happiness and hope. That had to be where her siblings were hidden, in the paintings of themselves. Could her brothers and sister be in this picture? Only one way to know for sure. Perhaps she could get all of them at once. Cora held her Red Soldier Talisman in one hand, and touched her siblings painted faces with a finger.

"Ah!" said the Queen, floating up beside it. "She has figured it out, I think!"

Cora tool a deep breath and said her spell:

"Fix, repair, heal, restore. Turn Bram, Elle and Acton back to how they were before."

She scrunched up her eyes, expecting some big flash of magic.

But there was nothing. Only silence.

"Bad luck!" laughed the Fairy Queen. "Wrong again!"

"You have to give me a clue!" Cora shouted. She'd guessed wrong twice. She had to be sure the next time.

"No more clues," the Fairy Queen said. "I've helped enough! A clever girl like my great-great-granddaughter should be able to work things out for herself."

There was some other strategy at work. Some other trick the Queen had played. But what was it? Cora whirled around desperately and barged her way back along the empty gallery and onto the landing.

Coriel flapped in her wake.

There were no more stairs, and no more rooms. "Bram, Elle and Acton aren't in this tower," Cora told the Fairy Queen. "You've cheated."

"They are," said the Fairy Queen. "You aren't looking hard enough. But hurry! Time's nearly up!"

Great-grandpa Otto's watch began to whir in Cora's fist, counting down the very last moments of Fairyland's solstice, and the bells in the belfry began to ring out the magical midnight hour of thirteen o'clock.

Bong. Bong. Bong.

The Fairy Queen accompanied the chimes with a song.

"Oranges and lemons, say the bells of St Clement's,

My stained glass is sparkling, say the bells of St Martin's."

Mama used to sing that same nursery rhyme to them. Mama...she would've known what to do. Tears streamed down Cora's face; she missed her mama more than ever.

There had to be one more hidden room, where Acton, Bram and Elle were, but she'd walked up the whole staircase and not seen one. "There must be a secret space in the tower!" Cora said to Coriel. "We need to find it!"

Bong. Bong. Bong.

"Right you are, my fulmar!" Coriel whirled around the top floor, her wings almost scraping the low glass ceiling.

"Nothing's hidden," said the Queen. "Everything's in plain sight."

"Up here!" Coriel called. Cora looked up. She glimpsed something through the see-through ceiling…the vague shape of another room. Of course – the *belfry! And the glass bells*…or perhaps…the *Glass-Belles!*

Bong. Bong. Bong.

They chimed on. But where were the stairs? Clutching her Red Soldier, Cora tried to remember the Stair Spell Coriel had told her…

"Glassy magic, crystal clear, make the floating steps appear."

At once, a hole appeared in the ceiling and a set of thirteen glass steps floated down from it. She ran up them and reached the tip of the tower, a glass belfry, whose four sides were embedded with large arches that were open to the elements.

The great grey full solstice moon hung in the nearest arch. Before it stood the Fairy Queen. Somehow she'd beaten Cora up there. On the floor around her were the scattered broken remains of a chandelier covered in glass roses with a unique glass star at its centre. It must've been the Wedding Chandelier, stolen from Fairykeep. It was just as Aunt Eliza had described it.

"One guess left," sang the Queen. "You can only save one of them!"

"That's not fair!" Cora cried.

"Nothing in life ever is," the Fairy Queen laughed, and Cora felt sick.

Bong. Bong. Bong.

called the three glass bells, in the centre of the belfry. Their chimes were so loud and desperate sounding, like a cry for help, that they made Cora's teeth chatter.

Twelve chimes gone. One remained.

"Which of these broken chandelier fragments are your brothers and sister, do you think?" the Fairy Queen asked.

"None of them," Cora said, clasping her Red Soldier Talisman in her fist, and heading straight for the three glass bells. She'd remembered her mama's words to her. *Don't let others define the world from their limited viewpoint.* And she knew what she had to do.

"NO!" yelled the Queen as Cora reached out and

touched all three bells at once, pressing one hand with the watch into one, one hand with the soldier into the other, and her cheek to the third, and she spoke her spell as the thirteenth chime began…

BO——

"Fix, repair, heal, restore. Turn Acton, Bram and Elle back to how they were before."

——NG!

There was a flash of light, then the three glass bells disappeared, and Acton, Elle and Bram stood before her.

"You found us!" they cheered, hugging Cora.

"YOU CHEATED!" the Fairy Queen screamed.

"No," Cora shook her head. "We made our fate anew, as we wanted it to be."

"Three in one is not fair!" the Fairy Queen snapped.

"Nothing in life ever is," Cora replied. "You said three guesses. You didn't specify how many names could be in each guess."

"Never mind," the Fairy Queen said. "The thirteenth chime was already chiming when you made your last guess, so you lose the bet. Now, give me the fifth shard, as you promised."

She raised her hands, and her eyes flashed silver with anger. Sudden dark clouds crowded round the belfry and the full moon. The four shards of the Glimmerglass Crown sparkled on her head, as she raked her hands across the sky, calling crackling flashes of lightning to her. She stroked and coaxed each one, until the sparkling silver shards wound around her fingers like tame electric eels, leaping excitedly in her palm. She clenched her fist preparing to throw the lightning bolts.

Elle, Bram, Acton and Cora stepped nervously round the side of the belfry trying to get away, as the Fairy Queen began to cast a spell:

"Static spiral, thunder clap, power thicken, lightning crack."

"What should we do, Coriel?" cried Cora.

"The fifth shard, my puffin!" Coriel hissed from her hood. "Use the fifth shard!"

Cora pulled the fifth shard from her pocket, just as the Queen threw her first lightning bolt at her heart. She held the mirror shard in front of her and the bolt of lightning hit it dead on.

It ricocheted off, as if the glass surface was a mirrored shield, and reflected back at the Queen, hitting her with full force in the chest, and knocking her against the parapet wall.

The Queen wasn't expecting that.

She tried to fire another bolt of lightning at Cora's head, but this time Cora was doubly ready. She held the shard in front of her face and the lightning bolt bounced off her again, rushing back at the Queen. It stung her right between the eyes with a massive electrical charge that lit up the belfry like a beacon of light.

The Queen screamed aloud in despair and fell, tumbling backwards over the parapet wall, her arms flailing wildly. She toppled from the tower, her hands scraping the edge of the wall and she tried to cling on for dear life…

Then she fell.

Cora, Acton, Elle and Bram ran to the place where she'd been and peered over the edge.

The Queen was still tumbling down the tower's sheer wall of moonlit, vertical glass, her petticoats ruffling like parachutes. The twigs, bones and horns writhed in her hair, and the four shards of the Glimmerglass Crown flashed on her head.

As she fell into the glass courtyard at the tower's base, the Crow Army, which circled the Well Between Worlds, scattered to let her pass.

The Queen let out a whooshing scream that echoed away to nothing, as she dropped into the long dark well shaft.

A second passed, then the crows rushed down the well behind her, off to the Dead Lands to feast on her broken remains.

The air around the Glass Tower was finally silent, still and clear, empty of the Queen's screams and curses, and the croaking crows.

Cora, Acton, Elle and Bram peered down the length of the cold, bare tower in relief, and saw Auberon and Hoglet tumble from the courtyard door at its bottom.

Auberon flapped across the courtyard, and Hoglet ran with him, their long shadows racing away in front of them, both keen to escape the tower.

When they reached the wall, the raven glided over it. Hoglet meanwhile put his hands on the glass and opened a door to let himself out. Cora couldn't be sure at this distance, but she could've sworn he was jumping for joy. As he left, he slammed the door closed behind him.

The power of that slam made the walls round the courtyard and the top of the Well Between Worlds collapse. In a sound like a whooshing avalanche, the courtyard walls tumbled to piles of rubble, and the well crumbled inwards, until there was only a dent in the glass courtyard, where the vile well had once stood.

"We'd best get out of here," Acton said. "Before the entire tower falls down!"

34

FAIRYLAND REPAIRED

Acton and Cora, Elle and Bram ran shakily down from the belfry via the floating glass steps and made their way back through the Fairy Queen's Glass Throne Room. All around them, stalactites were falling from the ceiling and stalagmites were erupting from the floor. Great long cracks had appeared in the walls since they were last here.

In the centre of the Throne Room, the crystal ball that the Queen had used to spy on her subjects lay smashed in a thousand jagged pieces on the floor. It seemed that Acton was right; without the Fairy Queen's spells to maintain it, the tower was beginning to crumble and break apart.

Quickly, they opened the great glass doors to the

cavernous hallway, where they found, to their shock and delight, that the glass statues of Fair Folk that the Fairy Queen had made had sprung back to life. The revived Fairies were dancing and cheering and hugging one another, their babbling joyful voices echoing around the hall. Cora and the others barely understood what they were saying, although the word *freedom* was shouted many times among the fizzing stream of excited chatter.

"You'd best come with us!" Cora shouted to everyone. "We think the tower might be about to collapse!"

Then the four Glass-Belles rushed onwards, followed closely by the Fairy Hordes. Coriel swooped ahead of everyone, down the many flights of glass stairs, to the base of the Glass Tower. All the while Cora clasped the fifth shard of the Glimmerglass Crown tightly and nervously in her hand. The faint glow of it lit everyone's way in the haze of the early dawn.

Only when they reached the Glass Courtyard, outside the Glass Tower, and found that there was truly no evidence of the Fairy Queen, or the rest of the crown, or the key, did Cora finally put that last broken piece away in the pocket of her red cloak. The moon was setting in the sky, and a rosy dawn was breaking. As the crowds of ecstatic unfrozen

Fairies tumbled out from the base of the tower, it swayed wildly on its foundations.

Acton took the Blue Soldier from his pocket, and knelt beside the dent in the glass courtyard, where the well had been. "We need to cast a spell to close the well, so the Fairy Queen can never return," he told the others. "And so there's no chance anyone else can send more cursed Lost Souls down there to the Dead Lands to be trapped against their will."

"Do you have a spell to do that?" Cora asked.

"No," Acton said. "But I suppose I can make one. How do you think it should start?"

"I know," Coriel twittered. "I heard Tempest cast such a spell once, twenty-six years ago. It must begin: 'Earth return, green grass grow'."

Acton nodded. He clasped the Blue Soldier and waited until he felt the Talisman humming, then he said:

"Earth return, green grass grow, keep this great evil down below."

At once mud smothered the hole, filling it in, and tufted grass, fresh green seedlings and wild flowers sprouted over it, until the patch where the well had been was no different from the rest of the earth around it. The spell didn't stop there, it engulfed the whole courtyard.

Plants cracked through the glass tiles. Tree branches

broke through the glass walls, and moss and ivy climbed the cracks in the slippery sides of the crumbling Glass Tower. Finally the place didn't look like it had ever been made from glass at all, but more like a mound made from the herbs, trees, bushes, flowers and an abundance of green plants, swaying in the early morning light.

Acton, Cora, Bram and Elle whirled around to see this new living hill they'd made, and as they did so they saw their great-grandma, Tempest the Storm Sorceress, riding on the back of their great-grand-uncle, Thomas the wolf, who was leaping in front of the fading moon and sailing across the dawn-tinged sky in gigantic seven-league leaps. Thomas and Tempest jumped over the hilltop and landed with a thud in the courtyard beside the four Glass-Belles.

"BRAVO!" Tempest shouted, climbing down from Thomas's back. "FAIRYLAND IS FINALLY FREE! SO ARE WE, AND SO ARE YOU ALL!"

Thomas the wolf opened his jaws wide to reveal a mouthful of yellow teeth and gave a joyful growl, that became a bark, then a roar, and finally a howl. AWHOOOOOOOOOOOOOOOOOOOOOOOOOO!

Then the rest of the animals, creatures and Fairies, who'd escaped from the Glass Tower, gathered around Tempest and Thomas and all joined in. Howling, and yelping and screaming and crying they laughed and danced together in one long, loud chaotic cry of approval that echoed in that fresh new dawn through all of Fairyland.

When everyone had finally finished rejoicing, and the rest of the joyful Fairies had begun to disperse, leaping over the crumbling, moss-covered walls around the tower that nature had ripped down, Tempest and Thomas hugged the children. Then Cora, Bram, Elle and Coriel introduced Acton to his great-grandma, Tempest, and great-grand-uncle, Thomas.

Acton was ecstatic to finally meet them. In a rush of breathless storytelling he and the others told the Storm Sorceress and the Wild Wolf about the strange things that had happened to them. Finally, Tempest said, "I think it's time you went home to Fairykeep Cottage. Your papa and your Aunt Eliza are probably wondering where you are."

She pressed her palm to her necklace and took a small brown seed from the Fairy Tree out of her pocket, and held it in her other hand. Then she spoke a spell.

"Fairy seed within my hand, become the doorway to England."

Threads of magic grew from the seed, shimmering between her fingers as if she was moving the very elements. The magic coalesced, opening into a doorway floating a single step above the courtyard floor. It was wide enough for the four children to pass though shoulder to shoulder.

When the magical doorway was at its widest and the children were ready to step through, Tempest hugged Cora, Bram, Elle and Acton in turn.

"You can visit us in our burrow house beneath the Heart of the Forest any time," she told each of them. "I suppose we needn't hide there any more, since the curse will be over, now that the Fairy Queen is gone, but over the past few decades I have made the space so cosy that it has started to feel like home."

"Does that mean the curse is lifted for us too?" Cora asked.

"And for Papa and Aunt Eliza and Kisi, at Fairykeep Cottage?" Bram added.

"It does," Tempest said. "The curse and the Queen are dead. They can't hurt anyone any more."

"And we'll live happily ever after!" Elle cheered, clapping her hands. "Every one of us, until the end of our days!"

"I hope so," said Tempest, "although problems might still come your way from time to time, they have a tendency to do that in this world, whether you're cursed or not. I have always said that happiness can't exist without sadness, nor trouble without calm, but I'm sure, after tonight's adventure, that all of you have more than enough magic, skill and hope in your hearts to deal with whatever life decides to throw at you. And so, goodbye…for now!" She kissed each of them in turn.

"Oh, I almost forgot to give you Otto's watch back!" Cora fished it out of the pocket of her red cloak. "Thank you so much for lending it to us, we would never have made it here in time without it."

"Then I think you should keep it," Tempest said, closing Cora's fingers back over the watch. "I can tell it wants to be with you."

Cora felt an immense well of pride that Tempest would trust her with her darling Otto's pocket watch once more. This time not only for an adventure, but for ever. She put it back in her pocket beside the shard of the crown. "What about this fifth shard?" she asked. "Should we keep that too?"

Tempest nodded. "It is safe to use now that the Queen is gone, and it will come in handy for you to open a door to Fairyland, if you ever want to visit us again."

"Goodbye little Glass-Belles," Thomas placed his paws on their shoulders. "And if you need us –" he added, licking Acton, Bram and Elle, on each of their faces in turn – "then we'll always be here to help."

He came to Cora last. And licked her face the longest. Because they had met first, Cora always felt she had a little more affinity with him than the other three. There was a question she'd been wanting to ask him all this time, since they'd first spoken. "Why did you decide to be a wolf for ever when you weren't born that way, Thomas?"

Thomas furrowed his shaggy brows and thought about this. "I tried out being all sorts of animals, but being a wolf was my favourite. So one night, on the full moon, I decided to stop changing back and forth between this and that, and became a wolf full time."

Cora thought it would be nice to be so certain of who you were meant to be that you could change yourself to become it. Sometimes she felt like twenty different people in a day, but she wasn't entirely sure which of them she truly was. Society certainly had its ideas, and various adults had expressed their thoughts quite forcefully. But Tempest and Thomas had taught her that other people's opinions about her didn't matter, when she knew the truth of who she was herself.

She smiled at Thomas. "You and Tempest were twins. Isn't it funny to start off the same and end up so different? You a wolf, and she a human."

"Change happens to everyone," Thomas said. "People grow into themselves as they age and have adventures. Siblings change too, but you must always see them for who they are and remember the love you feel for them underneath."

Cora felt that same love in her heart for her brothers and

sister, and in that moment she knew she would always feel it, no matter how different each one of them became.

"Goodbye, Tempest. Goodbye, Thomas." She kissed her two elderly relatives one last time. Then she stepped over to the magical doorway along with Bram, Elle and Acton.

"I think I might go with them for a little while, Tempest, my turtle dove," Coriel tweeted, and she leaped from Tempest's shoulder into the pocket of Acton's dressing gown.

"Goodbye then, Coriel," Tempest said.

"Take care of them," Thomas growled.

And the four Glass-Belles, with the little robin nesting in Acton's pocket, turned and marched through the magical doorway back to England, waving as they went.

35

THE BELLES' RETURN

Cora, Bram, Elle and Acton, with Coriel in his pocket, tumbled…

down

down

down

…through the magical doorway, and climbed to their feet to find themselves in the churchyard, standing before the gate that led to Fairykeep Cottage. They were all relieved to be nearly home. But sad to have said goodbye to Tempest and Thomas.

They passed the Fairy Tree, whose flowers were blooming, despite the cold. Blossoms sprang magically from its branches and floated free on the winter wind across the graveyard, to fall like pink snow on the Glass Family grave, where Mama and the rest of the family were buried.

"Goodbye, Mama," Acton said, touching the stone.

"We love you," Bram and Elle said together, and they touched the stone too.

"May the blessings of the trees, mountains, woodlands, streams, oceans and the untamed world be with you from now until for ever," Cora said.

"And may the blessings of the Greenwood be upon you…" Elle added.

"…wherever you may be," Bram finished.

The four of them walked up the frosty cobbled path through the graveyard towards Fairykeep Cottage. Bram opened the gate and they stepped through it into the cottage garden.

"If I grow up to be a novelist," Cora said as they walked across the frozen grass, "then I shall write about our adventure."

"Respectable women don't write novels," Bram said. "You'll have to call yourself something else."

"I think I'll use my own name, thank you," Cora said. "As Mary Shelley did. It's like Mama told us: we make our own fate, and part of that means being true to yourself."

Whatever name Cora used, Acton thought she'd make a great writer.

The wisteria on the front of Fairykeep Cottage was alive with buds, promising a great flowering in the spring. As they climbed the steps, the windows of the cottage seemed to sparkle with magic.

Bram pushed open the front door, and they stepped into the wide stone hallway. From there, Cora, Bram, Elle and Acton entered the drawing room, where Mama's picture of them all had reappeared on the whitewashed wall. It shone as bright as if it had been painted yesterday.

"Look!" Cora cried. Marino and Prosper's toys were on the shelves and Bob and Anna's Wedding Chandelier had returned to its hook in the ceiling, sparkling with sunlight as if it had just been polished. "Everything's back as it was in Mama's day, and better. Let's go and see if Papa is better too."

Cora rushed out of the door and up the stairs. Bram, Elle and Acton hurried behind her. Coriel leaped from Acton's pocket and swooped in their wake.

Cora had already reached the door of the Green Room. She knocked and, without waiting for an answer, barged in.

Papa looked up in shock. He was wearing his long coat, boots and hat, and was sitting all alone in Mama's rocking chair. It was an incongruous sight to see him dressed for the outside indoors. Acton, Cora, Bram and Elle rushed over to hug and kiss him in relief.

Teardrops streamed down Papa's face, his body convulsed with hiccupping sobs, and for a moment it seemed as if he was too overwhelmed to speak. "Thank heavens you're back!" he cried at last, when he'd finally caught his breath. "Eliza, Kisi and the whole village are out looking for you. I have been too, for the past three days! None of us have slept a wink since you disappeared. Where on earth were you?"

"Away with the Fairies!" Elle said.

"We saw Tempest and Thomas," Cora said.

"I saw Marino, Prosper, Otto, Bob and Anna, and gave them their True Names back," Acton said. "Then Mama and me tricked the Dead King in a game of riddles."

"And we fought our great-great-grandmother, the Fairy Queen for the Glimmerglass Crown and won," Cora said. "It was all terribly dangerous, but it means the curse is over, and Fairyland and the four other realms connected to the crown are free!" Then she remembered that Papa hated fairy tales, and so she stopped herself saying any more.

But Papa didn't seem fazed by any of that. "How funny," he said. "I only returned to Fairykeep Cottage an hour ago, because I felt sick with tiredness. I was in the Blue Room, desperately searching for fresh clues about where you might have gone, when a spark of light seemed to flash through the room from out of your mama's hand mirror on her desk.

That little light was so strong, that when I looked up again, it was almost as if stars were sparkling in the Blue Room.

"Their brightness blinded me for a moment, and I had to feel my way back in here, where it was dark, to sit in your mama's old chair and take some deep breaths. And while I did that, I thought about all my memories of you.

"Then – it was the strangest thing – it suddenly felt like rain was falling indoors, but when I brushed my face there was nothing there. And I had a sudden premonition, like a magic spell, almost, that you would be coming home today. So I decided to stay here and wait for you for a while."

"But if we've really been gone three days," Bram said. "Then it's…"

"Christmas Eve!" Elle interrupted. "How can that be?"

"I've no idea," Papa said. "But you being back for Christmas Eve is the perfect present."

He blinked back a bleary tear. His eyes were heavy and red-rimmed. Even their joyful reunion didn't seem to have cured him completely of his malaise. Then Acton remembered Mama's letter. He took it out and handed it to Papa.

"Mama wrote you this," he said.

"Where did you find it?" Papa asked.

"It's our gift to you," Acton said. He thought about telling Papa that Mama had given it to him in the Dead

Lands, but Papa had looked quite incredulous at the gabbled story they'd just told, and Acton knew that he probably wouldn't believe the truth about the letter, so he simply said, "It was in my things when I was unpacking."

Papa broke the candle-wax seal and opened the letter. More tears flowed as he read what Mama had written. "I'm crying too much to take it all in," he said to Acton. "Could you read it aloud? I'm sure everyone would like to hear her words."

Acton took a deep breath and read out the letter. It was not just to Papa, as Mama had said when she wrote it, but to all of them…

My dearest Pat, and my darling children,

When I was taken, the cursed darkness whooshed over you like an overwhelming cloud of sadness and, in your grief, a part of each of you has forgotten who you are and how to live.

You may not think of Fairykeep Cottage as home, but it is. A home is not the walls and doors and windows of a place, it's where your family are. And, for each of you right now, the family around you are as much in need of love and compassion as you are.

Cora, Bram, Elle and Acton, I always said you were Glass-Belles, clear and honest, beautiful and true, like the glass my family once made. But you are not delicate and fragile like those things. I see that now. You have grown strong and powerful, quick-witted, quick to learn and quick to laugh, and full of your own joyful music, so sing it loudly with each other!

Pat, you're a good man. Truthful and loving, silly, serious and funny all at the same time. You create beautiful poems and fabulous stories, and you cared for us, your family, and everyone in your community with a gentle, kind and detailed attention. I'm full of gratitude for the many wonderful years we had together. Look after our fantastic children for me, and make sure they grow up loved through and through.

I want each of you to know that you have my heart, now and always. So take a risk and start afresh. I know it can be scary when you've lost everything. It takes great courage to overcome your fear and begin again. I don't mean that you should forget the past, but honour it by embracing change with all your heart.

I know each of you can do this. You have that courage in you, I've seen it flourish a thousand times before. So go and make your fate anew, as you want it to be, and be assured that wherever you are, and whatever you do, I will always be with you. With all my love and hope,

Maria, Airam, Mama x

As Acton finished reading and handed the letter to Papa, the church bells outside the window began to ring. A minute passed. Papa sat back in his seat, sniffed, and wiped his face with his sleeve, then remembered he had a handkerchief in his pocket, took it out, and dabbed sorrowfully at his cheeks.

"Why don't you try and get out of your chair, Papa?" Cora suggested. "There are so many wonderful things to see."

"Mama's picture has returned," Acton said.

"And so have Marino and Prosper's toys, and Bob and Anna's chandelier," Bram added.

"I even have Otto's pocket watch, given to me by Tempest," Cora said, fishing it out of her pocket. "And this broken shard of the Dead King's crown." Though Papa didn't seem interested in either.

"And the Fairy Tree is in its full winter bloom," Elle chipped in. "Come, take a look."

"I don't think so, right now, children," Papa said. "I'm very tired." He kissed each of their foreheads once more. "But I really am glad that you're all back in one piece."

He closed his eyes and gave a deep sigh, clasping the letter in his fist.

"You'll come down tomorrow, won't you?" Acton asked. "On Christmas Day?"

"To see everything?" Bram said. "Fairykeep Cottage is gleaming!"

"She does look wonderfully like home," Elle said.

Papa didn't answer, only sat there in Mama's old rocking chair, with his eyes closed.

"We should leave you to get some rest," Cora said, putting the watch and the shard away.

She, Bram and Acton stood to go, but Papa spoke again. "I wish I could've seen Fairyland," he said. "The flowers and trees and everything there always sounded so beautiful in your mama's old stories."

"Come on," Cora beckoned to the others. "We should give him a minute."

But Elle wasn't ready to leave just yet. "You may not be able to go to Fairyland, Papa," she said, "but we can bring a little bit of Fairyland to you. A little of its wild nature, anyway." She took her Green Soldier in her fist, knelt and pressed her hand to the wooden floorboards, speaking a version of the spell Tempest had taught her.

"Wood, once seed, brown and dun. Grow like a sapling and seek the sun."

Nothing happened. For a moment Cora wondered if, perhaps, their magic no longer worked, now that they were back in England. But then a little gang of seedlings sprouted through the knotted floorboards. Quickly, she, Bram and

Acton joined in with Elle's spell, casting magic of their own to make a garden for their papa in the Green Room. Acton spoke his light spell:

"**Glow light, make darkness bright.**"

To make enough light to help Elle's plants flourish.

Bram spoke a Rain Spell to create enough water to make them grow strong:

"**Water crash, rain fall, make these trees and flowers grow green and tall!**"

Rain fell from the ceiling of the Green Room, just like in the old days of the Magic Weather Rooms. Finally, Cora spoke her Healing Spell, directing it around Fairykeep Cottage, so that being here together would heal Papa, Aunt Eliza, Bram, Acton, Elle, Kisi and herself of their woes.

"**Fairykeep Cottage, heal and restore. Let hope and love flood through your door.**"

As she finished, she opened her eyes and saw Elle's Fairyland flowers and foliage springing from the chest of drawers, the dresser, the cupboard and from between the floorboards, walls and under the bed. The curtains drew back magically of their own accord. The windows opened and birds flew in to join Coriel, who was perched in the branches of an indoor sapling tree. The birds landed on doorknobs and bed-knobs and the top of the wardrobe, shook the rain from their feathers, and, all at once started to trill and chirrup together, filling the room with their singing. Outside, the clouds lifted and sunlight from a sky bright-blue as a summer's day flooded the room, making a miniature rainbow in each of the four corners.

Finally Papa rose from his rocking chair and took a few steps, drinking everything in. Suddenly he raised his arm and began to twirl on the balls of his feet to the music of the birdsong, dancing an ecstatic jig among the unfurling vegetation. He looked radiant in the morning light, and the swaying leaves seemed to dance around him. When he at last stopped, he opened his eyes and saw Cora, Acton, Bram and Elle, standing in the magnificent indoor garden they had magically created, and a smile blossomed on his face for the first time in a long while.

"It's a paradise," he said. "Our very own Eden." And he put his arms around Cora, Bram and Elle and hugged them back properly this time. Only Acton hung back on the far side of the room, watching everyone for a moment like he was on the outside.

Then, suddenly, there were footsteps on the stairs, and Aunt Eliza and Kisi arrived, and bundled into the room with gasps of shock and surprise at the magic, and birds and plants, and the children returned. They were so overjoyed to see Papa smiling once more, that they rushed over and joined in the hug.

"We knew you were back when we passed the other Magic Weather Rooms in the hall," Aunt Eliza explained breathlessly. "There's a glorious sunset in the Red Room, a sirocco wind blowing in the Yellow Room, and stars shining in the Blue Room, but we had no idea that the Green Room would be this glorious! It's even better than in the old days!"

Acton could only agree. He was the last to hug his family and for a moment he stood alone and let the feeling of happiness wash over him like the rainwater. Then he kicked of his slippers and ran barefoot across the room into everyone's arms, and as he did so, the living carpet of grass and moss that covered the floorboards tickled his feet, and stroked his toes, and each of the wild seedlings in that waving sea of green grass opened their buds to let a thousand flowers of hope bloom.

Q + A with Peter Bunzl,
THE AUTHOR OF GLASSBORN

Tell us a little bit about your inspiration for Glassborn?
I love a book called *Jane Eyre* by Charlotte Brontë. After reading it, I became interested in the history of Charlotte's whole family.

Charlotte had two younger sisters, Emily and Anne, who were also writers, and a younger brother, Branwell, who was a painter. Their mother, Maria, died in 1821, when they were still very young, and their two older sisters died in 1825, four years later. From then on, they lived with their father, Patrick, who was a vicar, and their Aunt, Elizabeth Branwell, who looked after them and told them fairytales.

The Brontës would make up stories of their own too. About various places they imagined called Glass Town, Gondal and Angria. They would write these stories down as tiny newspaper articles, or in miniature books so small you'd need a magnifying glass to read them. Small enough to be read by Fairies, even…probably!

These four siblings, and their creative childhoods, were the inspiration for Cora, Bram, Elle and Acton in *Glassborn*. Though I chose to have two brothers and two sisters for my fictional family of storytellers, instead of three sisters and one brother.

How did you come up with the characters' names?

I like to collect odd names. The Brontë siblings all had interesting pen names. They had to use male names when they were published, because in those days respectable women weren't supposed to write novels. So, they each chose a name with the same initials as their real ones, and which showed they were related.

Charlotte's pen name was Currer Bell, Emily's was Ellis Bell, and Anne's was Acton Bell. Only much later could they use their True Names on their books.

When I had to make up names for the children in my story, I thought it would be fun to adapt the Brontë pen names.

I changed the first two slightly to Cora and Elle, because they were girls. But I kept Acton because it was such a weird name, and because I'd decided to make the youngest child in *Glassborn* a boy. I called the oldest brother Bramble, because it sounded a bit like Branwell.

Is Fairykeep Cottage based on anywhere real?

Fairykeep Cottage was inspired by the Haworth Parsonage; the real Georgian house where the Brontës lived. It still exists and is now the Brontë Museum. I visited the museum when I was researching *Glassborn*. Apart from an extension on the side, the layout of the main house is exactly the same as it was in Georgian times. Some of the Brontë's possessions, and some of their decor and objects are still in the house. Many of these sparked ideas and descriptions for *Glassborn*. Especially the two grandfather clocks; one in the study, and one on the stairs.

What other ideas influenced your story?

I love the Narnia books by C. S. Lewis. Just like the Brontë siblings, when he was a boy, C. S. Lewis, along with his brother, created an imaginary fantasy world. It was called Boxen, and it was full of talking animals.

My favourite books of his are *The Magician's Nephew*, and *The Lion, the Witch and the Wardrobe*.

When I was young, my mum made me a pop-up birthday card of the wardrobe, which opened to reveal a hidden, snowy wood, featuring the lamp post, the robin and Mr Tumnus.

Magicborn was partly inspired by *The Magician's Nephew*,

so I knew *Glassborn* would be inspired by *The Lion, the Witch and the Wardrobe*; a quest story, where four children visit a magical land where it is always winter and try to defeat a wicked Queen.

Another great quest story is *The Odyssey* by Homer. I used a few ideas from that ancient tale in my story too. See if you can spot them.

The Fairy Queen is a great baddie. What makes a good villain in a story?

A good villain needs to always be one step ahead of the hero and making their life difficult at every turn. They can be scary, gruesome, larger-than-life or quite subtle, but the most important thing is that they have to have their reasons for doing things. As the writer, you need to be able to see their side and create ideas and feelings for them that explain the choices they make, no matter how bad those choices are in the end.

ACKNOWLEDGEMENTS

I would like to thank everyone who helped bring this book into the world. Most especially...

My editor Rebecca Hill and my agent Jo Williamson for their sage notes and advice. Alice Moloney and Anne Finnis for their thoughtful additional edits. Katharine Millichope for her fabulous design. Sarah Cronin for her superb typesetting. Katarzyna Doszla for her stunning cover and interior illustrations. Leo Nickolls for his title lettering. Proofreaders Helen Greathead and Gareth Collinson for their considered comments. Publicists Fritha Lindqvist and Eve Wersocki Morris, and marketeer Hannah Reardon Steward, for getting the book out into the world. Everyone at Usborne Rights, Publicity and Sales who works tirelessly to sell the book here and in foreign territories. Lorraine's Lady Writers and The Forester Writers for your ongoing and continued friendship, writer dates and support. The S.C.B.W.I. and the S.O.A. great support spaces for writers at any stage of their career. The wider children's writing community of teachers, librarians, bloggers, readers and writers; it is always inspirational to meet up with you and hear about your creative endeavours. My partner, Michael for looking after me during the writing and no-writing phases alike. And finally, my emotional-support animals Bobby and Milo, whose barks, yips and meows are advice to take a welcome break from the book and play and mess around a little bit more in the real world.